T0197133

BIRDS OF TERROR

BIRDS OF TERROR

––––––– *by* –––––––

Noel T. Skippings

authorHOUSE°

AuthorHouse™
1663 Liberty Drive
Bloomington, IN 47403
www.authorhouse.com
Phone: 1 (800) 839-8640

Published by AuthorHouse 07/27/2015

ISBN: 978-1-5049-2412-2 (sc)
ISBN: 978-1-5049-2413-9 (hc)
ISBN: 978-1-5049-2411-5 (e)

Library of Congress Control Number: 2015911745

Print information available on the last page.

Birds of Terror

The forces of evil are rampant in the universe, but when there is a conflict between good and bad, right and wrong, and truth and falsehoods, undoubtedly good, right, and truth will prevail. The forces of evil, represented by bad, wrong, and falsehoods, can win battles only, but the forces of good, right, and truth win wars.

Evil begets evil, and must be destroyed at its roots, for fear that it springs up and disperses among the forces of good, right and truth. No problem should be too big to tackle, and too isolated and insignificant to ignore. A nation that is united must succeed and will succeed.

Acts of terrorism are being executed at first against government and public buildings, and eventually against private buildings and businesses. Investigations eventually revealed that trained birds are responsible for transporting the bombs that destroy establishments and kill people. It was now to be determined who was responsible for training the birds of terror, and subsequently, who was responsible for training that individual who trained the birds. Good and thorough investigations revealed the mastermind behind the cowardly and despicable acts, and law enforcement prevented him from assassinating the Leader of the country and his family, and destroying the People's House, where he lived. He was finally caught and prosecuted after the loss of many innocent lives.

This novel is thrilling, exciting, nail-biting, suspenseful and futuristic in plot. It prepares law-enforcement for what may happen or what is likely to happen in this climate of fear and intimidation, and what can be done to counter such dastardly and inhumane acts of terrorism. It is fiction, but a depiction of what can easily become a reality.

1

The police, soldiers, National Guard, and civilians stood on street corners, their guns pointed skyward at a flock of about one hundred birds. Bullets were heard all around as they took aim at the birds, trying to shoot them out the sky. Old men, women, and children ran for cover from the birds, fearing they were birds of terror, coming to bomb them. People screamed and wailed as they fled. Adults carried little children as they ran. Some children ran behind adults, trying to catch up. Feathers and dead birds fell from the sky as shots hit them. The birds started scattering and flying higher, trying to get out of the reach of the bullets, but about fifty birds were killed before the shooting ended. At least two loud explosions occurred in the sky among the birds. Those that survived disappeared. Some of the individuals fleeing the birds had fallen and were trampled by other fleeing individuals. At least three young children were bleeding as they searched desperately for their parents. It was total chaos.

Salerno Bondi smiled as he watched his birds fly around his single-family house. After a while, he opened the door, and they flew outside to get fresh air and some exercise. When they returned, he put them in their cages. Although he kept them in cages mostly for their own safety, they were free. He enjoyed the freedom that he and his birds enjoyed. It was obvious the birds preferred being in cages, because whenever he freed them, they returned and entered the open doors of the cages. Maybe they felt safer in the cages, or they preferred being there because they were sure of their meals. He and his birds had a unique relationship. It was a relationship envied by those who saw the behavior between Salerno and the birds. Some people wondered how he developed such a relationship with nonhumans.

Jayne Blulow had liked birds from when she was a little child. When she was about three years old, she asked her mother to buy a parakeet for her, which her mother did. She took care of that parakeet as if it were a baby. She kept the beautiful bird in a small cage. Jayne spent hours talking to the bird as if it were a human being and could understand what she was saying. After having the bird for a few weeks Jayne began to pat it, and the more she patted, it the more it seemed to like the patting and expect it. It was becoming obvious that when Jayne talked to the bird, the bird understood her more and more. It flapped its wings and skipped and jumped joyfully in the small cage. Everyone who saw that came to the unmistakable conclusion that Jayne and the bird understood each other.

After about a year, Jayne began to give it commands, and the bird would obey. She would tell it to sit if it was standing, and the bird would sit. She demonstrated to the bird how it should stand on one leg and then told it to stand on one leg. It did. When she told it to flap its wings, it would do so. Those who saw Jayne's interaction with the parakeet were flabbergasted. They could not understand how someone could get a bird to obey commands, especially from a little girl with absolutely no formal experience in training birds.

The parakeet was allowed out of its cage to fly around the room for exercise. But it always kept close to Jayne. When Jayne and her family were at the table eating, the parakeet was on the table close to Jayne and ate out of her plate and drank water out of her glass. If other family members tried to feed it, it would not eat from them unless Jayne told it to eat. It was obvious that Jayne and the parakeet had a strange and unbreakable connection with each other. Jayne sometimes treated the bird as if it were a human being, and the bird treated Jayne as if she were a bird. Jayne was always happiest when she was around that bird, and everyone close to her noticed.

When Jayne was fourteen, she asked her parents for more birds. Her first bird had died some time before, and she had the urge to train more birds. Her mother bought her six birds, and Jayne began to train them just as she had trained the parakeet. The six birds were different species, which she deliberately chose to see if other species could also be trained. The experiment was a resounding success. Some of the birds took longer than others to train, but in the end, it was a success. The birds could understand commands and respond accordingly. They were more trained than her first parakeet. Some of Jayne's family members asked her if she had any education in training birds since her first parakeet. They were surprised when she told them no.

When Jayne was seventeen years old, she met a boy in her class by the name of Salerno Bondi. He was a handsome young man who dressed very well and was well mannered. The boy's parents were from a different country, and he was more adjusted to their home country. Salerno's parents were not as well off as Jayne's parents, but he seemed satisfied with his status in life. He always asked Jayne if her country, which he called the host country, was attempting to conquer the world, which included his country, but Jayne said no. His country had different lifestyles, values, and cultural beliefs than Jayne's country. He always felt his country was the best example of what the world should be like and that others should follow it.

Jayne usually told Salerno her country was not only the mother of democracy, but also a country that gave everyone—including him—a fair chance at being what one wanted to be and doing what one wanted to do, and her country respected men and women equally. Deep down inside, Salerno realized what Jayne said was the truth, but because his parents and his people taught him otherwise, he refused to acknowledge it. He liked the freedom and lifestyles Jayne's country offered, but that was something he couldn't admit to his parents and his people. Had he done so, he would be considered a traitor and might have even been killed by his people.

One day, Jayne and Salerno were at the college cafeteria having lunch together. She told him of her love of birds and how she trained them to perform many acts. He could not believe her, so he asked her if he could come over to her house to see their tricks because he had developed a love for birds also. Jayne told him he could, and his visit was arranged for the following day. When Salerno saw what she had taught her birds, he still couldn't believe what he was seeing them do in response to Jayne's commands. To say he was impressed was an understatement. He asked her to teach him how to train birds, and she agreed.

Salerno spent many afternoons at Jayne's house, learning how to train birds. He was training the birds one day when an idea came to him. It made him smile. Jayne noticed him smiling and asked, "What are you smiling about?" He lied and told her he was smiling as he thought about how intelligent the birds were. The truth is that he was smiling because he had thought of how he could train birds to execute tasks he and his people would be proud of. He asked Jayne where she had bought the birds, and she told him. She then asked him, "Are you thinking about owning birds?"

He thought for a few seconds, unsure what his answer should be. Then he said, "No, I'm just enquiring."

****

At age twenty-one, Salerno had already successfully attended university. He and Jayne had parted ways and were out of touch with each other. The last time he had seen Jayne was when she was eighteen years old, and it was a brief, chance encounter. By then he had mastered training birds. He was now employed at an electronics store, making a fairly good salary. He was living in an apartment by himself as his parents had returned to their home country. It was time, he thought, to purchase birds and train them at another level. However, he thought that if he trained birds in an apartment, it could be suspicious because other tenants would always be around, and the landlord or landlady and the maintenance person might try to inquire about the birds, so he decided to purchase a small, reasonably priced house in a somewhat secluded location.

He found the ideal house after just two weeks of searching. It was on a cul-de-sac about half a mile from the nearest house, and the price was right. It was a cozy, one-bedroom house with a living room, an eat-in kitchen, and a full bathroom. Salerno was extremely excited as he walked around the house and the backyard. The backyard had many trees and shrubs, which were conducive to bird keeping and breeding, and gave the appearance of an aviary. Salerno bought wood and made several cages for birds, which he placed in the backyard. The cages were properly concealed from the road and other areas by the house and the trees and shrubs. The property was ideal for his plans.

At the beginning Salerno bought one dozen birds. They were all the same species. He thought that it would be easier to begin with one species because it may be better to train them. He began the training immediately, and it was going well because Jayne had trained him properly, and he was applying that training successfully. After a few weeks the birds were responding to commands in the manner that he wanted them to respond. They were standing on one foot and flapping their wings to commands to do so. They were turning around and around and singing to commands that he repeated again and again. One day when Salerno's friend and cousin Josef was at work, Salerno took two of his birds to Josef's house, and drove back and forth from Josef's house to his house about six times, allowing the birds to familiarize themselves with Josef's house and the course to and from the house. Every time he did that Josef was not at home.

Josef and Salerno were friends from when they were very young and when they lived back in their country. They are approximately the same age and from the same area in their country. Salerno decided to visit Josef alone. He left his birds at home. They were happy and excited to see each other and engaged in general conversation. Both

Salerno and Josef harbored the same dislike and hateful feelings for the host country, although the host country had given them an education and employment to help them provide for them and their families. Josef thought that the host country should not be allowed to exist. On several occasions one of Josef's friends by the name of Leon Chanley, who was not born in the host country told Josef that Josef was ungrateful because all the host country did for Josef, he, Josef, did not mean the host country any good and wished it harm. Two days earlier Leon said to Josef, "Josef, you are ungrateful. You are living in this country where you come to better yourself because life in your country is tough and unbearable, yet you have the gall to hate this country and its people. Whether you like it or not this country is the greatest country in the world. Its worst problem is better than your country's most positive attribute." Josef became infuriated and got up and left the room where he and Leon were sitting. He had said to himself, "I thought that Leon and I were friends. I should have known that no one from this country could be trusted. Leon can go to hell." Josef had no knowledge that Leon was not born in the host country. He vowed never to speak to Leon again unless it could not be helped. He told Salerno about what Leon had said, and Salerno asked him, "Are you still going to be his friend?" Josef looked at Salerno with wide open eyes and replied, "Are you crazy?" He went on to say, "Everybody from this country is alike. You see one and speak to one you see all and speak to all."

One day when Salerno visited Josef Salerno had two birds on his shoulders, and Josef asked him, "Man, what are these birds about?" Salerno smiled and said, "These birds are going to destroy the infidels." Josef could not understand and he had a puzzled look on his face. Salerno had a cynical smile on his face as he replied, "One of these days you will understand." As Salerno said that he stood up, shook Josef's hand and said, "Peace brother. I must leave now. Salerno then left with his birds perched on his shoulders. Josef was left wondering what Salerno meant by what Salerno had just said. After he could not think of a rational explanation for what Salerno said, he concluded that Salerno was just stating something that made no sense.

For several weeks Salerno took his birds to Josef's house and back when Josef was away from the house. As he traveled to Josef's house he would repeat "Josef, Josef, Josef," as he pointed to the house. One day Salerno strapped a note to one of the birds which read 'Josef, how are you today?' It was signed Salerno. He had a knot tied on the note that could be easily released by the bird using its feet to release it. He had taught the bird on several occasions how to release the note. After tying the note to the bird, he opened the door and said to the bird, "Josef, Josef, Josef," and sent the bird off. The bird flew away in the direction of Josef's house and after a few minutes it was out of sight. It was gone for approximately an hour when Salerno became concerned, thinking that it might have been involved in an accident or caught by someone. He became irritable and fidgety and started pacing the floor, when five minutes later the bird returned without the note. An hour later Josef called Salerno and apologized for not being home when Salerno stopped by.

Josef explained that he was delayed on the job because the relief worker showed up late. He asked Salerno "Is something wrong?" Salerno lied and said I wanted to discuss something with you, but that can wait." After Salerno hung up the phone he was jumping and saying "Yes, yes, yes." His experiment was successful. Salerno left some more notes at Josef's place that the birds delivered, and each time he would find an excuse as to why he left the notes. Surprisingly, not only did Josef not know that Salerno's birds delivered the notes, but he accepted Salerno's excuses. Salerno had used each bird at various times to deliver the notes. Although Salerno thought about telling Josef that the birds delivered the notes, he did not do so because he figured that if his birds were ever suspected of wrongdoing Josef might assist the authorities in determining that the birds belonged to him. In addition, he figured that even if he revealed his secret and plans to Josef, Josef might have not believed him anyway. Salerno vowed that he would not tell anyone his secret, and only he and his birds would be cognizant of their actions. His aim was to bring his enemies, the infidels, to their knees and terrorize them as much as he could, and he would do it covertly.

The following several weeks Salerno found a reason to send his birds to Josef's house to deliver notes, which Josef thought that Salerno had brought and left there himself. Every time the birds delivered the notes Salerno made sure that Josef was not at home. Josef asked Salerno again why he, Salerno, was leaving the notes when Salerno could have called him on the telephone, and Salerno told him that there is no privacy any longer with telephones, because law enforcement and others bug phones indiscriminately. Josef accepted that excuse, although he thought it was somewhat strange, because if someone did not do anything illegal then that someone would have to fear nothing. Salerno told him, "I constantly hear of the government or some other entity bugging people's phones and listening in on their conversations. I don't want that to happen to me." Josef replied, "That's true. I remember the Snowden guy who fled to Russia. He said that it happened to many people. I still think that he was a traitor. I will never turn on my country." Salerno was happy that he tricked Josef into believing why notes were left at his house, and that the motive was innocent.

After Salerno saw that his experiment with his birds was successful in the delivering of notes to Josef's house, he decided to expand his project. One day he took his birds with him to an old dilapidated building about three miles from his home. He took a photograph and drew a sketch of the building and made several trips back and forth to and from the building. After several practice runs he placed a small back pack about three inches by one and a half inches with pebbles in them, one on each bird's back. He put a red x to the front door of the dilapidated building on the sketch and instructed the birds to deliver the packages to the front door of the dilapidated building. After about fifty minutes the birds returned without the packages. He then got into his car and drove to the dilapidated building wondering if the birds had done as they were instructed to do. On his arrival at the building he was shocked and pleasantly surprised to see the two packages that he had strapped to the birds at the front door of the dilapidated building. He patted and kissed the birds and gave them an extra feeding of a stimulant laced food and drink. Whenever the birds were fed that they became really excited and appeared to be full of energy.

Although it was an undisputed fact, Salerno would not accept that his host country was the major superpower of the world. On several occasions Jayne told him that, but he would always try to challenge her on that. He had met Leon, his cousin Josef's friend, and Leon tried to convince him that the host country was the greatest country in the world. On one occasion Leon said to him, "Salerno, this country is the leader of all countries when it comes to peace, democracy, human rights and freedom of speech." Salerno became angry and retorted, "Then why is it always meddling in other countries' affairs?" Leon being a very argumentative individual said, "Any time this country intervenes in any other country's affairs, this country is invited to do so. The invitation is either from the people, or indirectly because of the abuses, lack of freedom and the injustice meted out to the poor people by the greedy leaders of that country. This country would not and cannot stand idly by and condone such behavior." "Nonsense," screamed Salerno. "Your country finds a reason for everything it does. It's a bully of the first degree." Leon determined to get in the last word, said calmly, "This country believes in peace and protecting those who cannot protect themselves. Unlike some other countries, it will not knowingly take the lives of innocent people." Salerno had heard enough, and just like Josef, he walked away infuriated, thinking that all the people of the host country and including Leon, were hypocrites, and out to destroy his people and his country.

It is a known fact that Salerno and Josef's people were extreme radicals who would do or say anything to protect their people and their country. Their beliefs and culture are different than those of Leon and Jayne's people's beliefs and culture. Salerno decided to visit his home country because he was away from his country too long. He missed his culture. He thought long and hard about making the visit, and when he made it he decided that he would be there for a few weeks. He felt that he needed cleansing and that he could get it only in his country, because the host country was too polluted and poisoned, so he called his family back in his home country and told them that he would visit them soon. He decided that he would inform Josef about the birds because he wanted Josef to care for them in his absence. Josef would not be told about his project with the birds, because Salerno wanted that to be his best kept secret. He spoke to Josef and Josef agreed to look after the birds while Salerno went abroad. Salerno told him what to feed the birds and when to feed them.

Back in Salerno's home country everything was quiet. His family was happy to see him again after not seeing him for a very long time. He received many hugs and kisses, and his little nieces and nephews gathered around him to see what he had brought for them. He gave them gifts that he bought in the host country that could not be obtained in his country. His bigger and older relatives received money from him. Everyone was thankful for what Salerno gave and expressed to him that they were happy that he was back home. Among the family members was one of his cousins by the name of Cunio, who was the same age as Salerno, but skinnier than Salerno. Cunio's family was very poor, and some days food was difficult to come by, which meant that he went hungry many days. Cunio and Salerno went outside under an oak tree and discussed life. After talking for some time Salerno said to Cunio, "Cunio, I have a plan to get even with the infidels."

Cunio knew who Salerno was referring to when Salerno said 'infidels'. That was a term that Salerno and his people used when referring to people like those from Salerno's host country. However,

Cunio was somewhat surprised when he heard Salerno refer to the people of the host country as 'infidels'. Cunio broke a twig from the hanging branch closest to him and appeared to be playing with it. There was silence for a while, then he said to Salerno, "How come you call them infidels when you live and work among them?" Cunio appeared to be genuinely confused, and Salerno noticed it, so Salerno patted him on the shoulder and replied, "Man that got nothing to do with it. You must look at the bigger picture. They will always be our enemies no matter what they do or don't do. "Cunio, still perplexed, asked, "But, is that right? Wouldn't it be best to live in peace than in war?" "There will never be peace," Salerno replied. Cunio could not understand how Salerno could think in the manner that he did. Still looking confused, he said, "Man I would give my life to live and work in your host country if I could. You see, I would be able to help my family. My father is ill and can no longer work."
"One day you'll understand what this is all about," said Salerno.

Salerno decided to get back to the topic and discuss a part of the plan to Cunio. He said to Cunio, "You live here, so you can tell me where I can find someone who is an expert in bomb making."
"Are you crazy?" Cunio asked.
"No," Salerno replied. "Please tell me who can assist in teaching me how to make bombs. Here, take this fifty dollars," Salerno continued. Fifty dollars was a lot of money in Cunio's country, and could go a long way in assisting him and his family to buy food. Cunio held out his hand and took the money from Salerno and folded it and put it in his shirt pocket. Still feeling guilty, Cunio asked Salerno, "Are you sure you want to do this?"
"Very sure," Salerno replied.
"Ok, come with me," Cunio said. He and Salerno walked down a narrow, dank alley until they saw a little house at the far end of the street.

Cunio knocked on the door of the little cinder block house and waited for a response. Suddenly a voice said, "Come in," and they entered.

Cunio appeared to bow to the man, which indicated that the man was a person of some stature.

The bomb maker was dressed in a black shirt and black pants with a black bandana wrapped around his head. He had on a pair of black shoes and black socks. His appearance was surely intimidating to say the least, as he sat on a small wooden stool in the center of the room. He appeared to be alone. Cunio addressed him as 'sir'. The man was looking down at the floor, and when he raised his head his dark piercing eyes stared straight at Salerno. He really had a gothic appearance. "What can I do for you?" the man asked. The question seemed to be directed at Cunio, although the man was still looking at Salerno, whom he did not know.

"This is my cousin Salerno who lives abroad in the mother of infidels' land. He comes to you for assistance. He will tell you exactly what he wants," Cunio told him. When Cunio mentioned the word infidels earlier, the man's interest peaked, and he said, speaking directly to Salerno, "You can call me AB." Salerno thought that AB was a strange way to refer to someone, but if that was the name that the man wanted be called then so be it. Maybe it was because of AB's involvement in freedom fighting, which the infidels call terrorism, that he did not want anyone to know his real name, Salerno thought. AB then gestured for Salerno and Cunio to sit, and they sat on two small wooden stools that were not too far from the door. It would not have taken long for one to notice that AB's house was sparsely furnished, even by Cunio's people's standards. There was no sign of a television or telephone. Dirty pots and pans were on a table on the Western side of the room. Photographs of heavily bearded men were hanging immediately behind AB. One of the photographs appeared to be of AB.

AB set with his legs wide apart and each hand on one of his legs. He had a black turban on his head that seemed to match his heavily bearded face and very thin frame.

"I'm here to seek your assistance sir," Salerno said in a soft, frightened voice. "Cunio told me that you can assist me."

"What is it that you want me to assist you with?" AB asked as he appeared to become a little impatient.

"I am embarking on a project against the infidels in the host country, and my project will involve maiming and destroying them with explosive devices, and I understand that you can teach me how to make and detonate these explosive devices." Salerno was about to continue speaking, but AB interrupted him by saying, "Yes, yes, that sounds very good." AB's whole countenance changed to one of excitement. Salerno continued, "My approach will be very novel. I am training some birds to deliver explosive devices to certain targets, but I have no expertise in the making of explosive devices. I would like also to know what your instructions will cost." AB smiled for the first time since Salerno and Cunio entered the room, and it was obvious that Salerno had aroused AB's curiosity.

"It would cost you nothing, as you are a freedom fighter for the cause. I am more than happy to be able to assist you in this just and noble cause, AB responded. Salerno was overjoyed that AB would be assisting him and that AB's assistance would cost nothing.

For the following two weeks AB instructed Salerno on how to make and handle small, compact, but very powerful bombs. AB thought that Salerno's project of using birds was a very ambitious and creative project, and was commendable and would be very difficult to detect if it were successful. AB allowed Salerno to experiment with the bombs by using them on old buildings and vehicles that were no longer in operation, and Salerno did a very good job. AB was proud of Salerno's ability to make and handle these explosive devices in such a short time. He even showed Salerno how to make and set remote switches on them. AB worked from an old building where he kept his bomb making tools, equipment, ingredients and electronic apparatus. He had televisions, clocks, and other electronic devices that he used in the detonation of bombs in that building. At the end of the two weeks of training AB hugged Salerno and wished Salerno luck in executing such a worthwhile project for his people against the infidels. When Salerno was being hugged by AB, Salerno felt a surge of unexplained power and energy that appeared to be coming from AB's body to his. That power surge, Salerno thought, was the beginning of a new phase of his life that he would need when he returned to his host country.

As Salerno and Cunio walked away, AB shouted out to Salerno, "Remember, the infidels are our everlasting enemies." Salerno turned his head around toward AB, shook his head in approval and waved as he continued walking. As he walked he thought of what he achieved in two weeks and how he would apply it for the rest of his life, for he could not only make small compact lethal bombs, but he could also package them and detonate them remotely from his computer. He knew that he would be a force to be reckoned with. He could hardly wait to return to his host country and watch the people of the host country live in fear as he unleashed his freedom birds on them. He thought that they were freedom birds because the birds would help to free his people from the grasp of the infidels. He knew that before he embarked on his project he would have to give the birds some more training, and this time he would train a greater number in the event that some of his birds were harmed or killed he would have back-ups.

Cunio said to Salerno as they walked, "Do you really want to do what you have planned? I understand that in your host country anyone can do and become whatever one wants to do and become. I would do anything to trade places with you." Salerno appeared to be disturbed at what Cunio was saying, and he was beginning to wonder if Cunio was sympathetic with his people's movement or he Cunio was a sympathizer of the infidels. He stopped in the middle of the street and turned toward Cunio and said, "What do you support, your people's struggle or the infidels' merciless killing of our people?" Cunio looked at him and said, "Why would you ask such a foolish question? You know I support my people." Cunio placed his hands in his pants pocket and turned away from Salerno and continued, "Salerno, we are family, and I will never, ever go against my people, but your host country has many advantages that you and others like you can enjoy and benefit from. Most of what you do and say is rhetoric and propaganda. If the host country is so bad why would people from all over the world want to live there? Man, people lose their lives almost daily trying to get to the host country." Salerno was about to become angry because he did not like what his cousin was saying about the host country being a country of opportunities.

As far as Salerno was concerned, Cunio should have hated the host country and its people even if Cunio thought that there was no reason to do so, and as far as Salerno knew, there were many reasons to hate them. Salerno started walking again and Cunio followed not knowing what Salerno would say next. He could not understand Salerno's rationale for being so hateful toward those who helped him and his family so much and in so many ways. Salerno patted Cunio on the shoulder and said, "Cunio, I think you must be very careful with what you say. Our people would not be happy if they hear you speak on behalf of the infidels."
"I'm not speaking on behalf of the infidels I'm only speaking the truth. Those people from the host country fought for their freedom and the freedom of many others. They helped many poor and impoverished countries." Before Cunio could continue any further, Salerno said, "Stop it, stop it. I think we should stop this conversation now." Both individuals remained silent for the remainder of the short walk. When they arrived at their house, they parted company without saying goodbye.

About one week later Salerno prepared for his return trip to the host country that he hated so much, and he could not believe that in two days' time he would be back on his job and ready to engage his birds in the ultimate training program. He loved his job and he loved electronics, because it was an exciting field to work in. For the three weeks that he was abroad he missed his job and his fellow employees. What he longed for most however, was to return to the training of his birds and to begin his project using the training that he got from AB. He thought about the things that Cunio said in favor of the host country and the host country's people, and found him, Salerno, believing and agreeing with Cunio. However, he told himself that he would agree with what the freedom fighters from his country of birth said, as they were older and wiser than he and they must know what they are saying.

The return flight back to the host country was very long, and he slept about three quarters of the journey. For the other quarter of the journey he thought about his ambitious and what he termed, infallible plan. When the airplane landed he arose from his seat, stretched and yawned, then took his luggage from the overhead compartment of the plane. Passengers were sitting, and some were standing in the aisle of the plane. While he was waiting for the passengers to begin disembarking he thought of his family back in his home country and how they were living in such poor and squalor conditions. He knew that if he were not living and working in the host country it would have been far worse for them, because although they were poor, they were much better off than many others in his country. The remittances that they received from him every month went a long way.

While Salerno was out of the host country for three weeks Leon was accepted for employment with the electronic company that employed Salerno. Although Leon had angered Josef a few times, Josef advised him to contact the electronics company in search of work, and Leon did it and he was hired. It was Leon's dream to work in the area of electronics as he dreamed one day of becoming an astronaut, and he knew that electronics would be the right area to get into. He had never divulged to Josef and Salerno that he was not a citizen of the host country, although he was a legal resident like Salerno. He made up his mind that he would tell them that he was not a citizen because he did not want to mislead them into thinking that he was. About five minutes after Leon entered his work place Salerno entered being the first day of his return to work after he returned from the visit to his country of birth. He had seen and spoken to Salerno but he did not really know anything about Salerno. They shook hands. When Leon met Salerno at Josef's house Salerno knew that Leon believed that the host country was the most perfect country in the world, and that it could not do or say anything wrong. In spite of that, Salerno thought that Leon was a nice guy. Leon knew from Josef that Salerno was very good at electronics, so when the supervisor told Leon that he, Leon, would be working under the immediate supervision of Salerno, Leon was very happy. Salerno said that he had no problem supervising and instructing Leon. Salerno showed Leon around the office and assisted Leon by explaining to Leon what Leon's tasks were and showing Leon how to perform those tasks. Salerno wondered if training Leon would be more difficult than training birds. As this thought crossed Salerno's mind, he chuckled.

"So, do you like this job?" Leon asked Salerno.
"Well, it's o.k., I guess. I've always wanted to be involved in electronics but to an even greater extent," Salerno replied.
"You have to creep before you walk," Leon responded. Leon continued, "I want to be working with the space program in this country one of these days." Salerno chuckled as he and Leon settled to engage in a set task.
At lunch time they sat at the general lunch table with other employees, but a little away from the others. An older employee was reading a science fiction book and seemed to be enjoying it as he ate a home-made corned beef sandwich. The corned beef appeared to be dropping from the bread and he did not notice it because he was preoccupied with reading the book. Two women, one of them was obviously a bleached blonde, and the other a brunette, were discussing their children's behavior. One of the women seemed to think that her two-year old was out of control and she did not know how to control him. Just as the other lady was about to give some advice on how to control the two year old, Leon asked Salerno, "So what is going on in your life? Do you have a life after work?" Salerno was busy trying

to hear the remedy or solution for the unruly two year old and he did not hear Leon, so Leon repeated the question. "I say what is going on in your life?"

Salerno apologized for not answering on the first occasion when the question was asked.

"Well, I go to the movies and play games on my computer etc.," Salerno replied, with his eyes transfixed on the two women who were talking about their children. He was not prepared to mention anything about his birds to Leon because he wanted that to be a secret, and because Leon was a sympathizer of the infidels. Leon tapped lightly on the table as he ate a banana. He thought that Salerno was not telling him everything, so he asked Salerno, "What about a girlfriend?" Salerno quickly responded, "What about it?" Leon said, "Do you have one?" Salerno chuckled and said, "Ha, no, I don't have a girlfriend. Women are too complicated. They don't know what they want and I don't know what they want." Leon thought that Salerno's answer was somewhat funny, so he responded, "It is said that you can't live with women and you can't live without them." Leon continued, "I was married, but the marriage did not work out. I had loved her dearly, but she became abusive and went as far as to state that she would bump me off." Salerno thought that he had heard enough about women so he changed the subject and asked Leon, "What do you think of this country?" Leon always longed for the opportunity to sing the praises of the host country, and this time would be no exception. Salerno continued. "Leon, you were born here, right." Leon thought that it was the proper time to tell Salerno that he was not born in the host country, but that he was given status to work and live there just like Salerno. He looked at Salerno and said, "Man, I was not born here, but I wish I was born her. This country is better than great. I love the country of my birth, but there are so many opportunities available to people living in this country. I honestly think that it is the greatest country in the world. It has its faults and problems, but nevertheless, it is the greatest. What do you think of it Salerno?" Salerno did not expect Leon to answer in the manner that he did. Deep down inside he was angry with Leon's answer, but he decided that he would not show it. Salerno hated pretence but thought that in the circumstances it would be best to pretend in order to help to further his goal. However, before he could reply to Leon's question the alarm went off that notified the workers that lunch time was over and it was time to return to work. He and Leon got up, cleared the table of their garbage, and returned to work.

For the remainder of the day Salerno thought about what Leon had said about the host country, and felt that Leon should have been ashamed of himself for praising the host country as he did. He wondered how Leon could praise the host country above Leon's country of birth. He expected a citizen who was born in the host country to speak of the host country in the manner that Leon spoke of it, but not one like Leon who was not born there. He was worried that because he had to work with Leon he could be hearing that kind of talk for a very long time. In any event he would not show his disgust and displeasure for what Leon said. By not showing his hatred for the host country to the infidels, he would not become a suspect in the event something went wrong with his planned project.

The birds were happy to see Salerno after he returned from abroad. As he neared the cages they flapped their wings, skipped about, chirped and sang. They were like his little children and he like their father. Josef told him that he, Josef, enjoyed feeding the birds, but Josef sensed that the birds had missed him while he was abroad. After work, and on his days off, Salerno continued with the training of the birds, come rain or sunshine. After all, it was essential that the birds be trained, and trained properly, because he could not afford for them to make mistakes. His success with his assignments depended on how efficient and successful they were at carrying out orders and observing the targets that they would have to strike.

Salerno decided that it was time that he named his project and a few names came to mind, but he settled for the name 'Operation Infidel

Destruction,' or Operation ID for short. He was satisfied that that was what his project would be about, and he was determined that he would live up to that name. His aim was to kill as many infidels as possible and destroy their buildings. He had resumed training of the two birds and eight additional birds that he acquired. He thought that ten birds were a good number to begin with in the event something happened to some he would have some remaining to carry out the assignment. The training was proceeding very well. The two first birds were undoubtedly more advanced in the training program than the others because they had weeks of training before the others. He continued sending messages to his friend and cousin Josef, who still did not know that birds were delivering the notes. Josef had discontinued asking Salerno why Salerno was communicating with notes, and he had accepted Salerno's first explanation.

It was time that Salerno extended the distance for the birds to train in the delivering and dropping of explosive devices, so he went much further and started to take photographs of various buildings, and he returned to his home and sketched the said buildings on a fairly large sketching pad. He would have the name of each building written on the sketch of the building in question, for example, if it were a sketch of the post office he would write post office on the sketch and then say repeatedly to the birds, 'Post office, post office, post office'. After doing that on several occasions for several days, he would then place several sketches of different buildings on the floor, one of which would be the post office, and say to the birds, 'Post office, post office, post office', and one by one the birds would move over to the several sketches and point out the post office with their beaks. One of the birds had some difficulty distinguishing the sketch of the post office from the other sketches, and Salerno noticed something remarkable. He was about to take that bird out of the project and work with the other nine when he noticed that two other birds began to assist that one in pointing out the correct sketch of the post office. He was flabbergasted and could not believe what he was witnessing. A few days later and after some selfless assistance from the two birds the bird that had the difficulty pointing out the post office began to point out the correct sketch. Salerno never imagined that he would experience birds assisting other birds in the manner that he saw them doing. After all, some human beings do not assist other human beings in that manner. He thought that maybe the two birds that assisted the other bird had sensed that he, Salerno, was about to remove that bird from the group, and that they had already become attached to that bird and did not want it removed from the group.

One weekend Salerno, Josef and Leon decided to visit one of the huge malls in the host country, and they sat at a table at the far Eastern end of a food court somewhat away from the other people sitting at the tables. There, they discussed employment matters and many other topics. The topic of the host country and their home countries arose. Josef and Salerno spoke highly of their birth countries, and admitted that life there was tough. Leon asked, "Why are women in your country degraded and not respected?" Josef became angry and retorted, "Women are not equal to men, and you know that. In this host country men and women are allowed to eat, socialize etc. together. That is an abomination." Salerno's lips were now quivering as he interjected, "I don't know about your little country, but in this country, men are allowing women to perform men's work and take over men's roles. Only in countries where infidels abide and rule this can happen." Leon smiled and shook his head in frustration. He could not believe that he heard what he had heard. He wondered how in this day and age people could harbor such backward and uncivilized way of thinking. Josef and Salerno watched him intently, anticipating what he would say about the host country and his own country. Salerno wondered if Leon would begin to sing the praises of the host country as he always did.

Leon knew that they were anxiously anticipating his response. He tapped lightly on the table with his index finger as he said, "I will begin with my country. My country is a small group of islands in the Caribbean. There, we treat men and women equally. As a matter of fact, most of the top positions are held by women. Anything that men do, women do, and sometimes better. We and the host country have many of the same values and principles, although we are little. That is the right thing to do." "Wait a minute, wait a minute," said Salerno. "Are the people in your country infidels also?" Leon responded by saying, "I don't know your definition of infidels, but if it means doing what the host country and my country are doing when they assist poor countries and give people like you jobs from all over the world, you can call us infidels any day." Leon went on, "The host country is a beacon for freedom, democracy, equality and respect for all. That is why you and I are here in the host country. I swear that in spite of some sickness that I suffer, if I am asked to represent the host country at home or abroad in any battle or war, I would go now. Believe me, I would."

Salerno's eyes became large and scary-looking as he listened to Leon. He was looking straight at Leon as he said, "Are you saying that if the host country asked you to fight against my country you would do so?" Josef was now looking directly at Leon anxiously awaiting his response. He wanted to know if Leon meant what he had just said when he said that he would fight for the host country anytime if he were asked to do so. Salerno, still looking at Leon said, "Answer me." Leon said, "Man, I mean what I said. You are my buddies, but this country stands for justice and peace for all. I will not be fighting you personally. I will be fighting a just cause, and for peace and justice. I will do it because it is the right thing to do. You must not take it personally. You want to hear the truth from me, and you should respect me for telling the truth." Salerno stood up fuming as he muttered, "Damn traitor" as he turned to Josef and said, "Let's go and leave this traitor alone." They got up and walked away from the table leaving Leon there.

Salerno and Josef's meals were unfinished. Leon sat there and finished his meal then he left alone. He was surprised that his friends had acted in the manner in which they did. He decided that he would still be their friend if they wanted him to, but he would keep his distance unless it was almost impossible to do so, for example, in the workplace. Leon knew that Salerno and Josef harbored radical thoughts, but he never thought that they would be so petty and unforgiving in their radical beliefs. He knew that their philosophy when it came to killing and harming innocent people and destroying people's properties was wrong, and as long as he lived he would not hesitate in telling them that.

The night following the dinner at the mall, Salerno thought about Leon's remarks at the food court in the mall, and decided that he, Salerno, had over reacted; over reacted only because he thought that his actions might have made Leon feel that he, Salerno, was a radical, and he did not want Leon to think about him that way. Salerno decided that he would speak to Leon the following day and apologize to Leon for what transpired the previous day. He would tell Leon that the manner in which he, Salerno, and Josef behaved was uncalled for, and would never happen again. He figured that the apology, although not coming from his heart, would placate Leon and might cause Leon to forget about the mall food court incident. Salerno called Josef and told him that it would be prudent if he, Josef, apologized to Leon for the incident at the mall food court. Josef said that he thought about it, and he came to the conclusion that both of them had overreacted. He promised Salerno that he would apologize to Leon.

Only two other persons were already at their workplace when Salerno entered. One of those two persons was Leon, who was already at his station beginning to embark on his tasks for the day. Salerno walked up to him and said, "Good morning bro." Leon stopped doing what he was doing and turned around, somewhat surprised to see Salerno standing close to him and addressing him as bro. He thought that Salerno might have still been angry from the mall food court incident. He responded, "Morning. How are you today?" Salerno was glad to know that Leon was not angry, although he thought that maybe Leon should have been angry because of his and Josef's behavior. Salerno said, "Man, I'm truly sorry for my behavior at the mall food court the other day. The manner in which I reacted was totally uncalled for. I thought about that ever since, and I want you to know that it would never happen again." He did not know what Leon would say. He wondered if Leon knew that the apology was only coming from his lips and not his heart. Leon smiled as usual and said, "Man I accept your apology. I thought about it and said that maybe you and Josef were having a bad day." Salerno always wondered how Leon was so cool and calm under pressure.

The only time that Leon seemed to be fired up was when Leon was defending the host country, and that, Salerno had a problem with. Leon did wonder if Salerno had a split personality because of the way in which he, Salerno, behaved at times. After Leon told Salerno that the apology was accepted, Leon extended his right hand toward Salerno and Salerno grabbed it and they shook hands. "We're still friends, right?" Leon asked him. Salerno squeezed Leon's hand and said, "Still friends." Their hands separated and Salerno walked off to his station a few yards from Leon's station. As Salerno walked away Leon wondered if the apology was genuine and sincere, or if Salerno made it only to please him, Leon. Leon was unable to determine whether the apology was sincere or not from Salerno's behavior.

When Salerno visited AB they tested some of the bombs that they made, and Salerno was happy with how they worked and how powerful they were. Evidently they could maim and kill and destroy huge buildings, and that was exactly what Salerno was looking for. He wanted to send a very strong message to the infidels, and let them know that they had home grown freedom fighters, or lone wolves, whatever the infidels wanted to call them. He knew that the infidels preferred to call people like him terrorists, but, like he always said, one man's terrorist is another man's freedom fighter. He was always surprised at how common the bomb-making ingredients were. They could be found easily in many local stores. Every week, for several weeks he purchased the materials and stored them in cupboards in his kitchen. If the average person saw them in his house that person would not know that the ingredients were bomb-making materials, and that was the way he wanted it.

The training of Salerno's birds continued constantly, because he did not want to commence Operation ID until he was certain that his birds were ready and wouldn't make any mistakes. The next training session involved making small packets the size of what the bombs would be, and strapping them to the birds, and showing the birds how to release them after delivery. This appeared somewhat difficult at first, but eventually the birds caught on and they mastered the skill of delivering the packets and releasing them. Every time the birds made a cold simulation dry run Salerno would reward them with extra bird food laced with a stimulant drug. The drug seemed to make the birds hyper and gave them a high level of energy. It appeared that they liked the drug and its effects, and might have become addicted to it.

One day while Salerno was training the birds he realized that he should have a small camera attached to them and monitored from his home so that he could actually trace and monitor their course and actions when they were sent out on their deadly missions or assignments. His experience in the field of electronics gave him an advantage to make that aspect of the project possible. He eventually found the right camera in a store that he could use for his project. It was a small camera that was sometimes used for underwater filming. He bought several of these cameras and rigged them to his computer at his house. The result was a resounding success and the reception was incredible. He could see the pictures clearly for several miles away from the birds. He could see clearly what the birds were doing when they were away from him. The small bombs could be detonated remotely just as AB had showed him. Salerno was now ready to begin Operation ID and wreak havoc on the infidels. It was time for the infidels to be taught a lesson. He decided that he would unleash untold havoc on the infidels, and he would never be caught because he saw his plan as being flawless.

Leon and Salerno were once again laughing and joking with each other just like old times. Sometimes they would call each other on the phone after work and they would chat for the longest. One day while they were on their lunch break having lunch, Leon said to Salerno, "I'm thinking about joining the army in this wonderful country. Why don't you think about it man? I really want to fight for this country. There are many terrorists in the world killing innocent men, women, and children. I know that wherever they are and whoever they are they'll be caught or killed by forces of this great country. They may escape for a while, but no wrong-doer can escape the long arm of justice of this country." Salerno shook his head negatively and said, "I cannot join an army because I'm a man of peace. I'm not a warmonger."

"Wait a minute, wait a minute," responded Leon. "This country and I are all about peace. This country has never and will never attack a peaceful country, whether it is democratic or not. It is only when a country's people's rights are being trampled on and those people cry out for help that this great country gets involved." Salerno continued shaking his head negatively and said, "That's not for me. You can fight a war that does not concern you, but I will not do so."

"Man, every war concerns us where a people are taken advantage of. We must face evil head on and destroy it mercilessly," Leon said. "Let's get back to work," Salerno said as he got up out of his seat and began to walk away.

Salerno could not understand why Leon was so dedicated to the host country in spite of not being born there. Sometimes it appeared as if Leon was more dedicated to the host country than to Leon's own country of birth, which dedication Salerno thought was weird and strange. Actually, Salerno thought that he remembered hearing Leon say that he loved the host country better than he loved the country of Leon's birth. If Leon said that, Salerno thought, Leon must be a fool. In any event, he thought Leon was stupid to think the way in which he did. Salerno wondered why Leon would want to go to war for the host country and support the host country. Salerno thought about taking

Leon's life whenever Operation ID began. "If Leon happened to be in a building that was targeted in Operation ID, Leon would have to die," Salerno said to himself. "Birds of a feather flock together. No pun intended. If Leon chose to be with infidels and think like infidels, then he is an infidel, and should die in the same manner as the other infidels," Salerno whispered.

There was a post office in the host country situated on Main Street and Jackee Street. It was about one and a half mile from Salerno's house. He wanted that post office to be his first target. He noticed that many birds were usually in the general area of the post office, and this, he figured, was an advantage because his birds would not appear out of place when in the company of other birds next to the post office building. He prepared ten little compact, but extremely powerful explosive devices just as AB had trained him to do. After that he made about five visits to the post office site with his ten birds in the car with him. He then took photographs of the post office then made a sketch of the post office from the photograph. He would then sit at his kitchen table, and with his ten birds perched on the table, and the sketch of the post office and sketches of other buildings lying flat on the table, he would say to the birds, "Post office, post office, post office," and the birds would use their beaks to point out the sketch of the post office. All ten birds pointed out the sketch of the post office on every occasion. He then marked in red ten points, each point in the form of an X on or around the post office as specific locations where he wanted the birds to release the bombs. He then assigned each red X to a specific bird and asked each bird repeatedly to point out its red X. Surprisingly, after a few attempts all the birds mastered their specific task. Salerno was now ready to begin Operation ID with his flock of killer birds. There was no turning back. All the dry runs and preparations would now be put into effect. His lifelong dream of intimidating and destroying the infidels would soon become a reality.

The following morning was bright and sunny with not a cloud in the clear, blue sky. Salerno awoke earlier than usual, not being able to sleep well that night because he thought about the operation most of the night. Nevertheless, he was feeling well and anticipating what was about to happen. What was about to happen would be history making, as no one had ever employed birds to attack an enemy. He fed the ten birds while they were in his dining room, giving them sufficient stimulant laced food and water. They appeared to be happier than usual, as if they knew that this day would be an historic and unforgettable day. After they ate and drank, he gently strapped the explosive devices and small cameras to them, with the easily loosened knots that he taught them how to get loosed. He then patted them and kissed all of them on the foreheads and said, "Go to the post office and deliver these packets." He opened the door and they flew away together, all in the same direction toward the post office. Salerno rushed over to his computer to monitor their flight path. After they got to a certain height and distance they leveled off.

The flock of avian bombers arrived safely at the post office in roughly the time that Salerno figured that they would take to get there. Each bird went to the location that was assigned it. Six of the birds were on the roof and four were on the ground at each corner of the post office building. No one was around on the outside of the building. The post office had just opened and some cars were parked in the parking lot, maybe the cars of the employees and one or two customers. Salerno watched intently as each bird went to its correct position and began to loosen the knots and gently released the packet of powerful explosive that it was carrying. He smiled with contentment, because so far, everything had gone as planned. As soon as the last bird detached its explosive device and set it down, they flew back together towards Salerno's home. Salerno knew that the post office opened at 8:00 clock, so he decided that he would wait until about 8:45 a.m. to program the explosive devices to detonate. At exactly 8:45 a.m. he detonated the explosive devices, after customers had entered the post office. He watched his computer for the 'successful' indicator to show. It showed seconds after the explosions and he jumped up, clapped and laughed and danced around the room merrily.

It was a busy day at the post office. It was the Christmas season and people were sending gifts abroad and collecting gifts and parcels, and also posting cards and regular mail. Salerno sat at his television awaiting news of the destruction of the post office building and possible loss of lives and injuries. About 9:00 a.m. the soap opera that was on the channel that he was watching was interrupted, and an announcer came on and said, "Breaking news. We have just learned that the general post office on Main and Jackee Streets has been bombed. We do not know the extent of the damage, or if any lives were lost. We have a reporter on the way there, and we'll keep you informed as the details come in." The announcer continued speaking. He said that it could be a gas explosion, but no one knew because details were still sketchy. About five minutes later the announcer said, "We have a reporter at the scene of the post office where the explosion was, and I must say, the building is totally destroyed. I cannot see how anyone can survive that." Salerno could now see the pictures of the carnage. He jumped up and pumped his fist in the air and shouted, "Yes, yes, die infidels." He rewarded the birds with extra food and stimulants, and they enjoyed their meal, flapping their wings and skipping around as if they were celebrating also.

The reporter at the scene of the bombed post office was speaking. He said, "What happened here this morning appears to be the work of terrorists. There are deaths, but we are unable to say how many people died. I can see the bodies of two men and four women. One of the women in a red dress appears to be decapitated. My God, what a scene." The reporter, an older man, walked to the Western side of the building, and as he got there he said, "Oh my God, there's a child and a woman who may be his mother and they are bloodied all over." The reporter's voice began to crack as tears streamed down his pale and gaunt face. The camera man turned the camera away from the reporter's face and the anchor at the television station began to speak. "Who would do something like this?" he asked. "It is very disturbing to see innocent men, women and especially innocent children slaughtered." As he spoke one could see the police, paramedics and firemen in the background at the scene. The area was cordoned off to prevent curious onlookers from getting in the way of the investigators and first responders. However, that did not prevent curious onlookers and busy bodies from gathering outside the cordoned area. Some of the onlookers were crying and others were talking about how sad it was to see so much damage. The onlookers could see at least two bodies on that side of the building.

An Afro-American man in his sixties stood outside the cordoned area talking to whoever would listen to him. He was saying, "Oh Lord, I just left from there, not five minutes before I heard a very loud boom. I could have been one of those dead. God is good." A policeman who was nearby heard the Afro-American man and took him aside and got the man's name, address and phone number, and told the man that the police would be contacting him for a statement. "No problem. I would be more than happy to assist the police in catching those murderous bastards that are responsible." A young man standing beside the same Afro-American man asked, "Did you notice anything suspicious while you were inside the post office?" The Afro-American man replied, "No, nothing at all. I didn't even see anything suspicious on the outside of the building. It's like it dropped from out of the sky." Salerno laughed when the Afro-American said that, because he knew that in a sense, the Afro-American man was correct.

The investigation of the destruction of the post office revealed that a bomb or bombs destroyed the said building, but the source of the bomb or bombs was unknown. An estimate of at least thirty six people had lost their lives in the bombing, and of that number, twenty six were men, eight women and two children. Later that day the chief of Police, the Mayor and the Governor appeared on television. They expressed their sympathy to the families of the deceased, and vowed to do what was in their power to catch those responsible for the bombing and loss of life. An hour later the Leader of the country appeared on television and gave sympathies from him and his family and his government. He said, "We will hunt down the killer or killers responsible for this dastardly act until we find him or them. No stone will be left uncovered. Those who commit crimes like these are spineless, degenerates. They are worst than cowards. To call them cowards would be bestowing honor on them that they do not deserve." Salerno smiled sarcastically as he listened to the Leader of the Country, and said softly, "They will never catch me."

The first assignment was completed, and Salerno could not believe that he had succeeded in executing the first act of Operation ID without a hitch. His opinion was that it was better than successful, and he could not wait to return to work to hear what Leon and the others would say although he would not be going to work until the following day. All the news channels were dealing with the bombing of the post office and the lives that were lost in that bombing. Experts on terrorism and explosives were on television being interviewed and giving their opinions. In at least one case, one expert was contradicting the other expert. For example, one expert said that it was most likely a suicide bomber who walked into the post office with a bomb or bombs strapped to him or her. Another expert said that it was possible that either the bomb was mailed to the post office or someone was trying to mail it from the post office and it detonated prematurely. Salerno laughed at them because he knew that they did not know what they were saying. He called them stupid infidels. While he was watching the news Josef called him and asked him, "Are you following the news?" and Salerno told him that he was following the news. Josef said, "Man that was something. It was cool." Salerno responded, "Be careful what you're saying. You don't know if your phone is bugged or tapped. Remember I used to leave notes at your door for the same reason. I will see you in person and we can talk about it." Josef remembered what Salerno had said when he was receiving notes from Salerno.

Everyone in the office was talking about the bombing of the post office when Salerno returned to work. One of the female employees said, "Those who did that are worst than dogs. They killed those two innocent children. What wrong could the children have done to them?" Salerno tried not to comment, and would not have commented if an elderly female employee did not ask him, "Salerno, what is your opinion on the bombing?" He shook his head as in disbelief and said, "It's so sad." At lunch time he and Leon sat together at the lunch table. Leon was evidently upset and distraught. Leon told Salerno that he, Leon, could not eat or sleep after he watched the slaughter of innocent people at the post office bombing. He said that when he heard of the two children who were murdered, he broke down. He went on to say, "Man, whoever did that should be tortured to death. Prison and the electric chair are too good for that monster or those monsters. I know this country, he, or they, if caught, will be given a fair trial. I know that if the bombing were in your country and the killers were caught the killers would be stoned or beheaded without a trial. I told you that this country is the best country in the world." Salerno wanted to become angry, but he knew that that would not be a good thing to do in the circumstances. He said, "Man, it's sad." Leon held his head down as tears fell from his eyes and he said, sobbing, "I know that I'm too old to join the army in this country, but I want to. This is the kind of violence and terrorism I spoke to you about. Can you imagine that those who did this are living in this country among us? Sometimes I think that this country is too democratic."

"Well, I hope that the police find some clues," Salerno said. Leon looked at Salerno and said, "Believe me, the killers will be found. I will bet you now, right here, investigators will find the killers. This country has the best investigators in the whole world."

Some of the investigators believed that the post office bombing was an isolated case. They doubted that there would be any more bombings, although they made it clear that everyone must remain vigilant. A federal reward, the equivalent of a quarter of a million dollars, was made for information leading to the arrest and conviction of those responsible for the bombing. It was felt that this huge reward would assist in flushing out the terrorists. Many tips came in but none panned out. Some of the tips were obviously false tips made by those who wanted to get their hands on the quarter of a million dollars, but instead of helping the investigation, their false tips were hurting the investigation and setting it back.

It was now two months since the bombing of the post office and the killing of people inside. Lives were returning to normal and there was a feeling that what happened was a one-time event by someone who probably held a grudge against another individual and thought that Christmas time was the best time for settling the score. It was thought that maybe the bomb was mailed in a Christmas gift packet or package. The conversation of the murders was now waning, although occasionally the deaths, especially of the two little children, would be mentioned in conversations. It was mentioned that one of the children was handicapped and was in a wheelchair at the time of the bombing. That child would not have stood a chance in any event. Occasionally Salerno and Leon would discuss the bombing, although almost invariably it was Leon who brought it up. On the last occasion Leon said to Salerno, "this country is too accommodating and lenient to non citizens. The more good it does for some migrants the more harm and evil some migrants do to it." Although Salerno disagreed with Leon, he did not tell Leon that he disagreed with him. A day after the bombing Salerno met with Josef, who had more or less stopped talking about the bombing to strangers. Josef was happy to see Salerno and Salerno was happy to see him. Josef now being alone with Salerno was free to express his mind on the bombing. He said to Salerno, "If I could meet the bombers I would congratulate them personally and let them know just how proud I am of them. Wouldn't you do that Salerno?" Salerno, while trying to keep a straight face said, "You know where I stand. If I could meet the bombers I would have a party for them, because they are my heroes." It was obvious that Josef had absolutely no idea that Salerno was the bomber, and Salerno wanted to keep it that way.

Approximately three months after the bombing of the post office the Chief of Police held a news conference to up-date the country on how the investigation was proceeding. He proceeded to the podium with a note pad in his hand, accompanied by one of his senior officers. Reporters were present and their cameras were flashing continuously even prior to his getting to the podium. As he got to the podium he placed the note pad on top of the podium, looked at those present and said," Good day everyone. It has been almost three months since the bombing of the post office on Main Street and Jackee Street by terrorists. I will now up-date you on how the investigation by the police is progressing. The Federal Investigations Department (FID) has also conducted its own independent investigation. Our investigation revealed the following: that the post office was bombed, and although we do not have definitive evidence, we believe that it is more likely than not that a bomb was mailed through another post office as a Christmas gift to someone, and it went through the post office on Main Street to be collected by an unsuspecting customer, and before it was collected it exploded. We cannot say who sent the bomb, where it came from or who was to collect it, but we believe that is what happened. We cannot do this partly because of the magnitude of the explosion which seemed to destroy all the components of the bomb. It was a very huge explosion. As I said, all the evidence has been destroyed either directly by the bomb or secondarily by the fire that resulted from the explosion. The investigation is still on-going, and I remind the general public that there is a reward of a quarter million dollars. If anyone out there knows anything about this crime please call the Crime Prevention hot line at this number. He recited a certain number to call. I will now take a few questions."

Reporters were shouting to be the first to get their questions to the Chief of Police, and he acknowledged a female reporter in a black low neck blouse and short green skirt who was standing at the front of the line in front of the other reporters. As she held the microphone very close to her mouth she said, "My name is Trudy McLock and I'm with WTAM Television. Can you say if the terrorists are from out of state?" The Chief of Police appeared a little puzzled as if he knew that that question would be asked. He knew that he could not answer it definitively but he decided that he would try his best. "Well, ah, ah, it is a sensible conclusion based on what little evidence we have. We know that the bomb exploded inside the post office, and the lone witness who survived, an older Afro-American man, said that he saw nothing inside or outside the post office just prior to the bomb igniting that looked suspicious." The same lady shouted, "Follow up, I have a follow up please." The Chief of Police did not want to deal with anything relating to that question any further, so he pointed to the male reporter just to her right. That reporter was a bald head man in a light brown formal suit with matching necktie and shoes. Before the male reporter could ask his question the same lady reporter who asked the first question shouted, "How do you know that the bomb was not in the post to be mailed from this post office at Main Street and Jackee Street?" the Chief of Police mumbled "You're very persistent," and refused to answer that question. He said, "Yes, the gentleman in the brown suit at the front."

The gentleman in the brown suit stated which news station he worked with then he asked: "How do you know that the bomb did not originate here and intended to be mailed from the Main Street and Jackee Street post office?" The chief of Police knew that he should answer that question, but he also knew that he really did not know the answer. It was essentially the same question that the first reporter had asked and he had refused to answer. He thought for a few seconds and said, "As I said, we believe from the evidence of a witness who had just left the building and was still on the premises when the bomb exploded, that it is most likely that no one inside the post office took the bomb there." Another reporter asked, "What are the chances of similar acts occurring in the future?" The Chief of Police went on to say, "Well, no one can predict what terrorists would do or would not do, or what they are thinking, but if I were to make an intelligent guess, I would say that it is unlikely to happen again. It appears that the bomb was for a particular person at a particular time." Other reporters were shouting out questions to the Chief of Police but he said that it was the end of the questioning because he had to return to resuming the investigation. He hurried off glad to get away from the reporters.

Salerno sat quietly at his television listening to the Chief of Police and the reporters as the reporters asked questions and the chief tried to answer the questions. He was glad that the Chief of Police decided to hold the news conference on a Saturday and tried to answer the questions, because he, Salerno, would be home from work and could watch and listen. Salerno believed that the Chief of Police had been totally fooled by him. It is further proof, Salerno thought, of how foolish the infidels are. Salerno further convinced himself that he could do a lot of damage to the infidels and never be caught. "I'm a genius," he said aloud. The next few weeks Salerno drove around with his killer crew of birds and took photographs of various buildings, and he eventually made sketches of those buildings, and put the names of the buildings on each sketch. He also visited the vicinity of a military base, which stimulated his curiosity. He could not get as close to the military base as he would have liked to or as close to it as he got to the other buildings, but nevertheless, he photographed it and subsequently made a sketch of it. The sketch was not as perfect as the sketches of other buildings, but it was sufficient for his killer birds, which appeared to be getting more and more intelligent and efficient. As he drove by the military base he kept saying to the birds, "Military base, military base, military base," and the birds seemed to bob their heads as if to say, 'we understand.'

A nocturnal attack would be a novel approach indeed, Salerno thought, as he considered the real probability of such an attack. He had the cameras with infra red capability, although he had never used them at night. He figured that an attack by night could really take the soldiers at the military base by surprise and leave them confused as to how they were attacked and who attacked them. He figured that at night only a handful of soldiers would be on guard, and that they would never notice the little birds. Even if the soldiers noticed the birds the soldiers would not think anything suspicious about them. This attack is a good idea, he thought to himself. In order to prepare for the attack Salerno made some practice runs by the military base at night while he said repeatedly, "Military base, military base, military base." He would return to his house with the birds and send them to the military base as a practice run, while watching them from his home on his computer. He was jubilant to see that they went straight to buildings on the base, off loaded the dummy bombs and returned home safely. He now felt ready for the second assignment of Operation ID. He decided to make the bombs twice as powerful as the bombs that destroyed the post office on Main Street because he wanted to be certain that he killed as many soldiers as possible, because it was these soldiers that the infidels used to kill and maim his people. This attack would be especially humiliating and shameful for the infidels because it would strike at the heart of their source of power and strength, and it would be on their own turf.

The bombs were prepared and attached to the birds very carefully. The infra red cameras were turned on and also attached to them. Salerno gave them some food with the unlawful stimulant, and they skipped around in glee as they demonstrated excessive energy. Whatever he gave them apparently gave them a kind of high that they experienced only when they ate it. He then kissed each bird on its forehead and said, "Military base, military base, military base," and opened the door as he watched them fly away in the direction of the military base. Each bird had its instructions where to place its bomb by watching the red X on the sketch. After about forty nine minutes of flying the birds landed on the base. Salerno watched that from his computer although it was not as clear as when they flew during the daytime. He could see them releasing the bombs in the exact locations that he had instructed them to be released. One of the birds apparently had some difficulty releasing its bomb, and as soon as one of the other birds noticed that that bird was having difficulty releasing its bomb, two of the other birds rushed to its aid and assisted in the release of the bomb that was attached to the bird. After the last bomb was released all ten birds flew off together for the return journey. Salerno was happy that the transport and deposit of the bombs were successful and went unnoticed.

The second assignment was well on its way, and Salerno had only to complete it from his home by putting in the password to detonate all the bombs. He wondered if he should embark on the detonation at night or early the following morning. His decision was that he would do it at night as more damage could be inflicted because at night most of the soldiers would be indoors either sleeping or doing chores. In the morning they would be in the yard on drills or exercising, and most of them would escape the blasts from the bombs. He decided that he would detonate the bombs at midnight. He sat at his computer and played some games to kill time until it was time to detonate the bombs. At 12 midnight sharp, Salerno put in the password in the computer to detonate the powerful bombs. This password was tantamount to pulling a switch or pushing a button. If the detonation was successful the computer would show the word 'successful' or 'success', on the monitor or screen. Almost instantly after he entered the password, the word 'successful' appeared on the computer screen. Although Salerno knew that the bombing was successful, nevertheless, he was not satisfied until he saw the news and heard the reporter speaking about the bombing. He thought that that was something that he had to improve on so that he could see what was happening at the scene of the target once his birds dropped the bombs and departed. Maybe at a later day he would have one of the birds drop off a camera in a strategic location of a target to fulfill that goal. It was something that he could not do too often because he would have to purchase too many cameras, and the stores may become suspicious if he purchased many of these types of cameras. He sat at his television playing games while he waited until the news reported the bombing, which he figured would not be too long.

At 12:15 a.m. a reporter appeared on the television and said, "It appears that there has just been a massive bombing in the vicinity of the military base on Military Road. Because of the reported massive extent of the bombing and because it was done at night when all or most of the soldiers would be indoors, it is expected that there will be many, many casualties." Cameramen and reporters were on the scene from about 12:27 a.m. wandering about trying to find out what happened. The bombed buildings were shown on television. Six buildings were totally destroyed, two other buildings had only two walls standing, and another two had its four walls standing but everything in the interior of the last four buildings was blown flat. As a matter of fact, the interior of all ten buildings was destroyed. Smoke and dust were seen still rising from the ten destroyed buildings with no signs of life evident in them. It was obvious that if people were in those ten buildings all of them had died. Soldiers from the remaining buildings began to gather around the destroyed buildings as if to protect them, when there was nothing left to protect. They had guns and other weaponry drawn and ready to fire in the event they were instructed to do so if the occasion arose for them to do so. They were told to be on the alert as there might have still been an imminent attack from the terrorists who had just blown up the ten buildings.

Huge flood lights lit the compound. There was total pandemonium on the base as soldiers were running to and fro and shouting commands and orders, and 'Yes sir' responses were heard. Some soldiers were stationed at the perimeter of the compound with orders to shoot anyone who looked suspicious. Sirens were blaring and fire engines and ambulances were rushing to the base to assist in whichever way they could. The whole scene appeared chaotic and disorganized. Salerno clapped, giggled and jumped up as he saw the damaged buildings and the confused and frightened soldiers. Some of the soldiers appeared to be very young and obviously had not experienced anything like that before. Reporters' voices cracked as they reported details of the destruction. One reporter said, "Words cannot describe the extent of the damage inflicted on us by two legged animals who call themselves human beings. If they are human beings, I am not a human being." Another reporter who stood as if in a daze said, "I'll just allow the camera to convey what happened. It can say much more than I can at the moment." On saying that, the camera man allowed the camera to move slowly around the morbid scene as the reporter wiped tears from his eyes and stooped to the ground with his knees bent.

Salerno felt that he struck at the heart of what the infidels stood for, because their so-called great defense which they always described as the best in the world had been not only penetrated but penetrated by one individual using birds to do so. If the soldiers could not defend themselves, how in the world, he figured, could they defend their country or anyone else? What he did, he thought, was an incredible feat. As far as he was concerned, he was better than the best army in the world.

A reporter had managed to contact the commander of the base and speak to him. The commander looked somewhat disheveled, maybe from just awaking and getting out of bed. The look in the commander's eyes was a look of fright and nervousness. The reporter said to him, "Commander, I know that this is an extremely difficult and troubling time for you, but do you have any opinion as to what transpired tonight?" The commander scratched his head and looked straight into the camera as he replied, "This is indeed a very sad day for us. It is very early for us to come to any kind of opinion, but I will assure you that whoever is responsible for this cowardly act will either be neutralized or brought to justice." The reporter attempted to ask another question but the commander thanked him and walked away. The reporter followed him still asking questions, but the commander refused to answer further questions. Finally, the reporter ceased from following him, and the commander walked toward one of the destroyed barracks.

Firefighters were sifting through the rubble trying to see if there were any signs of life, but there were none. Paramedics were moving around waiting for the injured, but there were none. All the soldiers from the ten barracks were dead. Another reporter followed the commander and asked him, "Who are you and what is your rank?" The commander turned around, and seeing that it was another reporter, said, "I'm the commander on this base." The reporter expressed his sympathy then asked the commander, "Sir, about how many soldiers occupied each of those ten barracks that were destroyed?" The commander was hesitant, as if he did not want to divulge that information, or at least as if he did not want to divulge it at the time to the reporter. Nevertheless, he decided to answer. "There were twenty five soldiers in each barrack," he replied. The reporter followed with the following question, "So you might have lost a total of about two hundred and fifty soldiers?"

"Well, we cannot say with any certainty how many men and women we might have lost, because some might have been visiting other barracks on the compound, or some from other barracks might have been visiting those soldiers on the destroyed barracks, or some soldiers might have been off base. I can't tell you momentarily."

"Do you have any idea how this might have happened?" The reporter asked the commander.

"No. investigations will have to be conducted properly before we can come to any conclusion," the commander replied.

Local and Federal investigators were on the scene with military investigators as all appeared to be working together to ascertain what had happened and who was responsible if anyone. Body bags were being carried with what remained of the dead soldiers, while those soldiers standing by were weeping for their fallen brothers and sisters. Some vowed to get revenge no matter what it cost or how long it took. As the body bags passed the soldiers the soldiers would stand at attention and salute. The whole scene was solemn and heart-wrenching. The investigators noticed that there were radar and surveillance cameras systems installed on and around the base, and they thought that valuable clues may be obtained from at least one of these systems. Three guards were at work that night in addition to the guards who manned the gate, the radar and surveillance systems. The guards stated that they did not see or hear anything out of the ordinary. They went on to say that no unauthorized individuals entered the base at any time. Had that happened, they agreed that they would have known. Some wondered if maybe one or more of the soldiers had brought bombs onto the compound with the intention of taking his or their lives and the lives of other soldiers. An investigation was conducted into this suggestion by examining the lives of all the dead and living soldiers, but nothing materialized from the investigation.

The total number of soldiers dead was two hundred and fifty. Their parents, families and friends took solace in the fact that they were asleep when the bombs exploded, and they most likely never knew what hit them. They died in their sleep. They figured that even if they were alive, their deaths were swift and quick, and therefore painless. A soldier who occupied one of the undestroyed barracks thought that the bombs could have been fired from drones flying overhead at the time. That, he said, could have explained why the soldiers on guard neither heard nor saw anything. If that were the case, opined another soldier, the radar system of the surveillance cameras might have detected the drones, but nothing was detected. The drone theory was therefore debunked or scrapped.

Funerals for the deceased were held in a cemetery for soldiers only, months after their deaths. Men, women and children cried openly. At one of the funerals a brother and sister who were soldiers and who were killed at the base, were buried simultaneously. The sister was twenty one years old and the brother was twenty three years old. The preacher conducting the funeral service said in his summon, "Only the Lord knows why these two innocent souls' lives were taken at such young ages. We must pray that those who committed this ghastly, cowardly act will be caught and punished." The sentiments of almost all of the mourners were that the murderers would not be caught, thus preventing justice from being done. The parents of the siblings were sitting stoically in the front bench closest to the caskets.

The deceased were their only children. The mother was holding a handkerchief in one hand and leaning on the shoulder of her husband, while he put one arm around her to comfort her. She whispered, "Why Lord? They were my only children."

The reward money increased to five million dollars. Everyone knew that the huge unprecedented increase was only because the most recent bombing was that of a military base, and because more people had died than in the post office bombing. The families of the deceased soldiers were happy that the reward money had been increased to that level as it could assist in flushing out the terrorists. The governor of the state vowed that justice would prevail and that the long arm of the law would reach out to wherever the terrorists were hiding and would bring them to justice. His words and the huge increase in the reward money gave the doubters hope that justice would be done and optimism that the terrorists would be caught and ultimately punished. The country's flag was flying at half staff in respect of the fallen soldiers. Everywhere one went one could hear conversations about the murdered soldiers. Many people blamed the army for not being alert enough to prevent such incidents from occurring. They said that the hierarchy in command on the base should either be court-martialed or tried in public in a civilian court of law. Those in command, in their defense, stated that they had adequate surveillance equipment, and that they could do no more to prevent what had happened from happening. They reminded the public that no one knew what really happened, and that the public should wait until the investigators did their work and completed the investigations before jumping to conclusions. They expressed their condolences to the families of the dead soldiers.

Meanwhile the army increased surveillance of that base and all other bases around the country. They were bent on ensuring that no similar acts or occurrences of terrorism would occur on the base. They were anxious to find out who and what had caused the loss of two hundred and fifty lives and the destruction of ten barracks. All the soldiers who survived were interviewed by all the investigative branches, as it was not ruled out that one or more of them could have been responsible for the explosive devices. Two of the live soldiers became persons of interest in the investigations because they had just returned to base about fifteen minutes prior to the bombing, and they were drunk. It was believed that they could have brought the bombs on the base either knowingly or unknowingly. The problem with that scenario is that at least two guards working on the night of the bombing, and another soldier who lived in the same barracks with the two suspects, saw when they entered their rooms and turned their lights on and off again. The soldier who witnessed this said that he was awake for a long time after the two soldiers entered their room and he did not see them leave their room again, nor heard their door opened or closed.

The investigators were now back where they started, with no clues and no suspects. Just like in the bombing of the post office, no evidence that could assist in determining what type of explosive used in the bombing was found. Some of the investigators thought that incredibly, all the components of the explosives might have melted or might have been blown up into extremely small indistinguishable pieces too small to be detected. The investigators wondered also if the components of the explosive devices were of plastic which melted quickly, or some other material which melted or burned very quickly. If that were correct, it would be something that they never experienced before. The investigation was becoming a daunting and unbelievable task. The radar and surveillance cameras footage was examined very carefully as the examiners went over and over them, but nothing that could assist them was seen or heard on the footage. The only reasonable conclusion was that one or more soldiers either knowingly or unknowingly brought the explosive devices on to the base and either deliberately set them off or the devices were timed to go off at the same time, or they were detonated remotely. That was the conclusion of all the investigative bodies that met and agreed that the Federal Investigation Department would deliver the findings.

However, there was a problem with that conclusion, because it meant that ten individuals each from different barracks had to take explosive devices into his barrack, and there was no evidence that ten soldiers had left the base or returned to the base.

The investigators made suggestions as how to prevent future attacks on the military bases, for example, they suggested that soldiers leaving and especially entering the bases be thoroughly searched, and that x-ray machines should be installed at the gates. They said also that better surveillance equipment should be installed with better and more lighting on and around the bases. The soldiers hearing that one or more of their own might have caused such devastation and loss of innocent lives were disheartened and sad. However, they got some comfort from the fact that the explosive devices could have been brought onto the base unknowingly. They believed that the findings of the investigators were wrong but they had no other reasonable explanation as to what occurred, so they reluctantly accepted the findings. Those live soldiers realized that they could have been one of the dead soldiers, and that if things did not change they might very well still be killed in similar fashion. The thought of that was frightening. The following week about half a dozen soldiers opted not to be soldiers any longer, because they feared that their lives were at risk, and no one knew what had happened and who was responsible. Bases around the country saw similar responses by soldiers. The army promised that it would do all that could be done to ensure the safety of soldiers on its bases. That assurance did not stem the flow of soldiers opting to leave the army. They felt that the bombing of the military base at Military Road was an act of terrorism, and that there was no protection, or insufficient protection for them as soldiers. Many of them decided that they would not risk their lives because they had families to provide for.

Leon was very angry over the fact that terrorists were bold and brazen enough to attack a military base in the host country. This strengthened his belief that the host country was too relaxed and lenient in deciding who they allowed in the country. He figured that there should be a limit, strictly adhered to, as to who should be allowed into the host country from countries known to harbor or accommodate or entertain terrorists, and furthermore, persons from those countries should be properly screened and searched prior to entering the host country. He believed also that all telephone calls, emails, faxes etc. should be secretly tapped into and screened by the host country with the stipulation that matters that were discussed that had nothing to do with security could not be used by the Department for Security. The host country should be allowed to do this to any and everyone, including diplomats, in the interest of national security. A country's security and the security of its people, are paramount to all other interests. Leon always said that he had no problems with his phones etc. being tapped because he knew the real reason for that being done was for the safety of all living in the country. He believed that those who had a problem with it had something to fear. If doing that would save a life then it was worth it and was justified.

One day Salerno and Leon were discussing the bombing of the soldiers' barracks at the military base. Leon told Salerno that the host country was too kind towards non-citizens. Salerno responded, "Man, you are not a citizen. You must be careful what you say, because right now you are attacking yourself." Leon hardly waited for Salerno to finished answering. He said to Salerno, "Yes, you are correct when you say that I am not a citizen, and I am aware of what I am saying. Many of these damn foreigners do not mean the host country any good. They are taking the host country's kindness for weakness. When the killer dogs are found I would pull the switch on the executioner's chair if I'm allowed to do it." Salerno responded, "Man, you got a lot of hate in your heart and this isn't even your country." Leon replied, "You don't understand. They are murdering innocent people and doing it in a country that reaches out to assist them and their families, so to say that I am angry is an understatement. Let me tell you something Salerno, even if you were the murderer or one of the murderers, I would kill you if I had the chance, because acts like the acts on the post office and the military base are done by cowards parading as men."

Salerno jerked his head up when he heard Leon say that he would kill him. His head was hanging down as he faced the ground as Leon spoke. Salerno's eyes opened wide as he said, "Leon, would you really kill me?" Leon told him that as it stood he, Salerno, had nothing to fear because he is not the terrorist, but that he swore by his God if Salerno was the terrorist or one of the terrorists, he would kill him, and that he meant that. Salerno trembled inside as he thought, 'If Leon only knew that I, Salerno, is in fact the terrorist.' Leon continued, "Man, you do not know how upset I am. People who would do something like that have no gratitude. Is this country perfect? No, but its imperfections are far better than the perfections of the countries of the murderous dogs." Their conversation ended here. Salerno could not stop thinking about that conversation with Leon, and what Leon said about killing him if he were the terrorist. Salerno figured that the infidels had brainwashed Leon into adopting their fallacious ideologies. At times he thought about trying to convert Leon to his beliefs, but he thought against it, because he thought that Leon was too steeped and set in his ways and the ways of the infidels. He wondered how Leon could say that the imperfections of the infidels are better than the perfections of his, Salerno's people. Salerno thought that Leon was presumptuous and was deliberately trying to anger him. However, he decided that whenever he was around Leon he would remain calm so that Leon's or any other's suspicion would be aroused as to who he, Salerno, really is. If they ever found out, Salerno would say that he is a freedom fighter and not a terrorist. It did not matter what Leon said or did, Salerno decided that he would not allow Leon to get under his skin, because Leon lived among infidels, and as the saying goes, birds of a feather flock together. If Leon walked like an infidel, looked like an infidel and talked like an infidel, Leon must be an infidel.

A government directive was sent out that all government buildings should have enhanced security in and around them. Surveillance cameras were installed on all of them with extra lighting added. Also security guards were placed at all the said buildings. Buildings that had guards already received extra guards. The government wanted to be certain that the security would be impenetrable. They wanted to send a message to the terrorists that they can and would be stopped, no matter what the costs. The investigators reluctantly agreed that there had been a serious breach of security at the military base and the post office, which resulted in the loss of many lives. Had the security officers at the gate of the military base been as vigilant as they should, the deaths of the soldiers and the destruction of the barracks could have been prevented. The bombing was totally avoidable, the investigators concluded in their final report.

As usual, after a bombing in the host country, so-called experts in the area of explosives and terrorism got on the media and gave their opinions and answered questions. On one particular day after the bombing of the military base, there were two experts on one of the television programs. They were expressing their opinions on the bombing of the post office and the bombing of the military base. One of the experts was an elderly female who had apparently already gone into retirement, and the other expert was a fairly young gentleman about thirty six years old. Salerno watched them to see how they would make fools of themselves and contradict each other as they invariably did. He was angry that a woman was on television speaking about men's affairs. He thought that she should have been at home looking after her grand children and cooking and cleaning the house. He wondered why the infidels allowed women to get out of control and perform men's jobs. Something like that could never occur in his country. In his country, women know their place in society, and if they did not, the men would teach them, sometimes in unkind ways.

The two experts were asked their opinions on what caused the bombings and who they thought were responsible. The young male expert was closer to the reporter in proximity than the older lady, so the young male expert began to answer the question first. He rubbed his hands together and began to smile as if involuntarily as he stared at the television host, and said:

"It is obvious that the post office bombing was done through the mail. By saying through the mail I mean either it was sent from another post office to pass through the post office on Main Street and Jackee Street, or it was about to be sent from the post office at Main Street and Jackee Street to another post office. I think that that is indisputable, and we all would agree to that. We must remember that there was an Afro-American man who was a witness at the post office on the day of the bombing, and he said that he did not see anything suspicious. The bombing of the soldiers' barracks at the military base was done by one or more soldiers of those barracks taking bombs onto the compound either wittingly or unwittingly. That is the only way in which that could have happened. All other probabilities were ruled out. I agree with the final findings of the investigators." The host asked him how he could be so certain about his answer and he said, "I am certain because those are the only reasonable and logical explanations of what might have occurred." The host then asked him, and "Who do you think is responsible for the bombings? Do you think the same person or persons are responsible for both bombings?"

"Well, that is a little more complicated to answer, but still the answer is fairly easy," the young expert answered. He continued, "I think that both bombings are not connected. The first bomb, that is, the bombing of the post office on Main Street and Jackee Street was more likely than not sent to an individual by an individual. It was personal. It was Christmas time and it was sent through the mail. It is only by chance that it did not reach its true destination. The second bombing was directed at the security forces, which was to send a clear message that this country is not as safe as we think it is."

The host wanted to hear what the lady had to say on the topic, so he said to her, "What is your opinion on this?" She smiled and shook her head from side to side as if to say I don't totally agree with the gentleman, then she confidently answered, "In respect of the post office bombing, there is absolutely no evidence that the bomb passed or was about to pass through the mail. It appears more likely than not that that is what happened, but that is not definitive." The host then asked her, "Well, do you have another explanation?"

"No, I don't, but I do not want us to tie ourselves down to explanations for which we have no proof. For all I know, the bombs could have fallen from the sky." The host and the other expert laughed aloud at that remark. The host then said, "Are you serious?"

"Yes I'm serious," she replied. "Who can say that a drone did not drop it on the post office?" she continued. The host and the other expert laughed again. They found what she said amusing. She continued with her answers and said, "As it pertains to the bombing of the military base, again, there is no evidence that those bombs were taken onto the military base by any of the soldiers, and because we do not know that, it would be an injustice to malign the soldiers' good names to such cowardly acts. Those brave men and women fought or were willing to fight for our country. I'm saying again, we cannot say that those bombs did not fall from the sky from a drone or drones." The other expert and the host laughed loudly again. The host then said, "Do you agree that your explanation is out of left field?" The female expert stood her ground and replied, "We must be careful in arriving at assumptions that are unsupported by evidence. That's all I'm saying."

Salerno was watching that program and was surprised that the female expert's answers were more on point than the male expert's answers. He still felt that a female should never be on television in the manner in which she was. Maybe if she were cleaning the offices in the television station she could get away with that, but not sitting next to a man and answering important questions. He knew that Leon would think that nothing was wrong with that, but it was another example of how the infidels got everything wrong by not letting a woman know her place and not putting a woman in her place. He figured that he understand why women in the world of the infidels were allowed to get into male topics; it was because it appeared that the female infidels were smarter than the male infidels. A caller called in and asked the young expert, "How can you say that is how the bombing of the post office on Main Street and Jackee Street occurred, when there is no evidence that it occurred in that manner?" The young male expert replied, "How can you say that it did not happen in that manner? There is no evidence that it did not." The host then told the lady expert that she did not say who she thought was responsible for the bombing. She said, very diplomatically, "It is difficult to say who is responsible. Somehow I think that both bombings are connected. No evidence of the ingredients or materials used by the terrorists was found in any of the bombings, and both bombings were mysteriously executed. Unlike my friend here, I think that both bombings are connected and were committed by the same individual or individuals." Salerno could not believe that a woman was so intelligent, and more so than her male counterpart. He thought that if the male infidels did not stop women from getting involved in men's affairs one day a woman would rule the host country, and that would be the biggest insult and shame on the male infidels and their country. One day when he and Leon were in conversation he wanted to tell Leon that, but he figured that Leon would have said that a woman leading the host country would be a good thing, because the men already messed the country up, and a woman could not do any worst. He knew Leon very well.

As the two experts gave their opinions on the bombings of the post office on Main Street and the military base, some officers from law enforcement watched and listened to them. Some of the officers agreed with the young gentleman and some agreed with the older lady. One of the officers said that he did not know whom he should believe, and that either of the experts might be correct. Another enforcement officer said that he was a staunch believer in UFOs and that it was possible that aliens came from another planet or from outer space and bombed the post office and the military base. An officer who heard him remarked, "Ron, come on, you know better. There are no aliens out there." The first officer known as Ron said, "How do you know that?" Their conversation was interrupted by a call that came in about a domestic disturbance between a man and his wife, and one of the officers had to respond to the call by going to the scene.

It was obvious that even the police were confused and uncertain about the bombings. If law enforcement were confused, then it could be expected that the general public would be confused. As far as the public was concerned, law enforcement did nothing and was doing nothing to allay those fears and worries. So far, there were no persons of interests or suspects in either of the bombings, and it was looking as if there would be none in the near future. Local communities formed crime watch and vigilante groups that were bent on taking the law in their hands if they caught the person or persons that were responsible for the bombings. Those groups vowed to exact their own justice on those responsible for the bombings. When the police heard about the vigilante groups they were not happy, because they knew that innocent people could be hurt and even killed if the vigilante groups suspected and accosted the wrong person or persons, and that the vigilante groups would be attempting to do the police's job. The Chief of Police took to the airwaves and tried to discourage the vigilante groups from taking the law in their own hands. He said that if they did so, and something went wrong, the groups would be held accountable and could be prosecuted and sued in a civil court of law. He said that if anyone had any information, or anyone they thought was a suspect, they should pass that information on to the police who are trained to deal with these types of maters.

No one had a clue as to who was responsible for the bombings. The birds were never mentioned as being close to any of the bombings. No one had suspected that there was only one person responsible for the bombings. He, Salerno, was proud to know that he was a lone wolf in the land of the infidels, inflicting severe damage and harm to them and their properties. He always said that if he ever did anything unlawful he would do it by himself, because anytime someone is involved in a crime with another individual, there is a chance that the other person might tell someone else about the crime. He used to say 'friend got friend'. He figured that the two or more perpetrators may have an argument and one might reveal the secret, or one might tell a best friend or his fiancée and that friend or fiancée might tell someone. That was one of the main reasons why he did not want a girlfriend, because he did not trust women. The only woman that he had some trust in was his mother, and sometimes he wondered if he could trust her. Josef was his only friend in the host country, and Salerno did not reveal his secrets to him. Although Salerno made Leon believe that he, Leon, was his friend, Salerno knew that Leon was not a real friend of his. Josef knew nothing about Operation ID and that meant that Salerno did not have to worry about Operation ID being exposed. Salerno could not afford his operation being exposed because he wanted to kill or maim a few more hundreds or thousands infidels, and destroy their infrastructure, buildings and businesses. He was beginning to realize that the project was easier and simpler than he first thought. The hardest part was the training of the birds, and an infidel, Jane, assisted him in doing that. He thought that infidels were so stupid, and did not realize when they are assisting in their own destruction. They always made it easier for someone to attack them, and many times they assist their enemies.

On Salerno's job it was time to name the employee of the year and everyone hoped that he or she would be that person chosen, because this title brought prestige and added income as an incentive for other employees. All the employees were gathered in the meeting room sitting in a semi-circle chatting and laughing. The air was thick with suspense as everyone waited to see who would be chosen as the employee of the year. The supervisor entered the room and greeted everyone as he took up his position at the front of the room. He stood at the podium and began to speak about work ethics and the commitment employees must have to their employment and employers. He spoke about being at work on time and performing at maximum capacity selflessly. After saying all that he said, "Some of you have really worked hard and tirelessly in this great company, putting the company above your own desires and interests. However, there is one employee who performed exceptionally well in every area, and who is of an exemplary character. It gives me great pleasure to announce the employee of the year. He is none other than Salerno. Let's give Salerno a round of applause."

Everyone started clapping as Salerno stood smiling and waving to everyone in the room. When Salerno arrived at the front of the room, the supervisor said, "Salerno, you will be well known in life. Your name will forever be engraved and etched in the history of this great country. Your contribution will always be remembered and mentioned on people's lips." He then invited Salerno to say a few words. Salerno was smiling as he held the plaque above his head waving it from side to side. He approached the microphone and said, "Thanks, thanks, thanks very much. Only in this beautiful country can someone like me achieve something like this. Anyone can succeed in this great country provided a person is honest and hardworking. Thanks again." Everyone clapped and hugged Salerno, and commended him on his achievement of the employee of the year award. He never knew that his fellow employees loved him so much. He could feel the sincerity in their expressions of congratulations, hugs and kisses, which made him feel badly because he knew what he had just said about the host country was nothing but lies, but if he had to lie and put on a façade, then so be it. He thought again and again about what he had just said and he could not believe how deceitful he had just been when he said what he said. Nevertheless, he did not feel too badly about it because he knew that he was trying to keep all eyes and suspicion off him. He did not want anyone to become suspicious about his project, so he thought that by sounding very patriotic for the host country it would deflect negative attention away from him. So far, he could see that it was working very well. He figured that he had just succeeded in his game of deceit.

About two days after he received the employee of the year award, Salerno met Jayne by one of the shopping centers in his area. They had not seen each other for a few months, and they were happy to see each other after a long time. She told him that she no longer trained birds, but that she kept two birds as pets. He told her that he no longer trained birds also because he had to put time and effort into his job. He was sorry that he lied to her, but he felt that he had to do so if he did not want anyone to suspect him in the event it was discovered that birds were involved in the acts of terrorism on the post office and the military base. She asked him about his job at Electronics Inc., and he told her that he had recently been named employee of the year. She congratulated him on his accomplishment and told him that she was not surprised because she knew that he was hard-working and he learned fast. Salerno wanted to keep up his façade of pretending that he loved the host country a lot, so he said, "This country is the greatest country in the whole world. I wouldn't want to live and work in any other country." Jayne agreed with him, adding, "I wish all foreigners think the way you do. People like the terrorists who bombed the post office and the military base are worthless dogs, and have no gratitude for what this country did for them." Salerno mumbled 'true', as he extended his hand to shake hers. They shook hands, said goodbye, and went their separate ways. He was satisfied that she had no idea who and what he really was. If she only knew that he was her true enemy, he wondered what she would say and do.

The Federal Investigations Department applied for and was granted permission to tap into phone calls, emails, texts, faxes and all other types of electronic communications, in an attempt to endeavor to find who the terrorists were who bombed the post office and the military base, and also in an effort to discover any future acts of terrorism. It was in line with what Leon was saying all the time. The responsible Department made many taps on these devices but they were unsuccessful in obtaining information that could assist them in their investigation. They would not have found anything on Salerno because he did not commit the bombings with anyone and he very seldom used telephones even if he had a partner in crime. What the Federal Investigations Department was experiencing in the investigation of these bombings was like nothing they had experienced before. There were absolutely no clues and no suspects or persons of interest in these bombings. They hated to admit it, but it was like they had reached a roadblock and they were uncertain as to which way to turn. There was suspicion about who bombed the military base, but there was no evidence to support that suspicion. As far as they were concerned this case was, if not the hardest and most difficult case they ever had, it was very close to the hardest and most difficult case. They decided to start all over from the beginning to see if they had missed anything. They did so, and once again they could not find the clue or evidence that they needed to jump-start the solving of this case. They decided to brainstorm and look outside of the circle to see if they could find any clues.

Meanwhile, Salerno felt totally invincible because no one had any idea that he and his birds were involved in the bombings. He had managed to trick the Federal Investigations Department, the local police, and other investigative bodies into thinking that the bombs were delivered by means other than his killer birds. They were not smart or intelligent enough to discern that he was the bomber and that he had used his trained birds to carry out the two bombings. This was in spite of those entities having very sophisticated devices for detecting ingredients and materials in shrapnel from bombs. He thought that he had proven that he was much smarter than the best investigators in the world, and he would prove that even further. One day while Salerno was at work he decided that he would further embarrass law enforcement by taunting them by phone. He knew that he had to be careful because phones could be traced to the owner of the phone and sometimes to the place where the phone was purchased, and that phones could be tapped.

Salerno purchased an untraceable, throw-away cell phone that he would use to begin the taunting of law enforcement, and would even use paid public phones that were at locations that were scarcely used and with no surveillance cameras around. His first call was on a Monday morning just before he left for work. It was made from one of his disposable untraceable, throw-away phones. He rang the police station and asked to speak to the Chief of Police on what he termed a very important subject. The Chief of Police immediately took up the phone and said, "This is the Chief of Police, How may I help you?" Salerno said, "This is the person who bombed the post office and the military base. You and your police are a bungling bunch of idiots who will never solve this case. There are more bombings to come." Salerno had first recorded his message onto a small tape recorder and distorted his voice so that it would be difficult for anyone to identify him. The chief of police had a habit of recording all in-coming telephone calls, and this call was no exception.

Immediately after the caller finished speaking the Chief of Police asked, "Who are you?" and before he got a response he heard a click and the phone was dead on the other end. The Chief of Police sat in his chair and played the message over and over trying to see if there was something that he could glean from the call that would assist him in determining who the caller was or where he was calling from. Although the person's voice was obviously distorted, the chief of Police knew that the caller was a male, and that he, the Chief of Police, might have just received his first real clue in the bombings. He called the head of the Federal Investigations Department and informed him about the phone call to his office, and asked him to come to his office as soon as possible. It took about five minutes for the head of the Federal Investigations Department to arrive at the Chief of Police's office. He rushed to the Chief of Police's office because he knew that he might be receiving his first clue from the terrorist himself. The Chief of Police and the head of the Federal Investigations Department listened to the recording from Salerno over and over, trying to listen for anything that could help in identifying the caller. They listened for any kind of sounds like trains, airplanes, farm tractors or animals, etc., in order to determine the location, but they heard none. They tried to decipher the voice to determine the nationality but it was too difficult to do so because the voice was distorted electronically. They determined that whoever the caller was he was very intelligent and probably knew something about electronics because the caller's voice was electronically distorted. They tried to trace the phone call but discovered that the phone that was used had a number that was untraceable. They decided that if they could get a criminal profile of the bomber that might assist them in narrowing down the possible suspects, so they turned to a criminal profiler from the Federal Investigations Department. The criminal profiler was a fairly young woman about twenty five years old.

The criminal profiler listened to the recording of the caller and determined that the caller was young and between the ages of twenty one to twenty five, and was a radical who hated this country. He went on to say that the caller fits right into this country's life style and is working among us. The bomber, the profiler said, is intelligent and deceitful, portraying himself as a person that he is not. Finally, the profiler said that the bomber would strike again. Salerno was twenty five years old. The profiler said that it would be difficult to catch the bomber because he is very careful not to make any mistakes. He went on to say that although the bomber appears to be killing for a cause, the bomber would not stop killing unless and until he is caught and that the bomber was most likely working alone. Although the profile could be helpful, it was a profile that could match hundreds or thousands of individuals, and would only be of assistance if a suspect was apprehended. Three days passed and on the fourth day the Chief of Police received another call from the bomber.

The chief of Police was excited because he knew that as long as he was communicating with the bomber there was a chance that the bomber would make a mistake. The caller said, "I will kill thousands of you then I will retire." The caller then hung up the phone before the

Chief of Police could say anything. Once again, the call was recorded, and the Chief of Police and the head of the Federal Investigations Department listened to the call repeatedly. The call was made exactly like the first call. There was no surrounding noise on the recording and the voice was electronically distorted. It appeared that the caller recorded the call in a quiet place like his bedroom, and that there were no trains, airplanes, tractors etc. close to where the calls were made. They viewed the caller as a brazen, bold and callous killer, who did not value human life at all. They believed that the caller was definitely the person that was responsible for the bombings.

Salerno thought that it would be prudent not to make any more calls because the more calls that he made the more chances he had of slipping up and revealing his identity. He stopped making calls and decided to keep a low profile the way he was doing prior to making the calls. That was a great disappointment to the Chief of Police, the Federal Investigations Department, and law enforcement on the whole because they believed that if the bomber kept making calls he would eventually make an error which could lead to his capture. They remembered that the criminal profiler said that the bomber was intelligent, and although the caller had made two calls, nevertheless, he proved that he was indeed an intelligent individual. His intelligence was manifested in deciding on the type of phone that he used, and in ceasing the phone calls before law enforcement determined who he was. After he stopped making the phone calls he decided that it was time to embark on his third assignment in the furtherance of Operation ID. He thought about the police station down town where the Chief of Police with whom he had just spoken, was in charge, and decided that it would make an excellent target. Salerno felt that the successful operation of that assignment would further embarrass and degrade law enforcement and prove that no one was immune from his attacks. It would be challenging and it would be defeating what stood for the pillar of protection and law and order, and he welcomed the challenge.

The police station was on a heavily used street, and many vehicles passed it daily commuting back and forth. Salerno passed it several times with his army of killer birds. He took photographs of it and sketched it out on his sketching pad. Every time he passed it he would say to the birds, "Police station, police station, police station." After he drew the sketch he placed it among several sketches of other buildings, even the sketches of the demolished post office and military base. He would then say to each of the ten birds, "Police station, police station, police station," and each bird would point out the police station over and over. Even the slow to learn bird pointed it out on every attempt except one. Salerno then placed a red X on ten locations on and around the police station using an indelible marker. Four red Xs were on the ground around the building and six were on various locations on the roof of the police station.

The following day Salerno went to work with a sense of pride knowing what his next assignment would be. As usual, he and Leon sat together at lunch chatting and talking about the job, and Leon once again congratulated him on being the employee of the year. Leon took the time again to remind Salerno of how great the host country is and how it is a special country. Leon said, "I told you that this country is the best country in the world. In what other country can an immigrant like you and me be named the employee of the year? You won that over citizens who were born and bred in this country. This is why I say again and again that I would give my life for this country." Salerno did not want to hear any of that talk, although he knew that any chance Leon got Leon would start speaking of the good of the host country, and Salerno did not want to show his antagonism toward the host country. He listened to Leon and said to him, "Did you hear my brief speech at the presentation of the employee of the year award?" Leon smiled, because he remembered Salerno's speech and thought that Salerno was really getting to like and appreciate the host country. "Man that was great. I'm glad that you are beginning to see this country in the same way that I see it." The smile left Leon's face and he became serious as he said, "I want to work in an area like policing or the army, where I can give something back to this great country, but I'm too old for both. It isn't fair to keep taking from this country and giving nothing in return." Salerno seemed to change his attitude somewhat, and he said, "Man you're not taking anything. You're working for what you get. It's not like you're on some kind of welfare program or unemployed; you're working."

Leon was now becoming confused and he wondered where exactly did Salerno stand. Leon said, "I know that, but this country is making many of my dreams and your dreams come true. You and I are able to take care of our families because of this country. I became a Realtor, I became a Night Auditor and I obtained a Degree in Liberal Studies, all because of the opportunities in this country. It saved many lives in my family, and I believe it saved lives in your family also, so giving my one life for this country is a small sacrifice or token of my appreciation for all that this country did for me." Salerno thought that he had heard enough and was not prepared to hear any more from Leon on the virtues of the host country. He said, "True. This is a great country." Salerno was glad that it was time to return to work as the lunch hour was over and the alarm sounded to notify them that the lunch time was over and it was time to return to work. As they walked off and prior to separating to go to their individual posts, Leon said, "I'm happy to see that you finally understand what I was saying and that you agree with me." Salerno whispered, "True." They then separated.

Although Leon appeared to believe that Salerno changed his views in respect of the negative criticism of the host country, there was something inside of Leon that was telling him that Salerno might not be speaking the truth, and that Salerno was only trying to bluff people into thinking that he loved the host country. Leon decided that he would watch Salerno carefully and listen to every word uttered from Salerno's mouth. He realized that people could change, but something was telling him that Salerno did not change his dislike for the host country. Salerno thought that he had fooled Leon and the others that he told about his love for the host country. He said that Leon and the other infidels were too gullible and pretentious. He thought that they were too quick to believe anything that someone told them. Salerno decided that as long as the infidels would believe his lies, he would continue to feed the lies to them and have them swallow them hook, line and sinker. He would have the last laugh after he destroyed hundreds, and maybe thousands of infidels, including Leon. It is sad that he would have to kill Leon also, but the fact is that Leon is an infidel, and all infidels must be destroyed in order for the world to be a better place, and there was no exception to that. He would watch the destruction of Leon, because Leon was spewing the same type of rhetoric that the other infidels spewed. "Leon's days are numbered," Salerno said softly.

It would be three days from today that the police station would be bombed and destroyed, with those inside at the time, killed. Salerno decided to have the birds practiced and trained for its destruction although they already knew where to go and what to do. They had made several dry runs at night and during the day. On the day set for the destruction of the police station many birds were on the electric wires along the busy street in the front of the police station. Some birds were in yards close to the police station, and some were in the police station yard. It was an area that birds frequented because there were many bugs and insects in the grass and the trees that lined the street. Other birds being present would conceal the presence of the killer birds and allow the killer birds to be inconspicuous. After Salerno drove home, he prepared the birds by giving them their favorite meal laced with the stimulant and some water to wash it down. They were lively as usual after they ate the stimulant laced food. Salerno then fastened the bombs and the cameras onto the birds.

The birds and cameras were the same color which acted as a means of camouflage, to make it appear that they were an integral part of or appendage of the birds. After fitting them with the equipment, he kissed each bird on the forehead and said, "Police station, police station, police station." He opened the door of his house and the birds flew off. He went to his computer and monitored their flight path. As they flew, some other birds were in the sky close by and they followed Salerno's birds. Salerno could see all that on his monitor from home. His birds led the way and they all landed in the police station yard together. As soon as the birds landed they began searching for food in the grass all around the police station. Salerno's killers pretended to be searching for food, but after a few seconds six of Salerno's birds flew on top of the roof of the police station while the other four took their assigned positions at various points at the base of the police station. They off-loaded their fatal cargo in mere seconds demonstrating that they had become experts at executing these types of operations. They were obviously professionals at what they were doing, and that was apparent. After all the bombs were detached and placed in their rightful positions, all ten birds flew off leaving the other birds feeding. Salerno watched them as they flew on their return journey.

When all the ten birds had returned, Salerno kissed them again and allowed them to fly around freely in the house after rewarding them with a meal laced with the stimulant. He then figured that it was time that most of the police men and women who were to be at work that day, would be there. He chuckled then put in the password to detonate the bombs simultaneously. Almost immediately he saw that it was a success because the success light came on denoting that it was successful. He would wait patiently at his television for the news of the explosions which he knew would soon come on. He would not have to wait long, for about ten minutes after the bombs were detonated a news flash came on the television screen stating that there was breaking news. He turned up the volume on the television and the reporter said, "News is coming into this station that there has been a bombing of the main police station. The details are very limited, but as we get more information we will make it available to you." The announcer remained on and almost immediately after his first release he said, "I understand that there has been some more information available. Wait a minute. This cannot be true, but the news now coming in is that the police station, the whole building, is flat. There is a cloud of smoke and dust." After he said that, another person entered the room where he sat and whispered something into the reporter's ear and the reporter could be heard saying, "Oh my God, are you saying that all who were inside the police station are dead?" He appeared too nervous and too shocked to speak any further. His face turned pale and his hands were shaking as if he suffered from some type of disease.

A female reporter entered the room and rushed over to the male reporter and took the microphone and resumed the story on the bombing of the police station. It was apparent that she was well trained and with much experience. She adjusted a chair that was beside the first reporter's chair and attached the small black cordless microphone to her blue and yellow blouse, and stared straight ahead into the camera and said, "We need to pray for the officers and the families of those officers that were in the demolished police station. These terrorists are going too far. We must apprehend the vicious murderers responsible for wreaking havoc on our people. These acts of terrorism are despicable and cowardly." As she spoke live photographs of the scene popped up on the television. Not one cinder block from the police station was left standing. It appeared as if the building was bulldozed. There was just a heap of smoldering rubble with smoke and dust still rising from the ruins. The reporter on the scene said, "My, my, how cruel can these bastards be?"

Police officers were at the scene with their sirens blaring and lights flashing. Ambulances and paramedics were also present. Politicians were gathering around with other members of the community. Police officers, men and women, were crying openly and two police officers were wailing. Some police officers were hugging each other as they cried, trying to give each other comfort. A short, fat male police officer was shouting, "Let's enter the building and save them. Please don't let them die." Another officer put his arms around the short officer and told him, "There's no building there, only the spot where the building was. It's gone." The short fat police officer had obviously lost his mind, because as the other officer told him, there was no building, only the spot where the building was. Two officers held on to the short fat officer as he tried to break free and run toward the smoldering ruins. A paramedic gave him an injection to calm him down and he became calm and quiet. They lay him on a gurney and he remained silent as tears streamed down his face. A young female police officer was crying and asking, "Why? Why?" She was pulling her hair out as she cried uncontrollably. A female from the crowd of onlookers walked over to the female officer and put her arms around the officer's waist and said, "You are weeping now but joy comes in the morning." The female officer said, "But where are my brothers and sisters that were in the building? I want to see them please." The lady who was holding the female office said, "Don't worry, they are in safe hands." Onlookers were crying and wailing. Paramedics were weeping as they tried to do their jobs.

The crime scene was cordoned off and all on-lookers, including the police, were outside the cordoned area. Detectives arrived at the scene and entered the cordoned area. One of the detectives said, "My, my, nobody could survive this." There was no sign of life. All that could be seen were body parts badly burned, blood and ruins from the building. They looked around for evidence but were finding it very difficult to find any. The coroner came and had the body parts collected and bagged and taken away. The crying and wailing intensified as the bags with the body parts were taken away. Police officers, paramedics and members from the general public were crying. People could be heard asking questions like, "What happened?" "Did anyone survive?" "How many officers were in the building?" An officer lay on the ground on his back screaming, "I want my friends, I want my friends." The whole scene was emotional. Politicians had already arrived at the scene and wanted to know what had happened. Someone who was passing the police station at the time of the blast said that he heard a great deafening sound, and he thought that it was the end of the world. His car windows were closed, yet the sound was incredibly loud. He said that it was so loud that it broke the back left window of his car. He said that he sped away in fear and returned only after he saw other vehicles speeding past him toward the blast. He said that when he returned to the scene he was struck to see the police station no longer existed. He asked, "What is this world coming to?" It started to rain and onlookers and police officers began to enter their vehicles for shelter and some dispersed.

Salerno was overjoyed at what he had just seen on the television. He managed to kill all who were in the police station at the time of the bombing although he did not know how many police officers were there at the time. The last two assignments, that is, the bombing of the military base and the bombing of the police station, were attacks on the fabric of the infidels' institutions. They represented the whole fabric and institution of the infidels. If he could succeed at executing those assignments he could succeed at any and all other assignments. He could not believe what he had just seen and heard on television. As he jumped up and down and shouted obscenities and words and phrases of jubilation he said, "Operation ID is a total and complete success. The infidels are falling like flies. I swear death to the infidels." He brought out a bottle of champagne and toasted to himself, saying, "To the mastermind of Operation ID." To say that he was proud of his success was a mild way of putting it.

While Salerno was celebrating his most recent victory the Chief of Police appeared on various news channels on the television. He appeared distraught and confused as if he did not know what his next move would be in attempting to find and capture the person or persons responsible for the bombing. It was announced that the Chief of Police would be making a short speech in relation to the bombings and that he would not be answering any questions. He wiped his teary and swollen eyes which indicated that he was crying. It was his first speech after the destruction of the police station and the murders of all the officers at the station at the time. He unfolded a white piece of paper and began to read from a prepared statement.

"I am lost for words at what happened to my dedicated men and women. Today is the saddest day of my life. I was to be at the police station at the time of the terrorists 'attack but I forgot my keys at home and I returned to my home to retrieve them. While I was returning to the police station it happened. We have lost eight brave police officers, three women and five men. Whoever is responsible will be brought to justice. My sympathies go out to their families. May their souls rest in peace and rise in glory." Tears were running down his face as he spoke. He walked away with his head down and wiping his face with the back of his hand as he left.

Surveillance cameras were mounted on the four corners of the police station but they were destroyed in the bomb blast. Investigators decided that surveillance cameras would have to be mounted on buildings or lamp posts across the streets from government buildings. Although the best investigators were assembled to investigate the bombing of the police station, after the investigators completed their investigations they found nothing to assist them in determining who or what caused the explosion. Those who might have been able to assist them were dead. Although there was no evidence, the investigators vowed that this case would not be a cold unsolved case. All the police officers from the destroyed police station who were not at the police station when it was destroyed, and their families, were interviewed. The investigators wanted to know if any of the dead police officers or their families received any threats within the last year or two, or if the police officers or their families had any altercation with anyone. They also investigated all arrests made within the last year or two by police officers of the destroyed police station, who were killed and those alive. Phone records and other electronic records of all the police officers of the destroyed station were checked. The investigators came up with nothing that could assist them in solving the bombing. They checked to determine if any police officers were radically inclined, but the results were negative. They asked the remaining officers and the Chief of Police if any officers had brought any packages or parcels to the police station recently. Again, the answers were in the negative. The person who was driving by the police station at the time of the blast was questioned in detail. He was asked if he noticed anyone, anything or any vehicle near the police station that appeared to be suspicious when he drove by it, and his answer was that he did not notice anything suspicious. No components or material from the bombs were found. Everything was obliterated. The fact that no components from a bomb were found was unusual and had never happened before. The terrorists appeared to be very professional in dealing with their explosives. They were deluding law enforcement, and the best investigators in the world.

The reward was increased from five million dollars to six million dollars. The investigators felt certain that the increase would cause someone to come forth with the tip or tips that they needed to solve the bombing. The truth was that no one had any tips or clues that could assist the investigators or the police in solving the bombing. However, the investigators believed that someone somewhere had some information that could assist, even if that someone did not realize that that the information was relevant. The investigators asked the public to think carefully and try to recall if they saw anyone acting suspiciously any time in the vicinity of the bombing. Hardware stores and other stores that sold materials and ingredients that could be used for making bombs were checked to see if any large amounts of those ingredients were sold to anyone. There was nothing on the surveillance cameras on the street on which the police station was or on any surrounding streets that could assist the investigators. Salerno had bought the ingredients and materials for the bombs in a state two states away from where he lived. They were bought at a small mama and papa hardware store where there were no surveillance cameras. Furthermore, the materials that he used were so common that their purchases would not have drawn attention. The investigators did not know what bomb making materials and ingredients to look for. They were at a disadvantage.

For some time the main conversation at Salerno's work place was about the bombing of the police station. Leon said that the terrorists had gone too far and that it was time that they are stopped. He blamed the host country for allowing those types of criminal elements without morals to enter the country. He told Salerno that because the matter involved national security, everybody's property should be searched without exception. Leon said that he knew that people would talk about violation of Human Rights, and that other entities would try to prevent it, but the drastic situation called for drastic action. Salerno said to Leon, "I think you are going too far. People have constitutional rights that must be respected." Leon replied, "I am aware of that, but when terrorists are taking innocent lives indiscriminately, the reaction must be proportionate to the action." Salerno shook his head in disbelief to what Leon had said because he saw where, if law enforcement were given legal authority to do what Leon wanted them to do, he would undoubtedly be caught.

Investigators from other states came to assist in the investigations to see if they could help in solving the crimes. They shared ideas and made suggestions to their counterparts. Drones and satellites were deployed and flown over and pointed at government buildings all over the country. Nothing unusual and no suspicious aircraft were detected. Nothing like the bombings had ever happened, and no one could understand how and why it was happening. It appeared as if an invisible force had demolished the post office, the military base and the police station. The different investigative teams could not understand why they could not find a single clue or receive a single tip. It was mind-boggling, to say the least. The bombings were not a freak incidence of nature or an attack from out of space, although some might have believed that. The investigators felt that there must be something that they were overlooking, but they could not determine what it was. Cameras were being installed in each corner of the ground on which government buildings were located, and across the street from government buildings. No cameras were installed on the actual buildings. This, the government thought, would save the cameras and the footage and would allow the investigators to see if anything suspicious would be caught on the footage. Security officers were also posted at all the government buildings around the country, with high-powered guns. The government was now certain that the security systems around the government buildings were impenetrable. They felt certain that there would be no more bombing. One of the investigators said that because they could find no evidence of bombings, maybe there were no bombings. He said that maybe something in the buildings' structure or some gas lines exploded. The others refused to believe what he said. They thought that it would be unusual and a weird coincidence for so many vital buildings to explode and incinerate in the manner they did.

The increased security seemed to be working because for six months the bombings had ceased, and Law enforcement officers were on the television speaking of how effective the enhanced security was. They said that maybe the terrorists had fled the country out of fear that as a result of the increased and enhanced security they would most likely be caught. An investigator from the Federal Investigations Department warned about being complacent. He believed that the terrorists were still around and had not left to go anywhere. He said, "We must not let our guard down. We must not rest until we find those responsible for the murders of our people and the wanton destruction of our buildings." The average persons did not know what to believe, as they were confused by the mixed messages that were sent by law enforcement. There were those who decided that they would not visit government buildings or go anywhere close to government buildings unless it was unavoidable. They viewed the government buildings as magnets for explosive devices or as time bombs. Government officials took to the airwaves to announce that everything was under control and that it was completely safe to visit all government buildings all around the country. That did not allay people's fears which were rampant and justifiable. They saw the risk of danger from visiting or being close to government buildings as being real and not worth taking.

Normalcy was returning to the people in the country. *It was a long period without incidents of bombings. The bombings were beginning to wane from their minds. After all, Thanksgiving holiday was rapidly approaching and they were consumed with that. People were thinking about travelling and drinking beer, eating turkey and ham and just having fun. There was no time for thinking about negative destructive things. While people were preparing for Thanksgiving, Salerno was planning his next assignment in furtherance of Operation ID. He knew that this would be a good time to execute it, as people would let down their guard to engage in celebrations and merry-making, and while they were doing that he would be scoping out buildings to see what building would be his next target. After some careful consideration he decided that the popular People's Mall would be his next target, because it would be crowded with people trying to take advantage of the discounted prices. This assignment would be different than the others in that it would not involve any government buildings and would not involve law enforcement bodies or agencies. It would also be the most difficult in a sense, because the mall is huge and the birds cannot enter the mall. If they did, they could be caught and the whole operation could be in jeopardy. He decided that he could have an explosive device placed at each entrance to the building, and some placed on top of the roof. These devices would be more powerful than the previous devices. He took his ten birds to the exterior of the mall a few times as practice. He did not have to do this as often as he did for the post office, the military base and the police station. They could find and destroy a target with only one visit. He did not have to make sketches of the buildings any longer, but he continued to do so. He made a rough sketch of the mall, concentrating on a particular area of the mall. This area had stores and a huge food court with several restaurants. He made plans especially for that area and concentrated on putting the red Xs in that area. Finally he and his flock of killers were ready for the next assignment.*

It was a cool Saturday afternoon and the mall was crowded with people of all races and from all areas. Salerno and his birds passed the mall before the assignment. There was hardly a parking space in the mall, and he was happy to see that. He knew that if everything went as planned, the casualty rate would be very high, and that was what he wanted. On his return journey home he bought some beer and food from a fast food restaurant. He decided that while his birds were executing the fourth assignment he would be relaxing and enjoying a few bears and a meal. The infidels would be caught off guard because warnings were given about government buildings only, so no one was thinking of privately owned buildings. This was further proof of the ignorance and stupidity of the infidels, who usually had a one track mind, he thought. He was now ready for the fourth assignment.

The mall was so crowded that people were bumping into each other. Some adults were walking with their young children and others had their babies in their arms. A couple had a pet poodle on a leash as they window shopped. Many people had gift bags and shopping bags with them that contained purchases they had just made, while others were just gazing in the windows and the stores as they walked by. Everyone appeared to be very happy with no troubles and worries on their minds. Thanksgiving meant a lot to them and they were going to enjoy it to the fullest. Shop owners were standing outside the doors of their stores trying to get shoppers to enter and take advantage of the discounted prices. One of the shop owners was saying, "Come one come all, I have the best prices in the mall." Some shoppers stopped and entered the store while others walked by not paying attention to what the store owner was saying. There was an area with games for young children to play. That area was full to capacity with about thirty children accompanied by their parents or guardians or other family members. The children were laughing and playing and making joyful noise. Some children were waiting until some of the rides became available so that they could enjoy them.

Salerno attached the explosive devices and the cameras to the ten birds that were about to execute the next assignment. They had just eaten their usual pre-assignment meal laced with the stimulant. He kissed them on their foreheads and said, "Mall, mall, mall," as they flapped their wings in excitement and in anticipation of what was to come. He then opened the door of the house and allowed the birds to fly off on their fourth assignment. They left in a north westerly direction toward the mall. Salerno went and sat at his computer and followed the flight of the birds on the computer. It took the birds about fifteen minutes to arrive at the mall. He watched them take up their assigned strategic positions and detached the explosive devices in their rightful places. As soon as they released the explosive devices they flew off together, heading back to Salerno's house where he awaited their return. He decided to await their return before he detonated the explosive devices, because he wanted to be certain that all of them were alright. Fifteen minutes after they detached and deposited the explosive devices they returned. Their return journey was shorter because they did not have the weight of the bombs and the cameras on them. He decided to put in the password and detonate the bombs, so he put in the password. On his computer screen he saw that the explosion was successful. He remained at his computer and searched the internet while his television was turned on as he awaited the news of the bombing to come on the television. Five minutes later a news flash announced that there appeared to be a bombing at the mall. As usual, the announcer said that details were sketchy, and that as soon as more details became available they would be announced. About fifteen minutes later a reporter was at the scene of the bombing milling around and trying to question persons at the scene. Unlike the other bombings, there were people with blood all over their bodies and shredded clothing. A woman's face was so bloody that her face could not be seen. All that could be seen was blood dripping down her face. Her blouse was torn and almost completely red, although it was apparently a white blouse.

Another lady was lying on the ground about twenty feet from the mall's entrance with one of her legs mangled. It appeared to be hanging on a thin piece of skin only. Paramedics and police were rushing into the mall as injured, bleeding shoppers were running out and being brought out. Some shoppers were holding onto others while some were lifting others out of the building. Just about everyone who came out of the mall was injured in one way or the other. The camera was pointed to the inside of the mall and one could see that the roof, or most of it, appeared to be missing and in a pile on the floor. The police were at the door preventing anyone but the first responders from entering.

A reporter tried to enter the building but the police stopped her at the door. However, she instructed her camera man to come closer in a certain direction. As the camera man did so, large slabs from the roof could be seen on the floor of the mall. Some shoppers were trapped under the slabs and mangled wires that fell from the roof. People were screaming, moaning and groaning, while others lay completely still as if they were already dead. Large pools of blood were seen coming from under the fallen slabs of roof, and loud screams were heard coming from that direction. Two women with blood all over their bodies were screaming and calling out for help. One of the women was saying, "Where's my child? Where's my child? Please move the roof and save my child. I want my child." Somebody rushed over to her and hugged her and tried to comfort her. Paramedics were bringing out casualties on gurneys. Some of the casualties on the gurneys were seriously injured while others were obviously dead. There was total pandemonium. As some paramedics walked pass the door, exiting with a dead individual, one of the paramedics could be heard saying, "There are hundreds of wounded and dead people in there." The police brought out the two women who were crying for their children. They were still crying. One of them appeared to be about to pass out as she began to wobble and look shaky. Two paramedics grabbed her and put her in the ambulance where they treated her. The other lady slumped to the ground outside the entrance, and was saying, "Why, why?" A lady who had just arrived sat down beside the crying lady and grabbed her in her arms, and said, "You will be alright."

As Salerno watched the television, he clapped and jumped up and down shouting, "Infidels die." Once again he was the victor. All the bragging and boasting about how well prepared the infidels were when it came to security was hogwash, he thought. As he watched the television, the reporter on site said, "I understand that at least three hundred adults and thirty nine children are dead. This is a tragedy of monumental proportions. Who could do something like this?" Bodies and injured persons were still being brought out of the mall. Heavy equipment had to be brought in to remove the slabs of roof off the bodies of the children and others trapped beneath the slabs. At least four reporters were at the scene. One of them asked a police officer "What caused this destruction?" The officer seemed perturbed as he said, "It is too soon to say, but it appears to be caused by some sort of explosive device." The reporter asked him, "Do you think that the same persons who are responsible for the bombing of the post office, the military base and the police station are responsible for the bombing of this mall?" The police officer, realizing that he should not say too much, said, "As I said, it is far too soon to say who is and who is not responsible." Later, on the nightly news, the Chief of Police was answering some questions. Someone asked him, "How come law enforcement did not warn private entities about the bombing? All I heard were warnings about government buildings." The chief of Police responded by saying, "When these sort of things happen, everyone should be cautious and protect ones property and oneself." Another person asked the Chief of Police, "Why can't the police find those responsible? They are paid to serve and protect and solve crimes." The chief agreed that it is their duty to solve crimes, but, he said, "The police cannot do miracles or magic. The police can only solve crimes when they have leads or clues that would assist them in solving crimes. That is why we ask the public to play its part and be vigilant and give us any information they may have about this or any other crime. The police are only as good as the community they serve." Some other questions were asked and the Chief did his best to answer them, but from the tone of the questioning it was obvious that the public were not satisfied with the performance of the police, especially in relation to the four bombings.

The day following the bombing of the mall people from all over went by the mall to view the damage. Everyone was talking about the bombing and the deaths of the three hundred adults and thirty nine children. The fear of leaving ones home and venturing out to government buildings and private businesses had increased. There were those who swore that they would remain at home and have home deliveries made whenever that was possible. The general public did not like the idea that there were no suspects and no persons of interest. Law enforcement was accused of incompetence and misleading the public. It was felt that if they did not have information to solve the bombings they should say so and not lead the public to think the police were on top of things. People were feeling very vulnerable because those who were paid to protect the public could not protect themselves. After all, the police station was bombed and eight police officers were killed, and the killers could not be found. It was suggested that a civilian posse be formed to hunt down the killers, but that suggestion was immediately discouraged because it was believed that people not trained in law enforcement may violate people's rights. One of those who favored the formation of a posse asked, "What difference does it make if we violate people's rights? Isn't that what the police do daily and the terrorists are doing to us now?" Tempers were flaring as the public was becoming agitated and very angry. There was a feeling that absolutely nothing was being done to stem the tide of murders by terrorists.

Investigators were sifting through the rubble of the bombed mall looking for clues. They spent hours working tediously, but like on the previous bomb sites, they came up with nothing. There were cameras mounted around the mall, and some of them survived the blast because the blast was contained to a certain area, and the mall was very big. The footage from the cameras was examined but nothing unusual was seen. This attack was mysterious like the others. If someone brought the bombs into the mall and set them down to be detonated it should have been caught on the cameras. It was believed that maybe an employee at the mall brought the explosive devices hidden in some clothing or a shoe box as merchandise for sale. This led to the investigators questioning all the employees at the mall and their families. The families and friends of the dead employees were also questioned at length. The families and friends of those who were killed but not employees at the mall were questioned also, but the investigators came up with nothing. Politicians were becoming concerned that the police could not solve these very serious crimes. They wondered what made these crimes so different from other similar crimes, when it is said that every criminal or most criminals leave clues at the crime scene, and that there is no such thing as the perfect crime, so why weren't the police solving the bombings. The Federal Investigations Department is supposed to be the best investigative department in the world, so why didn't they have a suspect as yet? Some wondered. The investigators made several visits to the bomb site before the rubble was removed, and took photographs of the scene. They questioned those who were at the mall at the time of the bombing, but no new evidence was forth-coming. Once again the question was asked if a drone could have possibly caused the explosion. This time that possibility was not totally ruled out. One of the investigators believed that this bombing may have been done by a copycat using a drone. Even if that were the case there should have been some shrapnel from the bomb at the bomb site. None was found and the drone theory was soon debunked. It was also believed that maybe a gas main probably exploded, but there was no proof that this was the case.

A year had passed since the bombing of the mall and the killing of three hundred and thirty nine people. It must be said that it may not be absolutely correct to say that the mall or the other three buildings were bombed because there really was no definitive evidence, or no evidence at all that they were bombed. Everyone knew that they exploded and were demolished or partly demolished, but to say that they were bombed would be a stretch without empirical evidence. Anyone and everyone would say that the buildings had to be bombed, because it was obvious that they were. The question that had to be asked was, "Who bombed the buildings and why and how were they bombed?" No one seemed to be able to answer those questions, and that bothered so many people. It appeared that those responsible for solving the crimes had given up trying to solve them. Although this appeared to be the case, it was not the case because they were doing all that they could to solve them. They were working assiduously and constantly to endeavor to solve what they termed 'terrible bombings'. They would not give up because the terrorists had struck at the core of law and order when they attacked men and women of the military and the police force. The investigators vowed that no matter how long it took, they would solve the cases of the bombings of the post office, the military base, the police station and the mall. That was their main priority, and they would remain unrelenting and steadfast in achieving that objective.

The decision was taken by Salerno to wait another year or eighteen months before he embarked on his fifth assignment. He figured that by waiting that long everybody's guard would be let down and some might think that the bombings or explosions were over, and either those responsible were imprisoned for other crimes, or had died or moved out of the jurisdiction. He thought that it was best to catch everyone off guard. During that period he had trained twenty birds to execute lethal assignments. That made a total of thirty birds that he had at his disposal to make Operation ID a success. He wanted to have some reserves in the event that his first ten birds got injured or were killed. He called that forward planning, unlike what the infidels did. His belief was that the infidels also reacted rather than being proactive by acting to prevent a certain course of action from happening. For example, the bombings had to take place and lives had to be lost and buildings destroyed before proper or adequate security could be put in place on and around government buildings.

After the mall bombing Salerno was promoted on his job because of his excellent performance. He was promoted over some of the born and bred citizens of the host country. Some of those citizens were reliable, but the truth was that Salerno was more reliable and dependable than they were. The employer felt that if there were one person that he could depend on and trust on the job it was Salerno, and he made no secret about that. Sometimes the supervisor would tell the other employees that Salerno was an exemplary person whom they should emulate, and by emulating him, they would become better individuals. Some of those employees did not take kindly to those types of remarks from the supervisor, but there was little or nothing that they could do about it because they wanted their jobs. The day after Salerno was promoted he and Leon were sitting down chatting. Leon had just congratulated him on his promotion and he thanked Leon. They spoke in general about the job and their lives and Leon said, "It appears that the spineless rats that did the bombings over a year ago fled the country. We don't need them here because they are only spineless dogs. I hate them with a passion."

Salerno listened to Leon as Leon spoke, then Salerno said, "They do not see themselves as spineless dogs. Maybe they see themselves as freedom fighters." Leon took offence to what Salerno said and responded, "Murdering innocent men, women and children are not acts of freedom fighters. What freedom do they want? If they want freedom there are better, peaceful means of fighting for it. I will support this country and countries like this country that supports freedom and equal rights until I die because it is the right and proper thing to do. We in this country are freedom fighters, but we do not go around maiming and killing innocent men, women, and children." Salerno knew that when he engaged in conversation with Leon it would most likely end in that manner. Salerno thought that he could gain some mileage on Leon on the equal rights issue, so he said, "You say that equal rights exist in this country, well why are you treated as inferior to another ethnicity?" Leon shook his head in disbelief and said, "I figured that you would mention this. This country has laws that tackle all types of discrimination. It is an offense to discriminate in many areas in this country, there are laws designed to protect me, but no one or no country or no law can stop an individual or individuals from discriminating against another individual. Only a few misinformed, stupid individuals discriminate. Even if I should depart this country to return to my country of birth permanently one day, I would still feel the same about this great country. In this country one is as free as the bald eagle." Leon had said enough and Salerno had heard enough and Salerno wanted to discontinue the conversation. Salerno said," Well if that is the way that you feel I cannot do anything about that. I love this country also." He did not want Leon to walk away thinking that he, Salerno, did not love the host country.

Salerno was angry that Leon would call freedom fighters like him and his people spineless dogs. He thought about that all that night until he fell asleep, and when he awoke that was the first thing on his mind. He made the decision that he would embark on his fifth assignment very soon, mostly because of the vitriolic and caustic attack by Leon on him, Salerno, and Salerno's people. That, coupled with the long period between the destruction of the mall, meant that it was time for another assignment to be carried out. Salerno drove around looking for a good target. He wanted a target that when it was attacked would create shock and fear in the public. He decided that he would attack the public hospital, where he could kill doctors, nurses and patients. He was sure that an attack like that would really hurt the infidels just as much as the other attacks or even more. It would surely be an attack that the infidels did not expect or anticipate. He knew the layout of the public hospital because he had been there for treatment on many occasions several months ago. Nevertheless, he drove by on a few occasions with his ten bird killers. Five of them were from the ten original birds and five were from the last twenty that were trained. He went through the same routine that he had gone through on the four previous occasions until he was satisfied that they were ready for the fifth assignment.

The day of the fifth assignment was a hot, sunny day. It was a Sunday and the trees were standing still as if there was no breeze blowing at all. It was a day for relaxing under the air conditioning or attending church services, or simply going to visit loved ones who were sick in the hospital. Salerno woke up early and fed his birds and made breakfast for himself. This morning he would be having a very light breakfast of corn flakes with milk. Usually when he would be embarking on or executing assignments, he would not eat much. Maybe the thoughts of the assignments caused him to lose his appetite. After eating his breakfast he brought the ten birds into his house and began to attach the explosive devices and the cameras to them. They were lively as they usually were when they were about to execute one of these assignments.

After the birds ate their stimulant laced meal and washed it down with some water they were chirping and skipping around with open wings as if they knew what they were about to do and enjoyed doing it. Salerno strapped the explosive devices and the small cameras onto them, kissed them on their foreheads and said, "Hospital." Lately while training them he thought that there was no need to repeat the name of the target more than once because they were getting better and better at what they were doing. As a matter of fact, he thought that maybe he did not have to say the name of the target at all, because the birds knew what the target would be. On saying the word "Hospital," he opened the door to let them out, and they flew away together in single file toward the direction of the public hospital. He shut the door a little and walked over to his computer with a cup of hot, instant coffee with milk in his hand. He put the cup of coffee on the computer table and began to play games on the computer while he watched the birds on the other computer heading toward the public hospital. They flew until he saw the hospital in sight getting bigger and bigger as they got closer and closer to it. Finally, they landed and took up their respective positions. When he saw that he stopped playing games and paid all his attention to the birds to see if they were doing everything correctly. He watched them closely as they released their explosive devices exactly where they were instructed to off-load them. As soon as the explosive devices were released the birds flew off on their return journey toward Salerno's house.

The bombs were strategically placed over the hospital and around the hospital compound, including the emergency room, the general ward and admissions. They were placed in what Salerno called 'strategic' locations where most damage could be sustained. The locations included the areas where patients were sleeping. The birds returned to Salerno's house and flew through the open door that Salerno had left open for them minutes after they deposited the bombs. He patted them, kissed them and said, "Job well done." They chirped and skipped around as if to say 'thank you'. He gave them some more stimulant laced food as a reward for their successful mission. It was an historic mission because it was the first time that all the original ten birds were not used to carry out an assignment. He was very proud of their performance, and knew that he had teams of killer birds that would last for a very long time and never be caught. He said, "I am too smart and too intelligent and brilliant for the infidels. All of them including Leon are idiots without vision. It is their Bible that says somewhere in it that 'where there is no vision the people perish. Now they will perish because they have no vision." He remembered hearing Leon say that some time ago about the people who Leon thought were responsible for the bombings, that they had no vision and that they would eventually perish.

On the computer screen in Salerno's house was the pass word that would detonate the explosive devices that were placed at the hospital. He laughed as he placed his right hand slowly over the mouse for the computer and guided the cursor onto the password. He left clicked the mouse as he said, "Die and go to hell you infidels." Shortly after that the word 'successful' appeared on the computer screen. He turned his television on and returned to playing games on his computer as he waited to hear the news of the explosions at the hospital. About nine minutes later the current program on the television ceased abruptly and a reporter interrupted and said, "We are receiving news that the public hospital was just blown up. The news is still coming in and we cannot confirm this report, but keep tuned in to this channel and we will keep you abreast of all developments in this matter." As soon as he finished speaking he said, "It appears that the initial report is correct. We are hearing that there is major damage to the hospital. At this stage there is no word on whether there are casualties." About twenty minutes later a reporter at the scene of the damaged hospital sent messages to the reporter on the television.

The reporter in the field said, "It looks like the invisible terrorists have struck again. I will from henceforth refer to them as the invisible terrorists because no one has ever seen them, and I believe that would be the case again. I am looking at the hospital and most of it is destroyed, as you can see. Concrete beams have fallen and the roof is non-existent. Stainless steel rebar can be seen protruding from the broken concrete. Concrete beams and columns are piled high on the floor, and presumably on top of people. Doctors, nurses, and patients are running from the damaged building out of fear that more concrete would fall or more bombs would explode. Some of them are bleeding profusely and others have to be carried." While he was speaking one could see a tall, skinny doctor with blood all over his white gown limping out of the emergency room door. As he exited he said, "Many of my colleagues are trapped inside. Please, please get some help for them." He was very distraught as he stopped to lean against a part of the hospital wall that was still standing. He appeared as if he did not know what to do next.

By this time the police and paramedics were on the scene scampering about. Cries for help were heard coming from inside what was left of the hospital, but it was difficult to get to them because the fallen beams and columns and portions of the roof were blocking the path to them. The general ward was completely destroyed. It would be a miracle if anyone was found alive. In all the chaos paramedics were entering the building cautiously and returning with wounded and dead bodies. They proceeded cautiously with every step they took, not wanting to cause any debris that was hanging precariously to fall and cause injury or death to them or anyone. Inside the building looked like a war zone.

As the wounded and dead were brought from the destroyed hospital Salerno was laughing, clapping and praising his god for what he termed his successful assignment. The more wounded and dead he saw the happier he felt and the more he rejoiced. As the wounded and dead were brought out the reporter said, "There's another, and another." At one stage he said, "I am tired of counting the wounded and dead." On a few occasions doctors and nurses were brought out on gurneys showing no signs of life, which caused people to believe that they were either dead or unconscious from fallen debris. For hours the wounded and the dead were brought out one after the other. It seemed as if that would never cease. It was a scene that Salerno enjoyed watching and could watch forever. He enjoyed seeing the panic and fear on the faces of the survivors, and the disbelief on the faces of the police and paramedics, on-lookers, and other first responders. People were being brought out with missing limbs and limbs just hanging. At least two headless bodies were brought out as an on-looker fainted on seeing them. No one knew whether it was the blast itself or whether it was fallen debris from the blast that had beheaded them. A police officer began to vomit when he saw the headless corpses, and another officer fell to the ground and went in a fetal position.

The whole scene was gruesome and incredible. However, the more gruesome it was the more Salerno felt that the fifth assignment was a complete success. He knew that the casualty count would be very high, and that was his intention. He wanted the infidels to remember his assignment and fear him whenever they talked about it, even many years after. He loved the fact that the reporter had referred to him as invisible, although he did not like the reporter using the word terrorist, because he always said that he was not a terrorist; he was a freedom fighter. Salerno thought that the reference to invisible was appropriate because no one had seen him or his birds commit any of the assignments. He believed that because he detonated the explosive devices from his home he would never be caught because he would never be seen. Even if the birds were caught, which he believed would not happen, the infidels still had no way of knowing that he was responsible. He was certain that he was committing what the infidels called the perfect crimes. An elderly nurse with what appeared to be a broken arm and a lot of blood on her chest said, "I heard a loud explosion that sounded like an atom bomb. It was deafening. I thought that it was the end of the world." Someone asked her if she saw the persons who were responsible for the bombs and she said, "No, and I'm glad that I did not see them, because if I had seen them I might have been locked up in prison by now because of what I would have done to them." The search and rescue mission went on for several hours, and when it was finished, the count for the dead and injured was, three hundred and twenty nine wounded and three hundred and sixty one dead. The wounded and the dead were all over the ground on the outside of the hospital as people gathered around with expressions of shock, anger and pain on their faces, wondering why law enforcement could not do anything to prevent and stop the carnage on the lives of innocent people.

The Leader of the country appeared on television and addressed the nation. His voice was cracking and his eyes were teary as he said, "My people, it is with a heavy heart that I address you today. Once again terrorists have attacked our country and our people, but please be assured that they will not get away with it as long as I am your leader. I repeat, they will not get away with it. My sympathy and that of my family go out to the families of those who were wounded and killed. We are not dealing with sane, rational and intelligent individuals, but with people who have no morals and no scruples, but they will be caught." Salerno watched and listened carefully to the Leader's speech, and thought that it was no more than crazy rhetoric that he expected to hear from the Leader. Salerno knew that the Leader had to appease his people, and that was what was being done by the Leader. Salerno wondered how he would ever be caught when the investigators had absolutely no evidence and no clues or leads as to who was executing the bombings. He thought that the Leader was saying only what the Leader's people wanted to hear, and not speaking from his heart when he said that the perpetrators would be caught and punished. Also, Salerno wondered how the Leader of the Country said that those that were responsible were not rational and intelligent individuals, because the award that Electronics Inc. presented to him proved that he was not only rational and intelligent, but more so than the people of the Leader's country.

Salerno did not like the Leader's choice of words that were used when the leader referred to those responsible as terrorists, because he, Salerno, was not a terrorist, and the infidels apparently did not understand that. He figured that if he were a terrorist, the infidels must be terrorists also because they bombed his people indiscriminately at times. He wondered what made him and his people terrorists and the infidels not terrorists. At one stage Salerno chuckled to himself and said, "It would be a good idea if I destroy the People's House." The People's House is a large, spacious residence that the Leader of the Country and his family occupied as their official residence. Every person who became the country's Leader after a General Election would occupy that house. Salerno knew that it would be an almost impossible task, but he figured that it could be done. Anyway, at the moment he would not consider it seriously. It was just a thought, and a fleeting one at that, as he had other things to occupy his mind.

The Leader of the country did not accept any questions, but one of his top Aides did. The Aide accepted a few questions from reporters, one of which was, "How come the Leader is so certain that the perpetrators will be caught?" The Aide replied, "With the sophisticated intelligence that we have in this country, it is not if they will be caught but when." Another reporter asked, "Do you think that the perpetrator is a lone wolf?" The Aide replied, "I do not know, but if it is the actions of a single individual, I think he should be called a lone skunk." The reporters laughed at that answer as the Aide closed his note book and said, "Have a nice day," as he walked away. Salerno became incensed over the fact that the Aide referred to him as a lone skunk, because he knew that a skunk, when it emitted its odor was the worst smelling animal alive, and neither he Salerno, nor his people smelled like a skunk. What that Aide said was to him, Salerno, offensive and the worst mistake that the Aide could have made.

Salerno vowed to get even with the country's Leader, the Leader's family, his Aide and all who resided or worked in the People's House. He thought that they were very insensitive to other ethnicities whose cultures differed. The decision to bomb the People's House with the Country's Leader and the Leader's family and others inside was now a real probability, and only because the Leader's Aide had referred to him as a lone skunk instead of a lone wolf. Leon and Salerno sat opposite each other at the lunch table as they ate and were about to discuss various issues. As soon as they were seated Leon began to speak about the hospital bombing. Salerno knew that this was about to happen but he did not care much because he wanted to hear what Leon would say about the fifth assignment on the hospital. Leon said, "Salerno, one thing I know for certain, and that is, good will conquer evil and right will conquer wrong. I want you to know that. Evil forces may prevail for a time but the good forces will bring them down to their knees. We in this country have no other option but to conquer those humonsters parading around as human beings." Salerno had never heard the term humonsters before, so he asked Leon, "What are humonsters?" Leon knew that he had coined that term and he had never used it before but he thought that it was a fitting and appropriate term to describe the terrorists that were killing people and destroying property without any reason. He noticed that Salerno was watching him and waiting for an answer, so he said, "Humonsters are those people who deliberately and wantonly attack and kill innocent men, women and children. They look like human beings but they act and behave like monsters. We have a saying that speaks about wolves in sheep's clothing, but they are monsters in human's clothing." Salerno appeared to be somewhat confused about what Leon had just said, because in a way Leon was calling him a humonster, although Leon did not know it. He noticed that Leon always came up with negative and degrading words to describe his, Salerno's people, which also applied to him, Salerno. After Leon explained what he meant by the term humonster, Salerno said, "Oh, I understand."

Leon continued talking about how the host country should carefully scrutinize everyone who entered its shores, even infants, because no one can be trusted. He said, "God could have made any country the leading country in the world, but he chose this country, and that is for a reason." Salerno being sarcastic asked, "And what is that reason?" "That reason is so that this country can be a beacon and a refuge and an example for democracy, freedom and justice. God bless this great country." As Leon spoke he turned his head away from Salerno, but not before Salerno noticed that Leon had tears in his eyes, so Salerno said to him, "Man, I notice that you are becoming very emotional." Leon wiped his eyes with the sleeve of his shirt and turned back to face Salerno as he said, "You don't understand. If someone has done all that that someone can to assist another how can that other repay that someone with hatred and evil?" Salerno thought that the question that was asked by Leon was rhetorical, nevertheless, he said, "That's life brother." Leon then reached for a white handkerchief that he had in his pocket, took it out and wiped his eyes, which were red by now. Although he figured that Salerno had seen him crying, nevertheless, he did not want Salerno to see him crying for fear that Salerno would think that he, Leon, was soft and not a real man. When he wiped his eyes with the handkerchief he had turned away from Salerno, but now he was facing Salerno again as Leon said, "All those helpless, innocent people lost their lives. The little children did not even live their lives as yet, and yet they were slaughtered worst than animals. Why? Why?" By now Leon found it very difficult to control his emotions, so he held his head down and sobbed openly. As he sobbed he kept saying "Why? Why?"

Salerno felt like telling Leon to go to hell where all the infidels would eventually be, but he knew that if he told Leon that, Leon might become suspicious, so he reached across the table, patted Leon on his shoulder and said, "I think I understand where you're coming from." Leon raised his head and said, "Enough is enough. It is time that we apprehend the evil doers. I will think long and hard to see if I can come up with any ideas that could assist the investigators. Two heads are better than one, and sometimes those who you least expect to assist may be helpful in solving crimes." Salerno became concerned on hearing Leon say that because he knew that he and Leon worked on the same job and they were usually engaged in conversations. Salerno wondered if he had ever said anything that made Leon suspicious of him, or if Leon had seen anything about him, Salerno, to make Leon suspicious. Salerno thought that he would try to throw Leon off course by saying, "Leon, what do you think about you and I doing a little detective work to see if we can find the people responsible for those bombings?" Leon thought that it was a good idea, but he wondered where they would start. He told Salerno that he would think about it. For the remainder of the day Salerno thought about what Leon said, and he was beginning to think that he could not trust Leon. He decided that before he allowed Leon to tell the investigators that he, Salerno, acted suspiciously or said something that sounded suspicious, he would kill Leon. Salerno decided to change his plan about the next assignment being the People's House, and chose Leon as the next assignment. He decided to use different ingredients and materials in the bomb that he would use to kill Leon. He did not care if the materials and ingredients could be determined. In any event, he would not be a suspect because he and Leon worked for the same employer, and as far as everyone knew, he and Leon were very good friends. Everyone on the job could vouch for that.

Leon lived about three miles from his workplace in a little one bedroom efficiency apartment. To get to and from work Leon would usually drive on the express highway instead of the surface streets, to try to avoid traffic jams. In spite of this, he would more often than not be delayed by backed up traffic and various accidents on the highway caused by speeding and inattentive drivers. Although he had to be at work at 8:00 a.m. he would always leave his home at 7:00 a.m. He did that almost invariably, unless something unforeseen arose that made him late for work. Salerno knew that he did that, and he knew the path that Leon would take to get to and from work, because he secretly followed Leon on at least three occasions. Leon drove an old navy blue station wagon that he had for about seven years, and which had more than its share of breaking down, especially when Leon really needed it. He planned to purchase a more reliable car some time later when he had some more disposable income, but at the moment he would have to use what he had. Salerno decided that in his attack on Leon, he would use only one bird to attack and kill Leon, and he would use a weaker bomb than those he used on the first five assignments. He chose a bird that he called Champ for the assignment. Champ was probably the smartest bird that he had. He decided that it would be easier to bomb Leon's car as opposed to blowing up the whole apartment, and furthermore, less materials and ingredients would be used if he blew up the car. He drove by Leon's apartment a few times for three days in the evenings, and pointed out Leon's car to Champ. He then made a sketch of the car and pointed to where Champ was to release the bomb.

Champ got it right every time, and he appeared jubilant every time he got it right. Salerno timed the bomb to be placed under Leon's car at 6:00 a.m. on a Tuesday morning, knowing that Leon would be in the car about 7:00 a.m. as was Leon's usual practice. Champ had the bomb at the scene on time, and he placed it exactly under the car where he was supposed to have placed it. After placing the bomb Champ headed back to Salerno. At 7:15 a.m. sharp Salerno put in the password and detonated the bomb. Leon almost would not have been in the car because he woke up late and had just entered the car and did not have the chance to shut the driver's door when the bomb exploded. He would usually enter his car, buckle himself in and say a little prayer every morning prior to commencing his journey to work. Before he could do that this morning, a loud, deafening explosion was heard throughout the neighborhood where he lived. The explosion set the car on fire immediately and the gas tank erupted from the full tank of gas that Leon had just filled the previous day. A large hole was blown in the floor of the car just below the front passenger's seat. The impact from the blast blew him straight out through the driver's open door and onto the shoulder of the road. He was on fire and screaming loudly for help. He was a human fireball.

At the time of the blast two off-duty police officers who were on their way to their favorite restaurant for breakfast happened to be passing by Leon's apartment. They lived not too far from Leon's apartment and would use this path every day. They had heard the loud explosion, and now saw Leon on fire and screaming for help, so they jumped out their car and rushed over to the burning car to see if anyone was inside. After seeing no one inside the burning car one of them looked over to the shoulder of the road and saw what he had first believed to be a mannequin on fire, and he realized that it was Leon on fire. Leon was now silent, apparently after going into shock. They rolled Leon over and over on the grass until they finally got the fire extinguished. From their experience of seeing many burnt victims, they knew that he had third degree burns all over his body. On the right side of his head just over his right ear there was a huge gash which appeared to expose some brain matter. His right leg was severed just above the knee, and was bleeding profusely, as he lay still. At first the two police officers thought that Leon was already dead, but one of them found a faint pulse after checking one of his burnt wrists. They tried talking to him so that he would not lose total consciousness. One of the police officers said to him, "Man, please stay with us. Please don't leave us. An ambulance is on the way and should be here shortly. You got to do it for yourself and your family." Leon was not responding.

The other police officer then asked Leon, "What is your name?" Although he asked Leon that question he did not really think that Leon would answer or was in a position to answer it. Leon tried to whisper his name but whatever he said could not be understood, as it was too garbled and too softly spoken. The officer who asked Leon his name cradled Leon's bloodied and burnt head in his arms as it lay in the officer's lap. The fire was totally extinguished. The officer was saying "Come on ambulance, come on." As Leon lay there he seemed to be gasping for breath and choking. The blood from the gash in Leon's head had soiled one of the officer's clothing. The officers kept talking to him in an attempt to prevent him from passing out, because they believed that if he passed out completely he might not survive. Leon could be heard groaning and moaning softly as the two officers remained with him trying to keep him awake. They were worried that he would die if the ambulance did not arrive soon. Shortly thereafter, the ambulance came, speeding with its sirens blasting. The paramedics were stunned to see Leon's condition, and wondered how he did not die before they arrived. Leon was placed in the ambulance with breathing devices hooked up to him. He was given about three injections. His blood pressure was very low and he had already lost a lot of blood. The paramedics determined that his chances of surviving were very low as they observed that he could not answer any of their questions and did not know his name. At the hospital the staff tried to stabilize him. He was given some blood to replace the blood that he lost. After running some tests on him the doctor hooked him up to many tubes and machines and determined that his condition was critical.

Salerno saw the report of the bombing of Leon's car about five minutes before he, Salerno, left for work. After Salerno saw the destruction of the car, he was certain that Leon could not survive the blast. He heard the reporter say that Leon was taken to Long view Hospital in critical condition. That was the hospital that Salerno intended to blow up first but later changed his mind and attacked the other hospital that was closer to him. He believed that it would be just a matter of time before Leon died. He smiled and said softly, "Another infidel will soon go to meet the king of infidels. Leon, you should have never become an infidel. You had the opportunity of becoming a freedom fighter but you refused." While Leon was fighting for his life the investigators were trying hard to find some clues at the scene of the crime. After a meticulous search they found some bomb-making material. They believed at first that it was the same bomber who bombed the other five sites, but after they found the bomb-making material, they decided that it was not the case, because the modus operandi of the bomber of Leon's car was different than that of the bomber of the other bombings, and also because the other bombings were buildings, unlike this one, which was a car.

law enforcement agreed that the bombing of Leon's car was not linked or connected to the other bombings, but they wanted to know who wanted to kill Leon and why did they want him killed. In trying to obtain this information the investigators started questioning employees on the job where Leon worked. None of them, not even his best friend Salerno, noticed anything suspicious. The investigators discovered that Leon was married, although he and his wife were separated. The investigators learned from Salerno that he and Leon were best friends and that some time ago Leon told him that Leon's wife had threatened to kill Leon and had pulled a gun on him. The investigators probed Salerno for more information but he said that that was all that Leon told him, and that he did not know if Leon was serious or not, but Leon appeared to be serious when it was said. The investigators were surprised to hear that, and thought that the tip that they obtained from Salerno might be a good tip. The truth is that Leon did not tell Salerno that his, Leon's wife, had threatened to kill Leon and pulled a gun on him. Salerno thought that if he put Leon's ex wife in the mix it would take any and all suspicion off him. Leon did not tell Salerno that Leon's wife pulled a gun on him. However, the investigators found what Salerno said as being very credible because they discovered that Leon and his wife had had a rocky marriage. Salerno was not the only person that told the investigators that Leon's wife had threatened to kill him.

There was at least one more person who gave the investigators that information. Leon's wife was subsequently interviewed and she admitted that their wedding was not the best and that they constantly argued and fought. She admitted that she had threatened to kill Leon out of anger with absolutely no intention of seeing that become a reality. She said that every spouse at some time in his or her marriage had threatened to kill the other spouse but that did not mean that the spouse who made the threat was serious. One of the police officers present said, "I never threatened to kill my wife and she never threatened to kill me." Another officer joined in and said, "What the officer just said applies to me and my wife also." Leon's wife shook her shoulders up and down and said, "Well, different strokes for different folks." The officers thought that it was a weird comment that she made, and that she was a good suspect in the attempted murder of her ex husband, Leon. However, without more evidence they could not take the suspicion any further. They decided that they would continue their investigations and not arrest her at this point in time.

The doctor attending Leon said that Leon would most likely be paralyzed, and that he was unable to speak because the deep gash to his head had damaged a great portion of his brain, and that could not be repaired. The prognosis was grim but in spite of it being grim, Leon would live, although he would be in a vegetative state. An attending nurse wondered if it would be better for Leon to be dead rather than being a so-called vegetable for the rest of his life. At first when Salerno heard that Leon would live he was very angry because Leon was just like the other infidels, and if he were like the other infidels, he should die like the other infidels. After Salerno discovered that although Leon would live, he would live in a vegetative state and not be any use to himself, Salerno was happy with that. He even thought that that condition might have been worse than Leon dying, because it meant that Leon would suffer and be punished for a very long time until he died. To Salerno, that was a means of torture, and he liked that. He was satisfied that Leon had learnt his lesson from saying the things that he said about the terrorists and the bombings.

About three weeks after Leon's car was bombed Salerno went to visit him in the hospital. Although he had heard of Leon's condition, nevertheless, he was still surprised to see the condition that Leon was in. Leon was lying on his back motionless and staring blankly into space, not being able to speak or hear. Spittle was drooling down the side of his chin and on to the pillow, which the nurse wiped off as soon as she entered the room. While she was in the room she had to wipe his face continuously to keep it from settling on the pillow and probably causing a stench. He could not recognize anyone, not even his so-called best friend, Salerno. One of the nurses attending Leon asked Salerno, "Are you related to Leon?" Salerno replied, "No, we worked at the same job and he was my best friend." "Oh, I can imagine how you feel," the nurse said. Salerno made a slight grimace as he stared at Leon and tried to make his visit and concern for Leon to appear genuine. When Salerno saw the nurse looking at him he closed his eyes and moved his lips as if he were saying a silent prayer for Leon. While he was doing that he appeared to be squeezing Leon's cold and lifeless hand. After Salerno opened his eyes the nurse said, "It's good that you prayed for him because he will need all the prayers that he can get if he is to get any better. Whoever did this to this young man has no feelings for his or her fellow human beings." Salerno was not prepared to hear more of that kind of talk so he Let go of Leon's hand and said, "Keep strong brother and hang on in there." Salerno then told the nurse to have a good day and he left the hospital. He was happy seeing Leon lying there helplessly in a vegetative state, and thought that Leon should have learned his lesson for supporting the infidels.

As he drove away from the hospital he thought of what the investigators said about the bombing of Leon's car not being connected to the other unsolved bombings, and wondered how they could be so stupid. They must have known that there were no bombings recently prior to the bombing of the post office and the other bombings, and suddenly there were the post office and the other bombings, so why couldn't they deduct that all the bombings were connected, he wondered. It was his intention to confuse the investigators into thinking that the bombing of Leon's car and the other bombings were not connected, and it worked. He thought that they would have been intelligent enough to figure out that the culprit might have been the same culprit in all the bombings, but the culprit might have used a different strategy to confuse the investigators into believing that the culprit was not the same person. Salerno exclaimed, "What fools these infidels are!"

Back at Salerno's employment the employees were grieving over Leon's near death experience and saying how sorry they were that something like that happened to him, knowing that he was such a nice person. Some of the employees wanted to collect funds to assist in his medical care, knowing that because of the extent of his injuries, his medical bills would be huge. One of the ladies by the name of Dellareese said that Leon was such a good, mannerly young man who would give anyone the shirt off his back. Another employee said that Leon loved this country. She said that she went to see him and she broke down and cried because she could not stand looking at him in the state that he was in. The other employees looked at Salerno as if they were expecting him to say something because he was the only one who had not said anything, and he was Leon's best friend. Salerno was caught off guard, but he managed to keep his composure and he said, "He is my best friend. It's too sad. I wonder who would do something like that to Leon." He thought that what he had just said was sufficient to placate those in the room, so he said no more.

The police held a press conference in which they decided to speak about the bombings. The spokesperson said that he wanted to clear the air about the most recent bombing which destroyed a young man's car and left the young man in a vegetative state for the remainder of his life. He went on to say, "The most recent bombing has absolutely nothing to do with the previous five unsolved bombings. I wish to state that categorically. They differ in several respects, and I will name a few of the ways in which they differ. Firstly, the person or persons who committed the previous five bombings bombed buildings and this culprit bombed a car. Secondly, the person or persons responsible for the five previous bombings aimed the attacks at several individuals and the person in the most recent bombing aimed the attack at one individual. Thirdly, the person or persons in the five previous attacks used material and ingredients that are untraceable, but that was not the case in the bombing of the car." The spokesperson paused for a while and said, "Although we have not found any fingerprints or DNA in any of the bombings, we are satisfied that the culprits will be found and punished." Most of the viewers were not convinced that the culprits would be found because it was a fairly long time after the post office bombings and the other four bombings and the police still did not have a suspect. After all, there were six bombings already and many lives had been lost, and yet the police did not even have a person of interest. So one wondered how the public could have faith in the police that the police would solve the bombings.

Five weeks after Leon's car was bombed and Leon was severely injured, a young man came forward and told the police that Leon's ex wife had contacted him some time ago about killing Leon, but he refused to do it. The police asked him if he believed that Leon's wife was serious when she asked about killing Leon, and the man said that he thought that she was very serious. The police were elated on receiving this information, and decided to conduct another interview with Leon's ex wife, who was surprised to see them for a second time after she told them that she knew nothing about the attempted murder of Leon. They asked her to come to the police station, which she did. They wanted to question her at the police station where they had full and complete control and where she may be a little intimidated by being at the police station as opposed to being in her own home. When she arrived they ushered her into the interrogation room.

Leon's ex wife appeared to be nervous and afraid as she sat in the chair at a small table pushed in the corner of the room furthest away from the door. She played with her well-manicured long fingernails as she wondered why the police wanted to question her again when she had no additional information for them. After putting her into the room they locked the door and left and went to another room where they monitored her for a while. They wanted to watch her behavior in their absence to see if she appeared nervous, restless, or somewhat guilty, or if she would say anything that may implicate her in Leon's attempted assassination. The police believed that she was involved in the actual attempted murder of Leon or that she knew who tried to kill him. They knew that she wanted him dead because Salerno and another individual had told them that she had said so. Salerno told them that Leon told him that she wanted to kill him and the other individual said that she came directly to him and mentioned that she wanted Leon dead. In the room she appeared to be restless and nervous and harboring some guilt. The police now felt sure from what they were told and how she was acting that she knew who tried to kill Leon and that she was most likely involved. They entered the room and began the interrogation. Two interrogators entered the room and began the interrogation. The first interrogator, a tall slender gentleman wearing a light grey suit sat closer to her than the other gentleman, who was shorter and a little fatter than the other. The taller gentleman began the interrogation.

Detective John: "First let me say that my name is John and my partner's name is Charlie."

Detective John: "First, let me read you your rights. You are not obliged to say anything, but if you do, whatever you say would be taken down in writing and may be used in a court of law. Do you understand that?
Mrs. Chanley: "Yes, I do."

Detective John: "Did you try to kill Leon?" She looked puzzled and in an awkward manner replied,

Mrs. Chanley: "Of course not."

Detective John: "Do you know who tried to kill him by bombing his car?"

Mrs. Chanley: "No. I do not."

Detective John: "Do you know Ossee Thess?"

Mrs. Chanley: "Yes, I know Ossee Thess."

Detective John: "Did you ever try to solicit Mr. Ossee Thess to kill Leon?"

Mrs. Chanley: "Oh my God. I might have said something like I don't mind if he is dead, but I didn't mean that. People always say things like that about other people and their spouses, but that does not mean that they want them dead."

She had begun to perspire and her countenance changed. She had honestly forgotten that she had once made a joke with Ossee Thess about killing Leon, but she was not serious. She and Leon had just had a fight and she was angry at the time and that is when she mentioned that to Ossee Thess. Now she realized that Ossee Thess had told the detectives what she said or he had told someone else what she said and that other person told the detectives. She did not think that Ossee Thess was the kind of person who would reveal something that she said to others. He was once trying to be her lover and she was thinking seriously about it, but she had a change of heart and did not go along with it. She wondered if that is what made Ossee angry and caused him to tell the detectives what she said about wanting Leon dead. The detective wanted a definitive answer because she had said that she might have told Ossee Thess that, so he asked her:

Detective John: "Did you tell Mr. Thess that you would like to see Leon dead?"

Mrs. Chanley: "Yes, I told him that in words to that effect, but I was not serious."

Detective John: "Do you know that Ossee Thess thought that you were very serious?"

Mrs. Chanley: "Well, I do not care about what he thought or thinks. I know that I wasn't serious."

During the investigations the police discovered that Leon's life was insured for One Hundred Thousand Dollars. They also discovered that it was Mrs. Chanley who had taken out the policy and she who was the beneficiary and that there was a double indemnity clause in the policy, which meant that if Leon died by accident the amount of one Hundred thousand Dollars would be doubled. She therefore stood to gain a lot from not only Leon's death, but from his death by accident. She had heard on the evening of the accident a report that Leon had died from grave injuries suffered from the bombing, so the next day she contacted the insurance agent about the policy. The detectives discovered this information and decided to ask her about it.

Detective Charlie: "Mrs. Chanley, are you aware that a life insurance policy was taken out on Leon's life?" As he asked her this question he watched her demeanor and noticed that her level of nervousness increased and she was perspiring more profusely than before.

Mrs. Chanley: "Yes, I think he had a policy."

The detective was becoming angry because he thought that she was being evasive with her answers. He thought that either she knew that there was a life policy on Leon's life or she didn't, and that she did know because she was the one who took it out and she was the beneficiary. He pulled his chair closer to her so that his face was right up to hers, and he continued with the questioning.

Detective Charlie: "Please don't be evasive and funny. Do you not understand my questions? I asked you if you were aware that a life insurance policy was taken out on Leon's life?"
She was getting scared as she could see that at least one of the detectives was becoming angry, and before she could answer, the first detective spoke to the second detective.

Detective John: "Come on Charlie. Don't be so tough on the lady. Give her a chance."

She did not know that they were playing good cop bad cop with her. She felt more comfortable and relaxed after she heard what detective John said to Detective Charlie. She believed that at least one of them was on her side, and was empathetic and sympathetic toward her. She thought that detective Charlie was very intimidating and unreasonable in the manner that he was questioning her. While she was engaged in deep thought detective Charlie said,

Detective Charlie: "I am still awaiting an answer."

She glanced at the other detective as if she was requesting and awaiting his approval for her to respond, and he shook his head as if to say 'go on and answer the question', and in a soft, frightened voice she answered him.

Mrs. Chanley: "Yes, I am aware that an insurance policy was taken out on his life."

The second detective then pounced on that answer and said,

Detective Charlie: "As a matter of fact it is you who took out that policy on Leon's life. Isn't that so?"

She was now realizing that she was being treated as a suspect in the bombing of Leon's car and causing the serious injuries to Leon, and that the detectives had all the relevant information about the life insurance policy. She crossed her legs as she responded,

Mrs. Chanley: "Detective, are you accusing me of bombing Leon's car?"

Detective Charley appeared to be angry as he retorted,

Detective Charlie: "I am not accusing you of a damn thing. I am asking you some damn simple and straightforward questions and you are refusing to answer them. You are getting on my very last nerve. Please answer the questions."

She felt as if detective Charlie was intentionally intimidating, demeaning, and belittling her, and before she could answer him, detective John interjected and said,

Detective John: "Don't be so mean with the lady. I think she is trying her best to answer you. Just give her some time."

As he said that he patted the detective Charlie on the shoulder. She decided that she would answer the question because of detective John whom she saw as a friend and who was always coming to her rescue from whom she called detective Pitbull Charlie. By now she had forgotten the question, so she asked detective Charlie,

Mrs. Chanley: "What was the question?"

She appeared embarrassed as she asked this question, although inside she was blaming detective Charlie for her lack of memory. Detective Charlie gasped as if he were frustrated with her behavior. He shook his head from left to right as he kissed his teeth in disbelief to what she was asking him, when she asked him to repeat the question. He decided to repeat it, so he said,

Detective Charlie: "I asked you if you are the one who took out the life insurance policy on Leon's life?"

Her voice was almost inaudible as she answered.

Mrs. Chanley: "Yes." She then continued, "But he was my husband at the time, and I will repeat, I do not know anything about the bombing of Leon's car." Detective Charlie, the second detective's voice had become calmer and quieter as he said,

Detective Charlie: "And did you check with the insurance company the day after the incident, thinking that Leon was dead?"

She began to tremble because she knew that she had done that and it was not a prudent thing to do. She realized that the detectives had investigated her properly. At this stage she was thinking that maybe she should have had a lawyer present, but she quickly thought against it, because she believed that if she had a lawyer present people might have thought that because she had the lawyer present she was guilty, and she was not guilty. She decided that because she had done nothing wrong she should have nothing to fear, so she decided that she would answer his questions without fear, because although he was a detective, he was only a man. She looked straight into his eyes and said,

Mrs. Chanley: "Yes, I did call the insurance company because I had heard that Leon was killed in the bomb blast."

Detective Charley: "Did you draw a gun on Leon?"

Mrs. Chanley: "No. I never did that."

Detective Charley: "If I tell you that someone said that you did, would that person be lying?"

Mrs. Chanley: "Yes he would."

Detective Charlie got out of his chair and whispered into the other detective's ear, then he turned back to Mrs. Chanley and told her to sit tight for a few minutes and he would be back. Both detectives left the room together.

Detective Charley and the other detective had a short meeting and discussed the interrogation of Mrs. Chanley. All present thought that she was in some way responsible for the bombing of Leon's car, and they believed also that the circumstantial evidence against her was strong and compelling. Firstly, there were two witnesses who reported that she said that she thought that Leon was better off dead. Secondly she took out a sizeable life insurance policy on his life. Thirdly, she tried to collect on the policy even while he was alive. Fourthly, she and Leon were constantly arguing, and fifthly, she was lying to the detectives and she was evasive in her answers. Detective Charlie thought that she should be arrested then and there and be charged with attempted murder or at least conspiring to murder Leon, but the detectives' superior thought that they should wait a little longer to see if more evidence would be forthcoming that would link her to the bombing more directly. Later her home was searched and her phone records were checked, but no new evidence surfaced.

The word got out that there was a suspect in the bombing of Leon's car, and on hearing this, the public felt better and started to see the police in a more positive light. Salerno wondered who the scapegoat suspect was and how the police arrived at that individual being a suspect. When he heard this he fell to his knees in his bedroom laughing, because he knew that whoever the suspect was, it was an innocent person. He thought that this was further proof that the infidels were foolish, incompetent, and did not know what they were doing. He wondered how the police could accuse a totally innocent person for acts that he, Salerno, had committed. He was anxious to find out who the suspect was and what evidence the police had against the suspect. He believed that what was about to happen to that innocent person was proof that many innocent people were falsely accused and convicted of crimes that they knew nothing about. He was engaged in these thoughts while he was watching a television program.

There was a break in the regular programming while Salerno was watching television. The announcer came on and said, "We have breaking news. We have just learnt that there has been an arrest in the bombing of Leon Chanley's car and Mr. Chanley's attempted murder. The name of the person responsible is Daksy Chanley, Leon Chanley's ex wife. I repeat, there has been an arrest in the bombing of Leon Chanley's car and the attempt on his life, and his ex wife is said to be the person that was arrested." Salerno was silent and surprised to hear that Leon's ex wife was the person arrested for Leon's car bombing and the attempt on his life. He started to wonder what evidence the police had on her, but he soon remembered that he had lied to the police and told them that Leon had told him that his wife said that she wanted Leon dead, and that she pulled a gun on him. He thought that it must have been some more evidence than that, and that the police should not have arrested and charged someone on that little hearsay evidence. Strangely, Salerno was beginning to feel sorry for Leon's wife because he knew that she was a woman and that she was innocent. However, before his sympathy increased too much he told himself that whether she did it or not and whether she was a woman or not, she was a damn infidel just like the other infidels, and all infidels were guilty and should perish. He believed that one day the infidels would blame an innocent infidel for the other bombings because he was too smart and intelligent to be caught.

The program that Salerno was watching on the television had resumed just after the announcement about Leon's wife being a suspect, and Salerno had returned to watching it as he ate potato chips. He was about to rise to go to the bathroom when he heard the announcer say that the Chief of Police was about to give a press conference at any minute. The camera then focused on the Chief of Police who was flanked by a detective and another police officer. The Chief of Police was dressed in his uniform as he walked briskly to the podium. He had a broad smile on his thin wrinkled face as he held a white notebook in his right hand. He opened the note book, looked at it and said, "I am more than happy to announce that we have arrested Mrs. Daksy Chanley, the ex wife of Mr. Leon Chanley, for the bombing of his car and the attempt on his life. We believe without a shadow of doubt that we have the right individual, and she will be brought to justice. I will not say more at this stage because I do not want to prejudice or jeopardize the case. For these same reasons I will not be taking any questions. Thanks, and have a good day." He then walked away followed by the detective and the other policeman. Salerno could not believe that the police had actually arrested an innocent woman. He knew that once she was arrested she would remain in jail until the trial, because the offences were very serious. He thought that the infidels' legal system was so fallible, and that instead of calling it the justice system, it should be called the injustice system.

Daksy Chanley's arrest was televised on all the news channels. She was dressed in a house coat with bedroom slippers on her feet, and her hair was not combed. It appeared that the police made the arrest very early in the morning while she was still in bed so that they could spring the element of surprise. Her hands were handcuffed behind her back as she walked with her head held down as if she were ashamed. Reporters had probably become aware of the arrest either by someone leaking it to them or maybe they found out on scanners that some of them possessed that could pick up police communications. The reporters were present, and one of them shouted out, "Did you really try to kill your ex husband?" She held her head up briefly, and it was then that one could see the tears streaming down her worried face. She stared briefly into that reporter's camera and said, "I did not try to kill my husband and I know nothing about it. The Lord knows that I am speaking the truth. The police have arrested the wrong person." After saying that, she held her head down again immediately as the police led her away. A policeman held on to each of her arms as they practically dragged her away.

Later the employees on her job watched the television coverage of her arrest in shock as some of them cried on seeing her in handcuffs and bedroom clothing. They could see fright and uncertainty in her bewildered face. One of her co-employees remarked, "My God, look how they're treating an innocent woman. I know that she is innocent. She is not capable of doing what they say she did." When the police got to their police cruiser one of the police officers helped to push her head down until she was seated inside the cruiser. She tried to wipe the tears from her face by leaning her face to the front shoulder part of her blouse while raising her shoulder. She turned her face from one side to the other, while raising each shoulder to wipe each side of her face. A photographer tried to take a photograph of her as she sat in the back seat of the police cruiser, but she quickly pulled her head into her chest and turned it away from the photographer.

The police cruiser drove away as she still had her head turned to the side, away from the photographer who was trying to take her photograph.
Daksy Chanley was subsequently arraigned for attempted murder, conspiracy to murder, and other offences in relation to the bombing of Leon Chanley's car and the attempt on his life, and she pleaded not guilty. A public defender was assigned to represent her because she could not afford to have a private attorney. Although her attorney wanted to believe that she was innocent, nevertheless, he told her that

the evidence against her was convincing. She had heard that public defenders did not put too much effort in their clients' cases, and now she was experiencing it herself. He said that he would do his best in representing her, but that she must not build up her hopes on an acquittal. She told him, "All my hopes are in my God, and I know that he wouldn't fail me."

Salerno decided that he would sit in on Mrs. Chanley's trial whenever he could. On the opening day of the trial Salerno was there sitting in the second row, not far from the defendant. He could see the right side of her face from where he was sitting, and sometimes saw her whole face whenever she turned around. It was the first time that he had seen her in person. He saw her on television when she was arrested and she looked far different now while she was in court. Her hair was neatly done, unlike when she was arrested. She had on make-up, which made her look much younger and prettier. She wore a light blue two-piece suit with matching shoes and a small matching purse. She appeared to be poised and relaxed as she and her state appointed attorney constantly whispered to each other. After the whispers she would usually look around the packed courtroom and smile. Her attorney was a short stocky, balding man who had a look of a professional and successful attorney. He had a reputation of attacking the prosecution's witnesses right from the beginning, in an attempt to intimidate them, and sometimes it worked.

The prosecutor and the other court staff had already entered the court when the judge entered. She was a middle aged woman with dark, silky, shoulder length hair. As she entered the court room the court clerk announced that everyone should stand, and all present stood until she entered and took her seat, then everyone sat. She looked through some papers that were already on her desk then asked the court clerk if the jury were ready. He indicated that they were and she told him to bring the jury in. The jury of seven men and five women entered the courtroom surveying the room as they entered. The jury appeared to be representative of the community because there were in addition to men and women, Caucasians, Afro Americans, an Asian, and Hispanics. After they were all seated the judge asked the prosecutor if he was ready to open his case, and he said that he was. It was when the prosecution opened their case that Salerno heard the evidence that the prosecution was relying on to convict Daksy Chanley.

After hearing the prosecution's opening evidence Salerno was convinced that the evidence was strong enough to convict her. He believed that if he did not know that she was innocent, from the evidence that he heard mentioned in the prosecution's opening address, he would have thought that she was guilty also. He admitted that the evidence was circumstantial, but he thought that it was a strong circumstantial case. It was amazing, he thought, how the infidels could fabricate and present evidence against an innocent person to make that person appear to be guilty. He heard of this, but now he was about to witness it for himself. He wondered why Daksy Chanley put herself in that position by the things she said and did. He realized that he had played a part of it also by lying to the police and telling them that Leon had told him that Daksy wanted to kill him, and that she had pulled a gun on him. Anyway, he took some comfort in knowing that the prosecution would not be calling him as a witness because they considered that his evidence was hearsay evidence and was not admissible. He never liked to lie but if the lie he was telling was against an infidel, he had no problem with that because he knew that his God would not punish him for that.

The prosecution began to call their witnesses that they relied on, beginning with Mr. Ossee Thess, who testified on oath that the defendant spoke to him about murdering Leon. He said that one day, about six months prior to the incident which destroyed Leon's car and seriously injured him, Daksy and he were at a restaurant downtown enjoying a friendly meal. He said that they were friends from high school days. He said that all of a sudden Daksy said words to the effect that Leon would be better off dead, and he was very shocked hearing those words coming from her lips. He said that for a moment he was dumbfounded and did not know how to respond to what she had just said. the public Defender asked him how he took those remarks made by Mrs. Chanley, and he said that he thought that she was as serious as cancer. Some of the jurors chuckled when he used that phrase. Ossee Thess' evidence was brief. After the prosecutor finished with him the state appointed attorney began to question Ossee Thess.

Under cross examination it was put to Ossee Thess that Mrs. Chanley did say words to that effect to him but it was only a joke and not to be taken seriously. Ossee disagreed and said that he knew that she was serious because she used those words after she told him that she and Leon had just had a big fight, and furthermore, she was not making a joke, because a joke is meant to be laughed at, and neither she nor he laughed at it. The prosecutor asked him if Mrs. Chanley ever used words to that effect to him or in his presence prior to that occasion or after that occasion, and he said, "She did not." After Ossee Thess completed his evidence, the prosecutor called an agent from the insurance company, who confirmed that Daksy Chanley was the person who had the life insurance policy on Leon's life written up, and she was the one who paid the premiums. The agent said that the policy was written about six months prior to the incident in which Leon's car was blown up and Leon was injured. He said that he heard about that incident on television the same day it occurred, but he had not heard that Leon had died. He was asked, "When was the first time you saw Mrs. Daksy Chanley after the bombing of Mr. Chanley's car?" and he replied, "The very next day about 9:00 a.m." One of the jurors gasped and shook her head from left to right, as two others who were sitting in the front row looked at each other with a look of disgust and unbelief.

The prosecutor asked the agent to tell the court the purpose of Mrs. Daksy Chanley's visit to his office on the day following the bombing of Mr. Chanley's car, and he said, "She came in and sat at my desk and I asked how I may be of assistance to her. She said that her husband was killed the previous day in a car accident. I told her that I saw the report on the news, but I did not know that he was killed. She assured me that he was, so I gave her some forms to fill in and told her that she would have to bring a copy of his death certificate when she returned with the forms." The prosecutor asked the agent what Mrs. Chanley's demeanor was like when she visited his office, and he said, 'She was calm, not crying, and seemed to be very interested in obtaining the money." The prosecutor then showed the agent a copy of the policy and the agent agreed that it was a copy of the policy for One Hundred Thousand Dollars, and that Mrs. Daksy Chanley was the beneficiary of that policy. He said that he was surprised that she would be checking on the policy so early and that he was somewhat suspicious about her. He was asked why he was suspicious about her, and he said because even if Mr. Chanley had died he thought that she should have waited a while before trying to obtain the money from the policy, as most people who just lost loved ones did. Some of the jurors were seen shaking their heads in disbelief as the agent spoke.

After the insurance agent gave his evidence the court took a twenty minutes break, and when it resumed, the detectives began to give their evidence. They spoke of the interview with the defendant and how she was evasive and even told them lies at first. They said that she did not want to admit that she had a life insurance policy on Mr. Leon Chanley's life, and did so only after she realized that they knew about it. They said that she did not want to admit that she had mentioned anything about wanting Mr. Chanley dead, and she did so only after they mentioned the name of Ossee Thess to her. Jurors were seen shaking their heads and looking at each other. After all the evidence was heard the prosecution closed their case and the defense called Daksy Chanley to the witness box to give evidence. She walked slowly to the witness stand with her head up and her eyes straight forward, as if trying to avoid direct contact with the jury which was sitting more to her left. She sat in the witness' chair as she played with her hair a little and tried to smooth out her dress under her.

All eyes were on Daksy Chanley as the courtroom was so silent that one could hear a feather drop. Daksy testified that she and her husband had some years of good times but things went sour after a while, and that she thought that both of them should take responsibility for that. She said that the marriage ended in divorce and that although she and Leon did not engage in much conversation after the divorce, she did not hate him, and that she wrote a policy of life insurance on his life because many spouses did that. She said that she did not try to kill Leon and she did not know anyone who tried to kill him because he was a likeable person. The state appointed attorney asked her if she knew Ossee Thess and she said that she and Ossee had attended the same high school and were friends for many years. She went on to say that she had made remarks to Ossee about wishing that her husband was dead or words to that effect, roughly six months or more prior to the accident involving Leon's car, but she was not serious when she made those remarks. She said, "At some point in time many people make jokes about wishing that their spouses were dead." When she said that people in the courtroom were heard laughing and murmuring, and the bailiff had to shout 'Order' a few times.

The jury were mumbling among themselves and shaking their heads in disbelief and disagreement about what she had just said. She was asked about the meeting with the detectives, and she said that she was scared and nervous, but she eventually told them the truth. The state appointed attorney asked her if she were evasive in answering the detectives' questions, and she said, "I don't think that I was evasive in answering their questions, and if it appeared that I was evasive it was only because I was nervous and afraid. I have never been in a situation like this before, so it is expected that I would be nervous. I am asking the jury to please believe me because I'm telling the truth and the Lord knows that I'm telling the truth. I am nervous and afraid at this moment." At this point she started crying and wiping her tears with the back of her hand, so the bailiff passed her some Kleenex. As she wiped her face she said, "I'm begging you for the last time please don't send me to prison. I'm not guilty. I would have never tried to kill Leon, and I do not know how to make bombs neither do I know anyone who makes bombs. I had a life insurance policy on Leon's life because that is something that every married couple who could afford it does."

The prosecutor started cross examining Daksy by asking her why she told Ossee Thess that she wanted her husband dead. She responded that she did not say that she wanted him dead that what she thought she said was that he might have been better off dead. The prosecutor asked her if that was not in essence the same thing, and she reluctantly agreed. He then asked her why she insured his life if she and he were no longer husband and wife, and she said that she thought that it was the right thing to do. The jury shook their heads as chuckling was heard coming from the people in the courtroom. The prosecutor continued his attack by asking her why she tried to obtain the insurance money while Mr. Chanley was still alive. She put her face in her hands and held her head down for a few seconds, after which she raised her head, removed her hands from her face and said, "It was a mistake. I thought that he was dead." The prosecutor told her that even if he was dead why not out of respect wait to collect the money.

She said that she wanted to get the money to assist with his funeral. The prosecutor grinned and said, "So you just came up with that." She disagreed that she had just come up with that. Finally, the prosecutor put to her that she was involved in the attempt to assassinate Mr. Leon Chanley and that she did it to collect the insurance money from the policy that she wrote on his life. She continued shaking her head in disagreement as he spoke, and laughed at him, and finally she said, "Sir, I did not try to kill Leon and I do not know who tried to do it. The Lord is my judge." The prosecutor sat as she began to walk back to her seat beside her attorney. When she got to her seat she held her head on the table and cried aloud. The judge took a brief recess.

When the court resumed the lawyers made their closing speeches. In this jurisdiction the prosecution addressed the jury first. The prosecution reminded the jury of all the circumstantial evidence, which when put together like a jig saw puzzle, formed an evidence puzzle which points to the defendant's guilt. He reminded the jury that they must not show sympathy for the defendant or for Mr. Leon Chanley. He said, "You must decide this case on the evidence, and I submit to you today that the evidence of the defendant's guilt is overwhelming. We do not have witnesses who actually saw what happened, and we did not find any bombs or bomb-making materials or ingredients at her house, but you must remember, no one will be that stupid to keep bombs or bomb-making materials or ingredients at his or her home. She was laughing while I was speaking. That says a lot. There is only one sensible and reasonable verdict, and that is guilty on all counts." He thanked the jury and sat.

In the defense's closing arguments, the public defender reminded the jury that this case was a purely circumstantial evidence case. He then explained what he meant by circumstantial evidence, and told them that there were no eye witnesses, no forensic evidence and no fingerprints that would link his client to the bombing of Mr. Leon Chanley's car. He said that the prosecutor relied on a statement that Mrs. Chanley made to one Ossee Thess as a joke, and the fact that his client took out a life insurance policy in Leon Chanley's name after they were no longer married, and that she inquired about the insurance money from the policy while her husband was still alive, and so soon after the incident. He said that she honestly believed that Mr. Chanley was dead and that nothing was wrong or unlawful in trying to get the funds from the policy as soon as she tried. After all, he said, "She was the one who paid the premiums. Mrs. Chanley is not guilty. She is an innocent woman who does not know how to make bombs and does not know anyone who makes bombs. Not many people know how to make bombs although one can go on the internet and learn how to. I bet if everyone in this courtroom is questioned about knowing how to make bombs, not one person in here would know how to make bombs, or would know someone who knows how to make bombs."

Salerno was a little uneasy and worried when he heard the Public defender say that, because he knew that he, Salerno, could make bombs and he knew someone who could make bombs. He hoped that no one would ask the one hundred plus persons in the courtroom if they could make bombs or if they knew someone who could make bombs. In any event, he figured that if he was asked he would not admit to the truth and no one would know that he was lying. When the Public Defender said that the judge smiled and chuckled and said, "Mr. Public defender you may be surprised to discover who in this courtroom could manufacture bombs. However, I will not permit that question to be asked in my courtroom." The Public Defender then said, "Your Honor Judge, I am only trying to make the point that the prosecution charged the wrong person. Members of the jury please find Mrs. Daksy Chanley not guilty. Find her not guilty not because I asked you to but because it is the right thing to do on the evidence the prosecution presented to this court." He made a little bow to the jury, smiled at Daksy Chanley and sat. As he sat she shook his hand and smiled as if to say thank you, you did a good job. She was evidently pleased with his closing argument and she felt that the jury was paying attention to him and what he said, and would find her not guilty.

The judge later summed up the case to the jury, trying to mention all the essential points that would assist them in their deliberations. His summing up was fair and balanced. At first he directed the jury on the law, telling them that he was the judge of the law, and he alone would determine the law, and that whatever he told them the law was, they had to accept it. He went on to say that they were judges also, but their role was different then his. He said that their role was that of judges of the facts, and that whatever they determined the facts were, everyone, including him, had to accept that. He said that the facts came from the witness box and not from the lawyers or anything they heard out of the courtroom. The prosecution had to prove the case against the defendant by proving it beyond reasonable doubt or by making the jury feel sure of the defendant's guilt. He directed them that the defendant had nothing to prove. After explaining the law involved, he went on to mention certain aspects of the evidence that the prosecution presented and certain aspects of the evidence that the defense presented, and continued by telling them what the defendant's defense was. His summing up was fair and well balanced, not taking any side, and pointing out the strengths and weaknesses of the prosecution's case and the defense's case. When he finished his summing up the jury left the courtroom to deliberate. Daksy watched them as they left in single file, and she was wondering what they had on their minds. She wondered if some of them had already made up their minds, and if so, what their decisions were.

While the jury were out deliberating Daksy and her lawyer chatted. The prosecutor left the courtroom for about half an hour. Daksy was smiling and appeared to be up-beat and confident that she would be victorious. She was thinking positively about the case and believing that she would win it because she knew that she knew nothing about the bombing of Leon's car. Her lawyer's positive attitude, calm behavior, and confidence gave her confidence that she would prevail. The prosecutor soon returned laughing and making jokes with his assistant. He appeared relaxed and like someone who was confident of victory. It was obvious that somebody would be victorious and somebody would be disappointed when the jury returned with their verdicts. There were five counts against Daksy Chanley, the most serious being attempted murder and conspiracy to commit murder. Her lawyer thought that if she could win only one or two of the counts against her it would be good if it is one of the most serious counts, or the two most serious counts, although he had a feeling that he would win with a complete acquittal because the prosecutor's case was weak.

The jury remained out deliberating for three hours and ten minutes, and finally they knocked on their door to signify that they had reached a verdict. All the smiles disappeared from the prosecutor's face, the public defender's face and Daksy Chanley's face. Daksy and her attorney appeared to be very nervous as the jury filed in silently. After all the jurors entered and were seated, the judge asked if they had reached their verdicts and the foreman said that they had. The judge then asked if the verdicts were verdicts upon which they all agreed, and the foreman answered that the verdicts were verdicts that they had all agreed. The judge then asked the clerk of court to let him see the verdicts, and the clerk of the court brought the verdicts to the judge folded on a white piece of paper. The judge looked at the verdicts expressionless as Daksy and her lawyer tried to read his face for an indication as to how the jury decided, but they could not. The public defender also tried to get an indication of how the jury decided by trying to read the judge's expressionless face, but that was unsuccessful. The prosecutor and the public defender glanced at the jury almost simultaneously to see if they could glean an indication of how they decided, but they were unsuccessful because all the jurors stared straight ahead as if they had planned to do that.

Daksy was afraid to look at the jury. However, at one stage she glanced at them through the corner of her left eye but they were not looking in her direction.

The judge then passed the paper with the verdicts on it back to the clerk of court and asked her to read the verdicts to the court, and she read them out loudly. She began to read, "On the first count of attempted murder against Daksy Chanley, we the jury find the defendant guilty as charged. Daksy thought that the clerk of court had said not guilty, as she was anticipating, so she gave a fairly loud sigh of relief and said, 'Thank you Lord.' It was only when her lawyer, seeing her reaction, whispered to her, "The clerk said guilty, but don't worry, there are four more to come." Her joyful expression changed to one of sorrow. After the clerk read the second count and said 'Guilty', Daksy did not remember any more of what the clerk said. A few minutes later she discovered that the jury had found her guilty on all five counts. Salerno wondered how someone who knew nothing about a crime could be found guilty of that crime. He concluded that the infidels' system of justice stunk and that he wanted no part of it. There were two other employees from Salerno's job present in court who came to see that Leon got justice. Unlike Salerno, they sat all the way at the back of the courtroom. They were elated at the verdicts and thought that Leon received some sort of justice.

The judge announced that he would set sentencing for two weeks from today's date as he had another matter to commence shortly. He informed the police that meanwhile, Mrs. Chanley would be remanded in custody at the central prison. After that announcement everyone rose and exited the courtroom. As Salerno left the courtroom he saw his two fellow employees who told him that they were in support of Leon, who could not be there. Salerno once again lied and said that he was there for the same reason and that he was happy with the verdicts. Just prior to walking out the courtroom door Salerno heard a loud shriek coming from inside the courtroom, and looked around to see where it came from. He saw Daksy Chanley lying on the courtroom floor and her attorney stooping over her and shouting for someone to call 911. Apparently the five convictions just set in and she realized that she was going to prison and that she could be going to prison for life or for a very long time, and she fainted and fell to the floor hitting her head very hard on the concrete floor, knocking her unconscious. The Public defender was frantically shouting "Call an ambulance she hit her head hard on the floor and it is bleeding profusely." The police officers in the courtroom were trying desperately to assist her as they unlocked the handcuffs from her hands that were handcuffed behind her. Even if she were conscious when she was falling she could not break the fall because her hands were handcuffed behind her. One of the police officers was on the phone speaking with 911 and begging for an ambulance to be sent quickly because it was an emergency. The Public Defender was slapping Daksy's face and saying, "Mrs. Chanley, Mrs. Chanley, can you hear me?" There was no response from her as she lay completely still and unconscious. A white piece of cloth was placed around her head to stem the bleeding, but the bleeding continued and soon the cloth was stained red with her blood.

The ambulance came speeding with its siren blaring as vehicles in its path hurried out of the way. It had hardly stopped when the paramedics jumped out with their life saving gear in their hands and hurried into the courtroom. They observed that Daksy was still unresponsive when they got to her. Immediately they placed the oxygen mask over her face and started giving her oxygen, and began to clean the wound to her head and bandaged it. It was a huge wound and it was still bleeding a lot. The paramedics lifted her onto the gurney and rushed her to the hospital. When they arrived at the hospital they rushed Daksy inside and the doctors began to work on her immediately. They ran a series of tests and did an MRI to determine if there was any brain damage. The MRI determined that she had a huge concussion to her brain which could have a devastating effect on her in the future if she survived. The doctors did all that they could to stop the swelling of her brain which had swollen a lot already. They had a small tube to the brain which they used to drain fluid from the brain and which should eventually reduce the swelling. After that they gave her some medication intravenously and waited to see how her body would respond. She remained unconscious for three days and when she regained consciousness she was unable to speak and walk on her own.

It was determined that the area of the brain that deals with equilibrium was very badly damaged, and once this area was damaged there was nothing that could be done to repair it. She received physical therapy daily to assist her in regaining strength in her legs, and learning to speak again. Her prognosis was not very good. Her doctors said that it was very unlikely that she would get any better, because the brain was a difficult organ to heal. Her sentencing day came and she was still hospitalized in a serious condition. The judge decided to postpone sentencing for another few months, thus giving Daksy more time to recuperate from her illness. When the adjourned date came she was much better than she was on the first day that was set for sentencing, and she was wheeled into the courtroom in a wheel chair by a close family member and escorted by the police. The judge expressed his sympathy for her medical problems and said that justice must be done, and should not be hindered by any subsequent events other than death. Salerno was seated in the second row again listening intently to what the judge was saying. The judge started speaking directly to her, telling her that she made a conscious decision to become involved in the bombing of Mr. Leon Chanley's car and attempting to take his life, and because of that the jury found her guilty and she had to be sentenced for the crimes that she committed. He said that she should not expect anyone to have sympathy for her because she showed no sympathy to Mr. Chanley, and that the crime was a senseless and brutal one. He went on to say that he did not believe that she actually planted the bomb, but he believed that she engineered and assisted in the planning of the vicious crime, and because of that he was sentencing her to thirty years to life. She began to cry and to say something to the judge but she was unable to do so. The judge then said while she was in the hospital she was essentially in prison and would have police guard twenty four seven, until she could be moved to the main prison. She was then taken back to the hospital crying and mumbling something that was inaudible. Her court appointed lawyer apologized to her and promised that he would file an appeal on her behalf to prove her innocence.

The media carried the story of what they called poetic justice in the Leon Chanley's case. They explained that it was Leon Chanley's wife, Daksy Chanley, who bombed his car and almost took his life. They said that he was in a vegetative state because of her, and since the bombing and trial of Daksy she fell in the courtroom and hit her head, and is now seriously injured and cannot speak and can hardly walk. They wondered if she was somewhat and in some way involved in the other unsolved bombings. One reporter said that he doubted that Daksy actually did the bombing of Leon's car, but the evidence was overwhelming that she was involved and she knew who did it, and that the jury felt the same way. He went on to say that because of her medical condition we may never know the full truth about the bombing of Leon's car and the other bombings. Not everyone thought that Daksy got what she deserved. There were those, although the minority, who believed that she was innocent. Those who did not think that she deserved such a stiff sentence said that she had already been punished by her mishap in the courtroom after she was convicted when she fell and seriously injured herself, and that to punish her further with such a long prison sentence was unconscionable and unreasonable.

Salerno was beginning to feel sorry for Daksy because she was not the one that he thought should be punished. He had just left the courtroom when she fainted and hit her head and was knocked unconscious. He heard the news just before he entered his car to drive off and after peeping into the courtroom he remained outside the courtroom in his car until the ambulance arrived and drove off with her. As the ambulance drove off he sat in his car in deep thought, wondering how such an advanced and progressive country like the host country could make such a grave mistake like the one it was making with Daksy Chanley. That only showed that the infidels were crazy and did not know what they were doing. He wondered how they could find her guilty when they had no proof that she planted the bomb or knew the person or persons who planted the bomb. There was no connection to her with the bomb. If they wanted to get you, they will get you, he figured. He believed that there must be many innocent persons in the infidels' prisons.

Daksy Chanley remained in the hospital for eight months after the mishap in the courtroom, after which she was transferred to the women's maximum security prison, where she was assigned a specialist nurse to assist with her physical therapy and to ensure that she received her medication on time. Her speech had improved tremendously. She cried just about every day in prison, and after some therapy her speech returned slowly. After that, whenever she could she would tell her cell mate that she was innocent and that she did not receive justice. Although the cell mate knew that most guilty persons who went to prison said that they were innocent, somehow she believed Daksy when Daksy told her that she was innocent. Many other prisoners did not believe her. One day a prisoner said to her, "Everyone who comes in here says that he or she is innocent, so it is not surprising hearing it from you." Daksy knew that it would serve her no good to become angry at what that prisoner said, so she remained calm and replied, "One day you will find out that I am speaking the truth, and you will believe me, one day."

Daksy decided that she would make her time in prison a positive stay by assisting others, so she decided to use her teaching skills to do so. She was a school teacher for many years so she decided that it would be best to assist prisoners who could not read and write and those who had limited skills in reading and writing. She even learned sign language to assist a prisoner who was a deaf mute. The prison superintendent was convinced that Daksy was innocent so he decided to assist her in any way that was legally possible, and he did so by first assisting in obtaining an instructor in sign language to teach her the sign language bi-weekly. After receiving some lessons she soon mastered the sign language and she was able to assist at least three other female prisoners with hearing and speech disability.

The police were elated because they had not only caught the person who tried to kill Leon Chanley, but they had managed to secure a conviction and long prison sentence for that person. The Chief of Police took to the airwaves and made the following statement to the public, "I am aware that the public heard from me on this matter, but I think that it is important for you, the public, to know that the police are constantly working to keep you safe. The criminals may run but they cannot hide. Mrs. Daksy Chanley thought that she could hide but we caught her and she is where she belongs. She can no longer hurt anyone." The Chief of Police's comments were aired on the evening news also, and when Salerno returned home from work he saw and heard it. He thought that the Chief of Police was nothing but a fake and a liar, and wondered how the Chief of Police could take credit for solving crimes that were not solved.

Although Salerno used the word 'crime', nevertheless, he hated that word when referring to what he did, because he did not see his actions as crimes, but as justifiable acts that would be done by those who loved their country. In any event, his main goal was to inflict harm on the infidels and keep suspicion away from him, and for this reason he thought that the Chief of Police was doing a good job in executing his, Salerno's, goal. While he pondered on the Chief of Police's statement, an idea came to him. He decided that he would write the Chief of Police and thank him for solving the bombing of his best friend's car and assisting in sending the culprit to prison. He sat at his dining room table laughing as he began to write, "Dear Chief of Police, it is with a great sense of pride and appreciation that I write to commend you and all those who were involved in solving the attempted murder of my dear friend Leon Chanley. That attempt on his life left me so devastated that I thought about taking my own life because he was my best friend, but you have caused me to regain my faith in the justice system and in life. I pray that you and your men continue to give excellent service to this great country." Salerno signed the letter and hand delivered it to the police station. When the Chief of Police received it he was so proud to receive such a positive feedback from a concerned citizen that he called a staff meeting and read it to all present, and after reading it he posted a copy of it on the notice board.

The Chief of Police remembered Salerno as Leon Chanley's best friend when the investigators questioned Salerno and his co-employees just after the bombing of Salerno's car. After the Chief of Police received the letter of commendation from Salerno, he wrote Salerno a note of thanks thanking him for his very kind remarks, and reminding him that he, the Chief of Police, and his men, would continue doing their best to rid the country of bad people like Daksy Chanley. Salerno showed the thank you note to all the members of his work place and stuck a copy of it on their notice board at his workplace. Salerno's supervisor was very proud of Salerno, and Salerno appeared to be overjoyed because the Chief of Police wrote him that note of thanks and because the supervisor was praising him. The truth is that Salerno was merely pretending, hoping that others would interpret his actions as love for Leon and love for the host country, which in reality, he hated both. The day after Salerno received the note of thanks from the Chief of Police the Chief of Police called him by phone and again thanked him personally. As soon as Salerno realized that it was the Chief of Police calling, he turned up the volume on the phone and put it on speaker so that all who were in hearing distance could hear what the Chief of Police was saying. He made gestures for the others to draw closer to the phone, which they did.

The Chief of Police and Salerno spoke for about three minutes, and when Salerno hung up the phone he was all smiles because the ruse on his part was working well. The Chief of Police's last words to him were, "Keep up the good works. It is people like you who show so much love and caring that make this country so great and successful." As far as Salerno was concerned, the police now saw him as a good person in the community who supported the police, and they would be looking at him in a positive light, and because of that he might never be seen as a suspect or person of interest in any of the bombings. This was a good feeling, so he decided that he would play the infidel's game better than they played it and win every time he played. He thought that it would be prudent to carry his con game a little further by visiting churches and being noticed in them. That was totally against his religion but he knew that the infidels put a lot of weight on religion although most of them were great sinners, even the preachers. The following Sunday he dressed in a dark blue suit with matching necktie and a black pair of shoes and attended the nearest church. It was a Pentecostal Church with a mixed congregation and a Caucasian pastor. The members and visitors appeared to be very friendly and deeply involved in their praise and worship. After the service, many of the congregation, including the pastor, shook his hand and thanked him for attending. His offering was one hundred dollars, which the pastor saw him put in the offering basket.

The person who collected the offering seemed very pleased when she saw the amount that he put in the plate. She gave him a wide smile and said, "God bless you." He attended the church on several occasions and gave generously every time he attended. He soon became well known by the pastor and members, who were now addressing him as 'brother Salerno'. On one occasion when the pastor was preaching he singled Salerno out saying, "Some of you need to be more faithful in your giving and your attendance like brother Salerno. He recently started attending church but he is attending faithfully and giving generously. Let's give a round of applause for brother Salerno." The whole congregation started clapping as Salerno stood, smiled and waved as he turned in all directions. He said to himself, "Suckers, you fell for my trap, and now you are entangled in my web of deception." Whenever church members or the pastor saw Salerno on the street or some other place they would say, "Hi brother Salerno." He had become well known to them and well loved and respected by them. It was what he had set out to do, and it was working so well. He prayed to his god thanking his god for making it possible for all his plans to go so smoothly. It was proof positive that his god was greater than the infidels' god, he thought, because through his god he was succeeding in all that he set out to accomplish.

Jayne Blulow the bird trainer, got employment with the local university to teach an experimental course on the training and caring of birds. It was intertwined with an environmental course and aimed at understanding birds so that human beings can better protect them and their environment. Jayne was enthusiastic about that course because it was right down her alley. She had not done any bird training for about one year although she still had two birds that were well trained and that she always interacted with. Her first batch of students was thirty five in number and they were just as enthusiastic about the course as she was. She had no idea that so many people were interested in the training and caring of birds. The classes were full of fun as they learned about the different species of birds, the behavior of birds and their feeding habits, etc. She told the students of her own experience in handling birds and understanding how intelligent birds were when human beings got to understand and respect them. After the first batch of students graduated Jayne went on to teach many more. It was obvious that she enjoyed the classes as much as the students did or more.

It was exactly one year and six months since Leon's car was blown up and Leon was seriously injured. His condition had not improved, and the doctors did not think that it would improve. The doctors wanted to disconnect the life saving device that kept him alive but his family refused to allow them to do it. The family always believed that one day Leon would come out of the coma when least expected and return to his normal self. His mother told the doctor who was caring for Leon that the Lord gave life and the Lord should be the only one to take life. The doctor tried to convince her that Salerno was alive only because of the life saving machine and if that machine were disconnected he would die immediately. He told her that Salerno was already brain dead, but Salerno's mother insisted that she would not consent to her son being deliberately killed by doctors. She said, "His wife killed him and now you doctors want to kill him. That is not fair. He is my child and I love him. You must remember the Hippocratic Oath which says 'at first do no harm.' Why do you want to harm him?" That ended the conversation on that topic.

For a while there was no more talk of the bombings that occurred prior to the bombing of Leon's car. There appeared to be no reason to fear further bombings because there had been no bombings for approximately one and a half years. Furthermore, the last bombing in which Leon Chanley almost lost his life was different than the other bombings, and the culprit, Leon's wife Daksy, was caught and convicted. It was believed by some that because of the long time interval between then and the last bombing in which Leon Chanley's car was bombed and he almost lost his life, that Leon's wife Daksy, might be the person who committed all the bombings, because since her conviction and incarceration there were no more bombings. They believed that this fact made her a viable suspect in all the other unsolved bombings. The police did not want to hear that because as far as they were concerned the bombing of Leon's car and the other bombings were not related. The bomber of Leon's car was tried, convicted and sentenced, and that was the end of that. The police did not want to hear anymore about those bombings being related because among other things, the materials used in Daksy's bomb were distinguishable, unlike the other bombs, and a serial bomber, like a serial murderer, usually did not change his modus operandi. It was obvious that this issue would not go away because there would always be those who believed that Leon's wife was the sole bomber of all the bombing incidents, or she knew those who committed all the bombings.

The People's House was huge with many rooms. There was a room in which the Leader of the Country and his spouse slept and one in which their children slept. There were offices for the Leader of the Country and those who worked from his office. The chief chef and other cooks and kitchen staff had a special area for them to relax and eat, and there were other rooms, like the room in which reporters congregated when the Leader was giving press conferences. The former Leaders of the Country had occupied the People's House and some of the rooms were named after them. The whole property was well protected by surveillance equipment and human guards who were always vigilant when doing their job. All over the compound were Federal agents and surveillance equipment, some not in plain view, and some on the roof of the building. Salerno knew that it would be difficult to enter the compound, and in any event, he would not want to enter it in the event that surveillance was checked, he would not want to see his car or him in the area on the footage. He even worried about driving by because he figured that the surveillance equipment might be pointed outside the compound in the streets surrounding the People's House, so he rented a vehicle and drove by with his killer birds as he pointed to the People's House saying, "People's House, People's House People's House." He drove by only once, but he had a post card on which the People's House was imprinted. The birds did not need to drive by more than once by then. They grasped concepts and tasks very quickly. He showed the birds the photograph of the People's House for about four months as he pointed out the locations where he wanted them to release the bombs. He placed red Xs on four points on the roof and six points on the ground around the People's House. The birds understood exactly what they had to do and demonstrated this by pointing out the spots where they were supposed to release the explosive devices. Every time they did so correctly. Salerno was satisfied with their performance, and he rewarded them with extra stimulant laced food every time they got it right. The reward encouraged them to be accurate.

One morning Salerno woke up and decided that the Tuesday of the following week would be the day that he would execute his seventh assignment. He knew that the birds were well prepared and ready to go, although he was aware that this assignment would be very challenging, but he knew that his birds could execute it successfully. He had exactly seven days before the execution of his seventh assignment, and he was anxiously anticipating the coming of that day. This assignment would have international ramifications as the government could be demoralized and destabilized if the Leader of the Country was killed. Without doubt this bombing would be the big one and the mother of all domestic bombings. It would penetrate what some of the infidels would call the impenetrable, because some of the best security in the world was at the People's House. By penetrating them he would be sending a message to the infidels that he is a force to be reckoned with, and that nothing and no one were safe from him and his birds when they decided to attack, destroy, and kill.

All day long while Salerno was at work he thought of the number seven assignment and how easy he and his birds would execute it. As the time drew nearer for the execution of the seventh assignment, the more tensed he became. On the day before the execution of the seventh assignment it was announced that the Leader of the Country was about to travel abroad the following day. That day was supposed to be the day of the execution of the assignment. Salerno became angry as he never saw it coming. He wondered why the announcement of the Leader of the Country's departure was made so late. Had it been announced a week or even a few days earlier he could have executed the seventh assignment earlier. He realized that the government might have announced the Leader of the Country's departure at a late stage for security reasons and for the protection of the Leader of the Country and his family. As a matter of fact, Salerno's foiled plan to bomb the People's House and kill the Leader of the Country and his family was a good example of why the Leader of the Country 's trips abroad should be announced as late as possible, and maybe not announced at all on some occasions. Although he was disappointed that he could not execute the bombing of the People's House as his seventh assignment the following day, he decided that he would look for another target which he would have executed in another week from today's date.

The following week Salerno drove around looking for another target to destroy. After driving around for about three days, on the fourth day he was driving by the international airport and he pulled off the road alongside the airport fence to watch the airplanes take off and land. It was then that the idea came to him to blow up some passenger planes while they were still on the ground, but with passengers in them. He went to his computer and checked the schedule for departures of some of the airline flights. He then took his birds to the airport fence where he could see the airplanes taking off and landing, and he pointed out the planes and said to the birds "Airplanes, airplanes, airplanes." He took some photographs of the airplanes while he sat in his car with the birds, and later made sketches of the planes on his sketching pad. He pointed out the wheel wells of the planes underneath the belly of the planes to the birds and placed a red X on the spot where each wheel well would be. The sketches that he did had the wheel wells opened. He even had a replica of a passenger plane with a wheel well that could open and close. Finally, the day came for the execution of the new seventh assignment. Usually when airplanes departed and landed, cars would be parked alongside the southern fence to watch them take off and land. Salerno parked about three hundred feet from the nearest car. He then released three birds with explosive devices and cameras strapped to them. As he released them he said 'Airplanes, wheel wells, airplanes, wheel wells, airplanes, wheel wells." He watched the three birds fly away toward three aircraft that were in line and preparing to take off. He watched each bird go to the belly of a different airplane and disappeared, and in a matter of minutes they flew back to his car minus the explosive devices. He kissed them on their foreheads and smiled as he gave them some of the stimulant laced food that he brought in a small zip lock bag for them.

The birds ate the food and flapped their wings as if they knew that the assignment was successful as they skipped around the front seat of the car. The airplanes were in the line for about twenty minutes, ready to take off. Salerno thought that he was waiting long enough so he put the password in his laptop computer that he had with him in his car. As he finished putting the password in he raised his head and looked toward the planes and immediately the three planes exploded simultaneously. The explosions were extremely loud and deafening, accompanied by fire and thick black smoke. The three planes were almost totally destroyed, and the explosions damaged other planes that were in close proximity to the three planes. Salerno started his car and drove onto the street slowly and drove away, trying not to draw attention to him. Most of the other vehicles that were parked by the fence left also out of fear that there would be more explosions. A few curious and fearless onlookers remained parked by the fence.

As Salerno drove home he listened to the radio in his car as he tried to hear the first report of the destroyed airplanes. He soon heard that some airplanes were blown up at the international airport in his city. The announcer on the radio was not certain how many airplanes were blown up and if they were blown up while they were still on the ground or after they became airborne. Salerno was clapping and shouting, "Yes, yes" as he drove away. He was surprised of how simple this assignment was and how smoothly it was executed. "Piece of cake," he screamed. "I'm on a roll and cannot be stopped," he shouted. As he listened he heard the announcer say, "The latest is that the airplanes were on the runway, that is, on the ground getting ready to lift off. It is feared that many might have lost their lives." Salerno clapped and laughed again as he shouted, "Infidels die."

After Salerno got home he went straight to the television in his bedroom where he could be more relaxed, and watched the news, where he saw photographs of the destroyed airplanes. He switched from channel to channel to watch the graphic, grotesque scenes. Strewn all over the ground were damaged suitcases, clothing, bodies and body parts. There was what appeared to be blood everywhere. What was left of one of the airplanes was on fire as a secondary explosion was heard coming from it, probably from the fuel tanks. Two individuals, who might have been passengers, were lying on the ground about thirty feet from the airplane that was at the rear. They were writhing and crying in agony from the pain caused from the injuries to their bodies. One of them had apparently lost an arm and the other was bleeding from his head. The police and the paramedics were already at the scene trying desperately to assist the injured. So far, the only sign of life was the two injured individuals that were not too far from the airplane at the rear of the other destroyed airplanes. Those two individuals were quickly placed in the ambulance and driven away.

It was now confirmed that no one else had survived the blasts. There were definitely no more signs of life and the police and the firemen stopped searching for the wounded. The first responders were gathered in one spot talking to each other and wondering who could have committed such a terrible act of terrorism. The announcer on one of the television channels said, "We do not know as yet how many people were on the three airplanes that were destroyed, but we understand that only two individuals survived, and they are in critical condition." About half an hour later the announcer said that the first airplane had one hundred and fifty persons on board, including the crew, and the second airplane had two hundred and forty one persons on board, including the crew, while the third airplane had three hundred and twenty two individuals on board, including the crew. Out of that number only two persons survived, and there was no guarantee that they would live because their injuries were serious. "It appears that at least a total of seven hundred and eleven persons lost their lives," the announcer said. "It seems like the invisible terrorists struck again, just when everyone thought that his reign of terror had ended. We now know that Mrs. Daksy Chanley is not responsible for the other acts of terrorism that are unsolved. However, that does not mean that she was not responsible for the attempt on her husband's life, or that she was not in some way involved in that attempt."

The police gave a very brief press conference in which they admitted that the destruction of the airplanes were acts of terrorism, and they reminded the public that so far there was no evidence that the person or persons responsible for the bombing of the airplanes are also responsible for the unsolved acts of terrorism. They contended that the bombs could have been placed in the suitcases with timers set to explode at a certain time, or set to detonate remotely by someone who controlled the remote switch. They reminded the public that no one should be fearful because the police would definitely solve these criminal acts. The police spokesperson left without answering a single question, but the Chief of Police fielded some questions later. Although some people tried to link the bombing of the airplanes with the other unsolved bombings, the Chief of Police dismissed that as utter nonsense. He said that it was too early to tell what happened, but they believed that bombs were placed in suitcases that were not checked at all or not checked properly by those persons who were supposed to check them and who were paid to check them. A reporter asked the Chief of Police, "If what you are saying is true, how come a bomb or bombs were placed on three different airplanes and different airlines?" The Chief of Police ignored the question by saying that he was not prepared to answer any more questions at this stage because the investigations are on-going, and that he did not want to jeopardize them.

The investigations of the bombings of the three airplanes took months as many persons were questioned and many clues investigated. Parts of the destroyed airplanes were tested and retested and the sites where the airplanes were destroyed were checked carefully for bomb-making material fragments. The airplanes were tediously put back together like a jig saw puzzle. No one would deny that the investigations were thorough. When the investigations were completed, it was determined that bombs or explosive devices had destroyed the three airplanes and taken the lives of the passengers and crew and seriously injured the two survivors. They went on to say that it was most likely that explosive devices were placed in suitcases that were either not checked at all or not checked properly, and that although the explosive devices appeared to be sophisticated and untraceable like those explosive devices that were used in the other unsolved bombings, it appeared that the bombings of the airplanes are not connected to the unsolved bombings. They said that extensive investigations were conducted and many people were questioned, and although the investigations are considered completed in a sense, the investigative bodies will still be open for any clues or tips that the public might have.

The majority of the public believed that the bombings of the airplanes were linked to the other unsolved bombings, in spite of what the Chief of Police said. The only problem that they had was that they could not understand how the bombs got on the airplanes if they were not put there in suitcases. They believed that the bombs might have been put in suitcases, but nevertheless, all the bombs were set by the same person.

It was amusing to Salerno as he listened to the inept police and aviation experts give their opinion of how the airplanes were bombed. He could not believe that they were nowhere near the truth as to what happened to the airplanes. It appeared that the untrained public had a better understanding of what happened, but the police did not want to hear the opinion of the general public. Although the investigations were closed officially, there was still no conclusive explanation as to what happened. After the investigations were closed the Chief of Police was heard saying that a disgruntled employee of the airlines could have placed the explosive devices in suitcases, when he was asked if he thought that a disgruntled employee of the airlines could have placed the bombs in suitcases. To some, this explanation was very credible, but still it could not be explained how a disgruntled employee of one airline could have placed explosive devices in suitcases on three different airlines. That was a very puzzling theory. No one seemed to be able to arrive at a credible explanation of what actually happened to the airplanes and how it happened. Some suggested that maybe one airplane exploded and the other two subsequently exploded from the heat and the power of the bomb of the first airplane. They said that it was most likely that that happened because the explosions affected only the three airplanes that were closest to each other.

After the three airplanes were destroyed all the other airplanes that were on the runway ready for takeoff were ordered to abort take off and remain where they were until further notice. Airplanes that were in flight already in the air were ordered to return immediately to the gates. One airplane was speeding down the runway to take off and it had to abort takeoff at the very last minute. The airplane stopped so abruptly that passengers started screaming because the pilot did not have time to explain to them what was happening. The airplane ran off the runway onto the grass, but no one was injured. The order to abort all flights and for airplanes that were already in the air to return to the nearest airports was extended to the whole country. Airplanes sat on the tarmac and runways for hours with passengers. Toilets on the airplanes were blocked and some running over onto the floor of the airplanes, while babies were screaming and passengers became irate. The temperature in the airplanes was becoming unbearably hot as bad odors were present throughout the planes. Finally, after about five hours, and in some cases more, passengers were allowed to disembark and buses took them back to the terminals. Some of the passengers were swearing and demanding the return of their money that they paid for their tickets, and vowing never to fly with those airlines again. Terminal buildings were jam packed with many angry passengers who wanted to get to their destinations. Fights broke out in the terminals among the irate passengers, and the police were called to restore order. Three passengers were arrested for disorderly conduct and threatening language. Babies were crying and wary mothers were exhausted and fed up. The police were beginning to feel the strain and stress from the angry passengers and screaming babies. Ticket agents were on the receiving end of verbal abuse, and an agent was grabbed by her collar by an irate passenger. The agent became scared and started crying. The atmosphere was tense and volatile.

Scenes at various terminal buildings around the country were viewed on television. It appeared as if the whole flying public had come to a standstill and was causing total chaos at the various terminal buildings. Meanwhile, Salerno was enjoying every bit of it. He kept saying to himself, "I can't believe that one man has caused all this embarrassment and chaos to so many people. I am so powerful." What surprised him even more was that no one had a clue that he was the person responsible for what was happening, and he was doing it alone. As he thought about this he remembered that the Leader of the Country's Aide had called him a lone skunk. Every time he thought of that he became infuriated and wanted desperately to destroy the Aide and all present at the People's House. Salerno knew that the day would come when he would have the opportunity to carry out that assignment which he would have done already had the Leader of the Country and his family not travelled abroad on the day before the seventh assignment was to be carried out. In any event he was very proud of himself and he was proving Leon wrong every day when Leon said that the bombers would be caught and punished. He was also proving the police and law enforcement wrong.

After the grounded airplanes were returned to the terminals around the country all the luggage was taken off them and they were searched for explosives. It was a slow, tedious task. No explosives or explosive materials were found. The searching took the whole day, so planes were not allowed to fly until the following day, which made the passengers more irate. Many of them slept at the airport and were smelly the following day because they were unable to take showers or bathe properly. All baggage handlers were questioned again and again by the local police after being questioned by the national investigative team. They were asked specifically about the luggage on the bombed planes, and they stated that they checked every piece of luggage carefully on those planes and followed the search with scanners and X-ray machines. They said that there were no bombs or explosive devices or materials in any body's suitcases, and that as it pertained to carry-on luggage, they could not vouch for that because they had nothing to do with that. Although the Federal investigations were officially closed, nevertheless, local investigations were still being conducted, and sometimes with a Federal employee.

The investigators were beginning to realize that the possibility of explosive devices entering the planes in the carry-on luggage was real because the carry-on luggage was not checked, and they could have had explosives in them. They concluded that this was the only means by which explosive devices could have been put on those planes. When the police said initially that the explosive devices were most likely put on the planes in luggage they were correct. The only slight difference is that the devices were put in the carry-on luggage. This is what the investigators final report said. The truth is that because the airplanes were so badly damaged it was difficult, if not impossible, to determine where the explosive devices were set or placed. All three airplanes were a heap of mangled metal. As to who caused the explosives to be placed on the airplanes, the investigators believed that it was the work of an irate passenger or passengers who wanted to get even with the airlines for some perceived wrong they did to him or her. The investigators maintained that the bombing of the three planes might have been done by a copy cat that was looking for attention. Security was strengthened in and around the terminal buildings around the country.

The Leader of the Country returned on his private aircraft the day before the three planes were bombed. A press conference was arranged with him in the press room of the People's House. He would up-date the country on his most recent journey abroad, and after that he would make a short speech about the most recent bombing of the three aircraft. Salerno was in his bedroom sitting on his bed when the Leader of the Country began to speak. He told the country about his visit abroad. He said that the trip abroad was a successful one but he was disheartened when he returned to find that only one day after he returned some heartless person or persons blew up three passenger planes and took so many innocent lives. He reiterated his promise to hunt down, capture and have those responsible tried in a court of law. He went on to say, "I know that it would not be easy, and some of you are probably saying that the bombings have gone on for so long and those responsible have not been caught. I want you to take it from me. This great country, the greatest in the world, will catch the terrorists responsible and bring them to justice. My family and I pray for those killed and send condolences to all the families and friends of those killed and injured." From the tone of his voice it was obvious that he was very serious and determined that he would catch those responsible and bring them to justice. Salerno listened intently to the leader of the Country's speech, and thought that nothing new was in his speech. As far as Salerno was concerned, the Leader of the Country was only rehashing what he and others, including Leon, had said, and all of them were idiots.

Every time Salerno thought of Leon he would begin to reminisce about what Leon said to him. He kept wondering why Leon was such a great supporter of the host country and he was not a citizen. Salerno knew what Leon said as to why he loved the host country and its people so much, but to Salerno, it did not make any sense. Salerno said to himself, "All the love that Leon has for the host country could not stop Leon from almost losing his life and becoming a vegetable." Salerno hoped that Leon had enough sense to understand that, because if he did not understand that prior to the bombing of his car, he might never understand it. He wondered if Leon felt that way about the host country after he was almost killed, and realizing that the host country could not protect him from the bomb. Salerno wanted Leon to know that he, Salerno, was only doing what he had to do to protect himself and his people from the unwanted aggression of the host country, but Leon could not see it. Salerno thought that as far as Leon was concerned, the host country could do no wrong.

After the flights resumed everything seemed to return to normal. The fear factor manifested by the bombing of the three planes was waning. The better and extra security in and around the airport terminals appeared to be paying off because there were no more bombings of airplanes. What the public did not know was that Salerno was eyeing another target; one that when successful, would astonish the world. His thoughts had returned to the bombing of the People's House with the Leader of the Country, his family and staff inside at the time. When this mission is executed it would please him more than all the other bombings combined. He knew that it would be an ambitious project, but he was well prepared to execute it with his killer birds. That assignment, which he was now calling his eighth assignment, would be the ultimate test of his superiority over the infidels, and their inability to stop him from reigning supreme, because the Leader of the People's House was undoubtedly the Leader of the world. The employees at Salerno's workplace discussed the bombing of the three commercial aircraft. They, unlike the police, felt that it was done by the same individual or individuals.

One of the female employees by the name of Veronica asked Salerno, "Who do you think is responsible for the bombing of the airplanes?" Salerno shook his head from right to left to right and said, "I don't know. It is too difficult to say." Another employee asked him, "Do you think that one individual is responsible for all the bombings, including the bombing of Leon's car?" This caught Salerno by surprise because he knew that everybody knew that Leon's ex wife Daksy Chanley, was convicted for that offense. That question made him believe that some of his fellow employees did not believe that Daksy Chanley bombed the car. Any way, he had to answer the question. He said, "No I don't believe that one person is responsible for all the bombing. You probably forgot that Leon's wife was found guilty for the bombing of Leon's car." An employee by the name of Peter said, "Come on Salerno, you and everybody know that Daksy Chanley was not involved in blowing up Leon's car. That was too sophisticated for her. Where did she get the bomb from?" Salerno replied, "I don't know, but she was convicted for it so she must be guilty." Salerno then looked at his watch and said, "Hey guys, it's time to return to work." The conversations ended and they returned to work from their lunch hour.

Salerno's co-employees discovered that he attended church regularly and paid tithes. They commended him for that and told him that he was a really good Christian. Some of them admitted that they were not good at attending church regularly and paying tithes. One of them said that by the time he paid his bills and taxes he did not have sufficient money left to eat a good meal, so paying tithes was out of the question. When he was called a good Christian he smiled and said, "Well, I try my best, although I must admit that I am not perfect." What his co-employees did not know was that Salerno hated Christianity and all those who believed in it. He thought that most Christian preachers were crooks who preyed on the poor and helpless and took the little money the poor and helpless had. In some instances the preachers even stole the people's properties and assets. What he thought was that the preachers added insult to injury by living lavishly, by owning huge houses, many expensive cars and in some instances some preachers have their own jet planes. He saw Christianity as one of the worst religions in the world because it encouraged preachers and its followers to become fraudsters and take advantage of poor unsuspecting individuals. He found this very ironic because what he had heard about Jesus Christ, the leader of Christianity, and the one from which Christianity derived its name, he was a pious person who did not indulge in extravagance, and he cared for and loved the poor. He heard the preacher in the church that he attended say Jesus said that if someone has two coats that person should give one of those coats to someone who has no coat. He never heard that their Jesus took the little that the poor had to enrich himself or his friends and family. Salerno thought that the advantage that the preachers took of the poor people was one of the greatest evils of Christianity. It was another failing of the infidels not to realize that he was only pretending to be a Christian to achieve his goal of destroying as many infidels as possible. He figured that if the greedy preachers could fool so many people by taking money and wealth away from them then he should have no problem fooling them by giving money to them in the form of offering and tithes. It was a reasonable proposition.

The staff at Salerno's work place decided that they would go to visit Leon in two days' time. It would be the first time that all the staff visited him at the same time. Salerno preferred not to visit him but he knew that if he did not visit Leon with the rest of the employees it would not look good, so he prepared to make the visit with them. When the day came everybody from Salerno's workplace met at the hospital at a certain time. All eight employees entered the room together where Leon was. A nurse was at Leon's bedside massaging his limbs and speaking to him although he could not understand and respond to her. He lay on his back motionless as he stared blankly into the ceiling. His eyes were fixed in one position with mostly the white of his eyes showing.

As they entered the room one of Leon's co-employees began to cry when she saw the condition that he was in. she had seen him before but she thought that he had improved since she saw him, but it appeared as if his condition had worsened. All of them talked to him although they got no response. They wanted to know how he felt, but he could not tell them. When Salerno said hello a single tear drop came from his right eye, which everybody present noticed. They wondered what that meant and why it happened only when Salerno said something to him. One of the ladies present thought that it meant that Leon was happy to hear his best friend Salerno's voice. Salerno did not know what to make of it. He wondered if Leon cried when Leon heard his, Salerno's voice, because Leon thought that he, Salerno, might have bombed the car. Salerno immediately dismissed that thought because he knew that Leon did not have the slightest idea that he, Salerno was responsible for the bombing of his car and his injuries. Some of the female employees from Leon's office touched Leon's hands and squeezed them hoping that they would receive a response from him, but there was no response. The oldest man from Leon's office who visited Leon was a deacon in his church. He asked the others to allow him to lead them in prayer for their friend and former colleague Leon, before they left. All eight of them held hands and one of them at one end of the line held Leon's hand as the deacon prayed. After the prayer they said goodbye to Leon.

After seeing the tear drop from Leon's right eye his fellow employees were convinced that he could hear them even if he could not respond. Even the nurse was surprised when she saw the tear drop from his eye because she had never seen that happen before. She thought that it was a positive sign, and she hurried off to tell the doctor that was on duty what she had just witnessed. When Leon's colleagues returned to their cars in the hospital parking lot they stood there for a few minutes, and one of them said, "I think that he is only suffering. Why don't they just pull the plug and take him out of his misery?" The deacon quickly responded, "Oh no, that decision should be God's, and God's alone, not man." One of the other ladies said, "I agree. Maybe he will come out of the coma one of these days. If they end his life prematurely that could not happen." Salerno listened as they spoke, and wondered how Leon could be so lucky to survive the bomb blast. If it was not luck, he thought, then Leon's God must have been watching over him, because his life was miraculously saved.

The lady who cried when they entered Leon's room was the last to speak. She said, "I pray to God that the devilish bastard who put Leon in that condition burns in hell. He or they are the worst demons in the world." The others present agreed with her, and one of them said, "We must get back to the office," and they headed to their cars and drove off from the parking lot. All the way back to the office Salerno thought about the visit to the hospital. He would have preferred to see Leon die in the explosion than to see him in that condition. He thought that it was very unfortunate that Leon ended up in the condition that he was in, but that was life, and life was not fair. He wondered why Leon had caused that to happen to him. If Leon had not kept telling him about how great and wonderful the host country was, everything would have been alright. Leon had to be taught a lesson, and he, Salerno, would be willing to do the same to any of his co-employees if they acted and behaved in the manner that Leon did.

After the bombing of the hospital renewed pressure mounted on the police to solve the unsolved bombings. A crime watch group brought pressure to bear on law enforcement to solve the unsolved bombings sooner rather than later. The crime watch group believed that the terrorists had reached a new low when they bombed a hospital with sick, helpless patients. The governor of the state promised to do all within his power to capture and punish the terrorists that were responsible for the bombings. Law enforcement decided to go over the evidence for the third time from the beginning to the end. They believed that there might be some evidence at one of the bomb sites that they overlooked, or in some of the rubble from the bomb sites. They had used a huge vacant building like an aircraft hangar to store all the exhibits from the bomb sites. They sifted through the evidence very cautiously for a very long time but they did not find anything that could assist them in solving the outstanding bombings. They found some components of the bomb at the scene in the bombing of Leon Chanley's car, and that is how they knew that the culprit or culprits in that case and the culprit or culprits in the other cases were not the same. In the unsolved bombings it appeared as if the person or persons involved had used some materials in making the bombs that incinerated or wasted away once the bombs were detonated. The investigators had never seen anything like this before. If what they said were correct, the terrorists were ahead of law enforcement, and it would make it extremely difficult for law enforcement to solve these types of cases unless there were eyewitnesses, which would be unusual. They would only be solved if someone caught the terrorists in the act, or someone leaked information that could lead to their arrests. The terrorists' tactics and strategies were becoming more and more sophisticated and undetectable.

Another troubling issue was the fact that law enforcement did not know how the terrorists obtained the bombs and how they got them to the locations where they were detonated. There are suspicions, for example, in the bombing of the post office that the bomb was sent through the mail, but there is no concrete proof of that. Surveillance cameras from all the post offices around the country were examined to see if anyone acting suspiciously was posting any parcels, and people were questioned at length, but no evidence to support someone sending the bombs was ever found. Likewise with the airplanes bombings, there was no definitive evidence that bombs were taken on board the airplanes in carry-on luggage or any other luggage, although that seemed quite plausible. After the bombing of the airplanes, all luggage was carefully searched prior to it getting on the planes. Surveillance cameras were set up on the inside and outside of post offices and packages screened prior to acceptance for posting. Military bases had high powered surveillance cameras installed, and the private possessions of all soldiers were searched on leaving and entering the bases. There were no exceptions. The same procedure applied to police stations because the possibility could not be ruled out that a rogue police officer introduced the explosive device into the police station because of a grievance he had with someone who worked in that police station. There were those who wondered why these measures and precautions were not taken before so many people got injured and before so many lives were lost.

Back at Salerno's work place the employees were trying to get their lives back to normal after the bombing of Leon's car, but it was not easy as almost every day someone would mention Leon's name and tell a joke about him, or mention something Leon said or did. About two days ago, Mary, who worked about five feet away from Leon, was talking with Salerno and another employee. She said, "Salerno, I can recall you and Leon talking one day and Leon said, 'Salerno, when those terrorists dogs are caught I will be right there to see them in court, and I will shout, God bless this host country and down with the forces of evil.'" Salerno remembered that conversation very well, so he said, "Yes, I remember that." That was all that Salerno said. He did not worry about that day because he knew that that day would never come. Salerno thought about his next assignment, which would be assignment number eight, which was supposed to be assignment number seven, but the Leader of the Country and his family left the host country to go abroad on business. They were back and it was time to execute the next assignment. After this assignment he would put all other assignments on hold for at least five years, because he figured that he would be travelling and attending university. He figured that his final assignment should be a climax, and bombing the Leader of the Country's residence, the People's House, was definitely a climax that could not be topped. As far as he was concerned it surpassed the bombing of the military base and the police station, although some would disagree with him. Bombing of the People's House would send a message that when the freedom fighters wanted to strike a target they would be unstoppable and no one could stand in their way. This assignment, he thought, would be the mother of insults to the infidels and would convey the scant disrespect that the freedom fighters have for them. It would also demonstrate the weaknesses of the infidels and the strengths of the freedom fighters.

The ten killer birds spent a lot of time practicing the routine for the eighth assignment to destroy the People's House and kill the Leader of the country. Their practice was flawless, as it had to be, because Salerno would not settle for anything less, and he could not afford to make mistakes when executing this assignment. Finally they were ready to go on their mission to destroy the People's House and the Leader of the Country and all present at the time. Salerno had called in sick explaining that he thought that he had a stomach bug and as a result he was suffering from a serious bout of diarrhea. This day appeared to be one of the best days of the year, as it was a sunny day but cool, with a bright blue cloudless sky. He arose early from bed and although he did not sleep well that night, nevertheless, he was wide awake and anxious to embark on his most important assignment. All that night he tossed and turned thinking about what he was about to do the following day, and how he would make international news.

The streets surrounding the People's House had their usual traffic and curious pedestrians. As usual, some of the pedestrians were tourists who came from their various homes and countries to see the People's House, and they were peeping through the iron fence trying to get a glance inside the huge and well-guarded yard. Some hoped that they would even get a glimpse of the Leader of the Country himself. Others were taking photographs of the People's House from outside the iron fence. Guards were seen patrolling the compound and two were stationed at the gate. Salerno strapped the explosive devices to the birds then he attached the small cameras to their bodies. These bombs were more powerful than all the other bombs so far, and if everything went well, would cause more damage. After the explosive devices were attached to the birds he gave them some stimulant laced food, and after they ate he kissed them on their foreheads and said, "The People's House, the People's House the People's House." He opened the door and they flew out together heading toward the People's House. He estimated that their returned journey would take approximately an hour if everything went well.

Other birds were in the sky on that day, apparently enjoying the good, clear weather. Some of them were playing in flight, some appeared to be flying aimlessly, and some were following their leaders. Soon, the ten birds who would be executing the eighth assignment were among the other birds heading in a Westerly direction towards the People's House. Salerno rushed to his computer to follow his avian killers as they embarked on their deadly journey. After fifteen minutes of flight he noticed that his ten birds were in front of all the other birds and the other birds were following them. About half an hour after the ten birds departed from Salerno's house they arrived at the People's House and six landed on the ground surrounding the People's House while four landed on the roof. The other birds that were not a part of the assassination team landed on the grounds of the People's House and started looking through the grass for food. There were two guards on the roof of the People's House at the time that the four birds landed. One of the guards was very observant and noticed that although there were at least about fifty birds only four landed on the roof, so he watched the four on the roof. As he got closer to one of the four birds he noticed that there was something strapped to it and the bird was trying desperately to release the object that was strapped to it. The guard drew this to the attention of the other guard and they both started chasing the four birds away.

By now, all four birds were trying to release the strapped objects but the guards chased them off before they could release whatever was on their backs.

Meanwhile one of the two guards had called to the guards on the ground surrounding the People's House and told them to chase all the birds away immediately because some of the birds were carrying something. All the birds flew off quickly except the killer birds which seemed to linger as if they wanted to make another attempt to discharge their cargo. Finally the guards decided to fire off shots at the birds as the birds tried to return to the roof. One of the shots hit one of the birds and there was a huge explosion as feathers went flying all over the place. The guards ducked not knowing what would follow. As soon as that happened the army was notified and two fighter jets were scrambled, and in no time they appeared over the area of the People's House. The Leader and his family and staff were notified and they were rushed to prepared bunkers under the People's House for their safety. The fighter jets had never had to confront killer birds before and were not sure how to handle the situation. They stayed a good distance away from the birds because they feared that the birds would attach themselves to the planes and blow up the planes.

Meanwhile Salerno saw that his eighth assignment was failing. He could not afford for the remaining birds to return to him because he figured that the army would follow them and discover that he was the mastermind, so he decided to destroy them. He put in the password and destroyed the remaining birds. There were a huge explosion and feathers and other debris from the birds flew all around. The fighter jets pulled back. Black smoke from burned body parts and feathers filled the sky. After Salerno took the decision to destroy the birds he sat down in his chair at his computer and cried. He could not believe that ten of his birds had lost their lives at one time and all because of the infidels. His birds and he were like family and he knew that he would miss them dearly. He was now grieving and angrier than he had ever been in his life, so he vowed that he would get even with the infidels for the pain and suffering that they had caused him. What made him even angrier was the fact that the infidels had made him kill his own birds. As far as he was concerned, that was unforgivable. It was a good thing that he had more trained birds. He had never prepared for a situation like that because he thought that the infidels would never detect his project, but they did, and he had to deal with it.

The Leader of the Country and his family were notified of all the events that unfolded involving the killer birds. He could not believe it. He said that it sounded like a movie about alien birds attacking human beings, but he was assured that it was very real and that it was only because of the guard on the roof of the People's House who saw the birds before they off-loaded the explosive devices that he and his family were alive. The National Security Team was alerted and an impromptu security meeting was held to determine what to do in the future with threats of the type by terrorists that used birds and other animals as carriers of explosive devices. At the meeting the National Security Chief agreed that the country was faced with a novel type of threat which no one had foreseen. It was a threat that if it went unnoticed and undetected could have caused untold damage and a great loss of life. It was agreed that it should be published that everyone must be on the lookout for all birds because it was just discovered that birds were carrying explosive devices. People were told to remain indoors unless it was absolutely necessary to venture outdoors, and if they sighted any birds they must try to drive the birds away and call the police.

The investigators began their investigations on the compound of the People's House as they began on the roof and moved to the ground surrounding the People's House. About fifty to eighty feet away from the People's House, in the direction where the killer birds flew, the investigators saw hundreds of feathers and the remains of dead birds, but there was no evidence of bomb-making materials or bomb-making ingredients. It was obvious that the person or persons that were responsible for the explosive devices had used material and ingredients that were untraceable and undetectable. It was now determined that the explosive devices that were used in the unsolved bombings were carried by trained birds that were about to bomb the People's House. It was concluded also that without a shadow of doubt birds were responsible for delivering the bombs to the bomb sites of the unsolved bombings. The problem was how to deal with the birds carrying explosives. It was agreed by the police that anyone who had a license to carry a firearm could shoot at any bird in sight that was believed to be a threat. Guns were sold by the dozens every hour, even to those who never fired a gun before. Children were being given target practice so that they could learn how to shoot and assist in shooting at birds that were perceived to be a threat.

Salerno was still grieving. He cried all day after his birds were killed and asked his god why did his birds have to lose their lives. His eyes were swollen from crying for his birds, and he refused to eat for some time. He asked for two weeks' vacation, which he was entitled to, and it was granted. He decided to use this period for grieving, but if he thought that he should use part of it to exact revenge, he would. Although he had more trained birds that could execute more assignments, he still missed the ten birds that were killed, because he was very attached to them. Every time he thought about the deaths of his birds he began to cry and would go into a fetal position in his bed rolling over from side to side. He found it hard to accept that ten of his birds were killed and all at the same time. He wondered how the infidels could be so cruel and so mean by not caring about the lives of his birds. They had scrambled fighter jets to fight his birds as if his birds were other infidels that they were confronting. He swore to his god that revenge would be brutal and swift, although he knew that it would be difficult to execute another assignment successfully with his birds because everyone would be on the look-out for birds carrying explosive devices, but he decided that he had to try, and he knew that he would succeed because he was smarter than the infidels. He managed to sit up in bed with a towel that he used to keep wiping the tears from his face. He wanted to watch the evening news to see what would be said about the foiled assassination attempt of the Leader of the Country and his family and staff.

At 6:00 0'Clock sharp the news began and the first story was about the attempted assassination of the Leader of the Country and his family. The reporter said, "Today there has been an attempt to assassinate the Leader of the Country and his family by using killer birds carrying explosive devices. It is believed that the same method was used to blow up the post office, the military base, the police station, the mall, the public hospital, Leon Chanley's car and the three airplanes. However, the person or persons behind those bombings are still at large. The public is asked to be on the lookout for birds carrying explosive devices." When he finished that announcement he had two individuals on the show who were giving their opinions about the attempted bombings and the birds with the explosive devices. One of the guests was a spokesperson from the office of the chief of Police. He was asked by the reporter, "So what's next?" The spokesperson said, "We are asking the public to be on the lookout for those birds of terror that are terrorizing our people. It is crystal clear that those birds were properly trained and although all of them were killed we believe that there are more already trained for these missions of terror, and even if they are not already trained, more will soon be trained." The other individual interjected and said, "And the trainer of these birds is a murderer and a terrorist. He killed at random and for no obvious reason. We know that he hates the citizens of this country." The reporter said, "I noticed that the speaker just said that Leon Chanley was a victim of the terrorist. If that is so why is Mrs. Daksy Chanley spending time in prison for the bombing of Leon's car? I believe that it was done by the birds of terror and their trainer or trainers. What do you think?" The spokesman from the Chief of Police office responded very quickly by saying, "No, no, no. I guess I was misunderstood, because everyone knows that his wife was convicted by a jury of her peers and sentenced to prison for a very long time. That bombing is in no way connected or related to the other unsolved bombings." The reporter said, "But have you considered the possibility that she could be wrongly convicted? Many who followed the case believe that she was wrongly convicted." "Oh no, she was not wrongly convicted," the spokesperson replied. "What do you think sir?" the reporter asked the other individual who was seated and seemed to be enjoying the conversation between the reporter and the spokesman from the Chief of Police's office. The other gentleman who represented a group called Citizens for Justice, or CFJ, replied, "Based on what I have heard, I do not think that Mrs. Daksy Chanley bombed her husband's car or knows who did it. Although that bombing was directed at a single individual, unlike the other bombings, I think that the birds of terror are responsible. Forgive me for using your term birds of terror," he said to the Chief of Police's spokesperson. The reporter said, "I agree wholeheartedly with you, and I love the term 'Birds of Terror', I think that it is appropriate."

Salerno watched the whole exchange and thought about the different opinions held by the chief of Police spokesperson and the other two individuals. He found it strange and amusing that the individual that was wrong was the Chief of Police's spokesperson, the one who should have been the most correct. Salerno was not sure what his next move would be, but there was no doubt, as far as he was concerned, that he still wanted to assassinate the Leader of the Country and the Leader's family and destroy the People's House, but he was aware that the chances of that happening after the foiled attempt were very small and next to impossible. Whenever he thought about that he became very angry with the infidels who prevented that from happening on the first attempt and who caused his birds to lose their lives. As soon as he thought about the birds losing their lives he started crying again and he said, "They meant so much to me. Why did the infidels cause them to lose their lives?" He thought that now that the country knew that his birds were responsible for at least some of the bombings, he would have to keep a low profile with his birds. He was satisfied that no one should be aware that he was still training birds because only Jayne knew and he told her that he stopped training birds for over two years ago.

As Salerno thought about the deaths of his birds his anger grew, and he decided that he had to get even and he had to do it then. He did not care what his targets were, whether they were men, women or children, because as far as he was concerned, their lives were no more precious than his birds' lives. As a matter of fact, his birds' lives were much more precious than theirs because his birds were innocent and executing the will of freedom fighters, while the lives of human beings were fulfilling the will of the infidels. He was ready to commence and unleash a different style and tactic of attacks on the infidels as a means of revenge for the killing of his birds. One night he took a single bird with him and pointed out a school to the bird. The bird seemed ready after a few practice runs so he strapped a powerful bomb and a camera to the bird on a Monday morning when the school would be packed with children.

The bird flew very high until it got close to the school then it dove like a hawk or eagle diving to grasp its prey. In no time it landed on the top of the school and released its powerful bomb and flew off hastily after releasing it. Salerno followed that on his computer. He was very surprised to learn that no one had seen or intercepted the bird. It had made a safe landing, deposit and escape. He thought that there would have been impenetrable security around the school, but that was not the case. When the bird was far enough away from the bomb he detonated it, and it made a huge sound. A great hole was made in the roof of the school and the roof fell on little children and their teachers. Children and teachers were running from their classes screaming and shouting for help. The classrooms that were affected most by the bomb were almost completely destroyed. Classroom furniture was blown apart and into teachers and children, some of whom were impaled by parts of the furniture. The classroom floor and walls were plastered with blood from those injured and killed. Teachers and children were trapped below the rubble.

First responders came soon after the explosion and began to recover the bodies and attend to those who were injured. The recovery and rescue efforts went on for some time as bystanders looked on curiously crying and chatting with each other. The police kept them far away from the actual scene to prevent the public from interfering in the investigations. Parents arrived screaming and trying to get through the police barricades, but the police took their names and addresses and telephone numbers and stopped them from doing so. Some of the parents were shouting, "Where is my child?" The police told them that they were trying to get to the bottom of what happened. As the bodies of teachers and children were brought out, screaming intensified from those present. One of the parents was on the ground crying and saying, "Lord, where is my child? I want my child." About an hour after the accident the first responders were engaged only in a recovery effort because all those who had survived from those two classrooms were safely outside the building. Later it was disclosed that there were fifty injured and one hundred and sixty dead. Most of the dead were children.

The Chief of Police took to the airwaves and warned the public to arm themselves and shoot any bird that was seen. He said that he would have a meeting with the governor and the mayor and ask for the army, the National Guard and the police to be placed on every street corner with their guns pointed to the sky. He wanted all licensed gun owners to protect themselves, their properties, and their families by being on guard twenty four seven with their guns pointed toward the sky. Two days later the streets were filled with soldiers, National guardsmen, police officers and civilians carrying guns that were aimed at the sky. Someone shouted "birds," and when they looked up there were two birds flying about three hundred feet above. All of a sudden there were flurries of bullets fired in the direction of the birds. The sounds from the different caliber guns sounded like a war zone. As the shots were fired young children that were playing outside hurried inside and cowered under their beds. Some mothers ran inside their clothes closets and hid, while others ran outside not wanting to be inside the house, apartment, or a building, in the event the birds placed bombs on top of those structures. Bullets were heard all around. The police saw a bird flying high and aimed at it and fired and shot it down, and to their surprise they discovered that it was a bald eagle.

The following Sunday Pastor Brown was having service in his mega church when two birds flew into the church, apparently fighting or playing. Pastor Brown's sermon was entitled 'We should fear nothing but God.' The birds flew into the church through the main entrance door and went to the ceiling. As soon as they entered Pastor Brown saw them because from where he stood to preach he was facing the main entrance door. Pastor Brown had just reached to the point where he said, "I cannot believe that grown men and women are afraid of little things like spiders, roaches, rats and birds." At the same time he mentioned the word 'birds' he saw the two birds fly inside the church. He dropped his Bible and started running to get to the side door. He tripped over his robe and tried to get up again, but by then others had seen the two birds in the ceiling and made the alarm. The whole congregation was now running toward the two exits screaming in panic as they ran. An old lady was trampled trying to get out the door, and she later died from her injuries. Pastor Brown got up off the floor and ran to his parked car screaming, "Lord, don't let your child suffer." Some of the congregation ran off leaving their cars behind. It was discovered that the two birds were Morning Doves playing. Pastor Brown had to be hospitalized for a slipped disc in his back, and three other parishioners had minor injuries.

A day later the police were on television asking the public if they knew anyone who trained birds and that if they did they must call a number that the police gave out. About fifteen minutes later the police started receiving calls from many young people, all mentioning the name of one Jayne Blulow, stating that she taught a class on the training of birds and caring for birds at the local university. The police contacted the university and the Dean at the local university told them that Jayne Blulow did teach courses on the training and caring of birds, and the Dean gave the police Jayne's phone number. The police phoned Jayne and asked her if she would be willing to come to the police station so they could ask her a few questions, and she agreed. She appeared at the police station not knowing why the police wanted to speak to her, because as far as she was concerned she had done nothing wrong. When Jayne entered the police station the police escorted her to the interrogation room and began to question her after the detectives introduced themselves. "I understand that you taught classes at the local university on the training and caring of birds," one of the detectives said to her. At first she appeared to be scared and nervous, but after the detectives began to talk about the course she taught at the local university on birds, she became more relaxed.

As a matter of fact, Jayne enjoyed speaking about birds, and she was willing to do so at any time and any place. She smiled and replied to the detective, "Yes, I did. Why, did something happen?" The same detective asked her, "Were you following the news lately? Did you hear about the attempted assassination of the Leader of the Country and his family by trained birds?" Jayne looked surprised at what the detective said. She could not believe what he was saying, and she was beginning to become scared and afraid again because she knew if what the detective said was the truth, she would be a suspect because she trained birds. She twisted in her chair and tried to look directly in the detective's eyes as she said, "I do not follow the news much because there is too much bad news nowadays, but I heard a little something about it." The other detective asked her, "Do you know anything about the birds that were trying to assassinate the Leader of the Country and his family?" Jayne became serious and began to shake her head in the negative as she said, "Sir, you're barking up the wrong tree. I have never had a traffic ticket in my life." The same detective said, "Do you mind if we search your premises?"

Jayne was now very concerned because she felt that the detectives thought that she was involved with the birds of terror, and that was something that she did not want to be associated with. She was hoping that the detectives would visit her premises immediately so that they could rule her out as a suspect. She replied, "Sir, let's go right now." The first detective told her that he wanted to ask her a few more questions before they searched her premises. The same detective went on to say to her, "What we want to know is, do you have a list or lists of persons that you taught in that class?" She was too happy to provide them with anything that she had that could assist them in solving the crimes and removing her from their minds as a potential suspect, so she replied, "Yes, I do. The university should have lists of those persons also." The first detective asked her, "How far did your training of birds go?" "Well, I can tell you," replied Jayne. "It did not go as far as training birds to kill or assassinate people and destroy property."

The detective continued with the questions by asking her, "Do you know if any of your past students might have trained birds to carry and drop explosive devices?" Jayne did not know for certain if that happened, but she doubted it, because as far as she could recall, none of her students appeared to be criminals or have criminal minds. She told the detective that she did not know of any of her students who engaged or would engage in training birds to commit criminal acts. The detectives then agreed to follow Jayne to her premises although they were doubtful that she was involved with the birds in criminal acts. She walked out the police station to her car that was parked in the parking lot and they followed her. All three got into their cars and drove to Jayne's premises, where the detectives conducted a thorough search of the interior of her apartment and the exterior, but they found no evidence to implicate her in any of the bombings. She had only two pet birds that appeared to be old and feeble and could not execute any assignments like the birds of terror conducted. She gave the detectives copies of the lists of students that she taught the course of bird training and caring of birds. The detectives thanked her for her cooperation and left, telling her that if they required any further information from her they would contact her.

The lists contained two hundred and forty names, and the detectives believed that any one or more of those persons on the lists could be responsible for the training of the killer birds and the execution of the deadly attacks. It would take some time for the detectives to question all the persons on the lists, but it had to be done. The questioning of Jayne's past students who did the course in the training of birds commenced, and each student's apartment or house was searched, but nothing was found to connect them to the birds of terror. None of the students seemed to have any knowledge of the explosives or anyone who might have been involved in the making or delivery of it. The investigators were now confused and not sure where to turn. They had taken weeks to question everyone, and they believed that the questioning would have been successful, but that was not the case.

The guard that was on the roof of the People's House and spotted the bird with the explosive strapped to it was considered a hero and given a medal for his bravery. He was praised as the person who possibly saved the lives of the Leader of the Country and the Leader's family and staff. Everywhere he went he was congratulated and hailed as a hero. People would shake his hand and call him the hero of the day. Some even suggested that he should contest the up-coming election for Leader of the Country. He did not think that he had done anything that would warrant such great attention and commendation. Any time anyone approached him on the subject he would say that he was just doing his job and that he was proud to do it. He was put in charge of security at the premises of the People's House, and also put in charge of training for all the guards. It was accepted that had it not been for his keen sense of awareness, the outcome could have been different. Security was improved in and around the People's House by installing higher definition surveillance equipment, and better radars were set up around the compound.

There was total chaos in the streets. Pedestrians were running and looking into the sky, and everywhere birds were seen the pedestrians would shout, "Birds, I see birds." Children screamed as they ran, either being dragged by their parents or trying to catch up to their terrified parents. In some cases parents had their babies in baby carriages which they pushed with speeds as if they were in a speed carriages race. Some were running into buildings and some were running out of buildings. On the other hand drivers were speeding on the streets to get to where they were going, out of fear that a bird or birds might land on or under their vehicles and release explosive devices to kill them and destroy their vehicles. They were driving erratically, and that caused several vehicle accidents, which could have been avoided. The drivers were tooting their horns incessantly in an attempt to endeavor to get off the streets. Two drivers were involved in an accident involving a grey pick-up truck and a small blue car. They exited their vehicles and started arguing, blaming each other for the accident. The driver from the small blue car punched the driver from the grey pick-up truck in his nose and blood started gushing from the truck driver's nose. They began to fight and suddenly someone shouted, "Birds overhead," and the two men looked into the sky and saw a flock of birds flying over. The two drivers jumped into their vehicles and sped off going in different directions, not acknowledging the police car that was coming to break up the fight between them.

Fighter jets flew with high powered surveillance equipment, examining every bird in the sky. The pilots of these jets had special orders to shoot to kill and destroy any and all birds that appeared to be carrying anything suspicious. When pedestrians heard airplanes flying overhead they had a sense of security, knowing that the aircraft were fighter jets flying to protect them. However, they also became afraid also, because they figured that where there were fighter jets in the sky there was a possibility that birds of terror were not too far away. Commercial passengers' aircraft were sometimes escorted by the fighter jets. If a bird or birds were seen on anyone's premises the birds would be shot or stoned and the police would be called. The fighter jet planes were equipped with special weapons that could fire hundreds of pellet size bullets that could kill hundreds of birds simultaneously. Some of these guns were used by the soldiers and police who were on the ground firing shots at the birds in the air. This type of weapon was successful in killing many birds with one pull of the trigger. The weapon was called a Multi-Spray Gun or MSG.

Salerno was aware of the Multi Spray Gun and saw it as a threat to the survival of his birds and the success of his assignments, so he decided that at least for now he would send one and no more than two birds out on a mission, and he would adopt a different method of releasing and depositing the bombs. He decided that he would make an automatic, remote release switch and attach it to the birds so that he could release the bombs remotely wherever and whenever he wanted to drop them. In that way, his birds would expose themselves to less risk by not having to go to a site to deposit the bombs. He figured that if the birds did not have to go physically to the People's House, they would have been alive today, because he could have released the bombs from high in the air above the People's House. He manufactured the automatic remote release switch or ARRS and tested it repeatedly by allowing the birds to carry little harmless packages, and he would trigger the switch remotely and the packages would be released. He was now ready to apply it to an assignment.

One day there was a huge baseball game at the national stadium with at least thirty thousand spectators present watching the game and cheering for their teams, when suddenly a flock of birds flew by overhead. One of the players on the field looked into the sky and shouted, "Birds, birds, run." All the players, referees and spectators began to run. The players were running in all directions on the field. Some headed for the bleachers as some of the spectators that were sitting in the bleachers ran to the field. Most of the thirty thousand spectators headed for the single exit which was too small to accommodate all of them, so people were crushed and trampled trying to escape as they shouted and screamed. Some adults had taken their young children to see the game, and after the adults behaved in such a frightened manner the children panicked and began to cry. A spectator had his six year old son on his shoulders as he tried to escape, but before he could get to the exit the child was knocked off his shoulder and trampled. Spectators had fallen to the ground while they tried to escape, and other spectators were walking and running on the fallen spectators' bodies. It was complete pandemonium. The birds flew straight to the now empty field and landed as if in search of insects or other bugs for their meal. Some of the birds flew to the parts of the bleachers that were now vacant, where they feasted on leftovers of popcorn, bread, hotdogs etc. In some cases there were whole meals not yet touched. Those birds were well fed from eating those meals that the frightened spectators ran off and left. As the birds flew to the bleachers the spectators who had not yet escaped from the bleachers screamed louder and louder and pushed harder and harder to escape.

Fights broke out among the fleeing spectators. A woman took off one of her stiletto shoes and hit another woman in the head with it, and the woman who was hit in the head started bleeding. That caused those two women to begin fighting as people were trying to push their way pass them. Meanwhile, on the outside of the stadium the spectators who had already exited the stadium were either in their cars or trying to get to their cars. Those who were already in their vehicles sped off with their tires screeching. Some of those who sped off got into accidents with other vehicles. Two pedestrians were knocked down and run over by some of the speeding cars as the drivers tried to speed off from the parking lot. The police and paramedics were called and came to try to restore order. The army and the National Guard came and began firing shots at the birds that were still around. By now, many had realized that the birds were not birds of terror, but a flock of hungry birds looking for food. A police officer got on the PA System and announced, "The birds are not birds of terror. They are only birds looking for some food. Please return and enjoy the game." Only few persons heard him, and in any event, the majority of spectators had already left and did not return.

The rampage at the national stadium was televised as millions watched it. Salerno was watching it from his bedroom. He laughed and laughed as he watched the chaotic scene at the national stadium that a flock of innocent birds caused. Those birds had instilled fear and confusion on the foolish infidels, and the birds were unarmed. He wished that those birds were his birds, and that they were armed. He realized that if that were the case he could have killed thousands of infidels. While he was thinking about that, a thought came to him. He realized that there would be another ball game at the national stadium in the next two weeks, so he decided that he would prepare two birds to attack the stadium while the game was going on. He knew that the game would not be as big as the last one, but nevertheless, there would still be a few thousand spectators present, and he could test his new Automatic Remote Release Switch or ARRS, where he would release the bombs remotely so that the birds would not have to be physically present on the target to release the bombs. He marveled at how he continued to manage to outsmart the infidels and how they were not thinking ahead, but rather reacting to what he did. He thought that it was one of the infidels' greatest weaknesses.

After the stadium scare everyone was talking about how the birds of terror were causing so much fear and chaos in the country. People wanted to know what could be done to allow citizens to return to the normal life that they had before the birds began to wreak havoc. They said that it was very unfortunate birds were controlling the lives of grown men and women and that the politicians were doing nothing about it. It was weird how the blame for the birds of terror was being passed around to various individuals at various times. At first, and still now, to some extent, the police were blamed for not being able to solve the attacks of the birds of terror, but now some individuals were blaming the politicians.

Time came for the second ball game at the national park. The crowd was understandably smaller than the last ball game. That was because the two teams that were playing were not as popular as the two teams that played on the last occasion, and also because although the birds that invaded the ball game were innocent, nevertheless, people were still afraid to attend. At this game there were only about eight thousand spectators present. The game began and there were shouting and screaming by supporters of the various teams. The sky was dark and overcast, unlike the day of the last ball game. On the premises and surrounding the premises were police, National Guard and soldiers, and some civilians had brought their guns to the game with them. About one hour into the game some weather birds flew over heading straight for the stadium. It appeared that the birds already knew that whenever there was a game at the stadium they would find food. Salerno knew this also, so he had shown two of his birds the stadium a few times and trained them to fly over the stadium. He chose today to allow them to carry out another assignment. This assignment would be unlike the others in that he would use his newest gadget, the Automatic Remote Release Switch or ARRS to detach the bombs from the birds in flight and let the bombs drop onto the stadium. He was very anxious to execute this assignment and experience its success.

Salerno released two birds, each carrying a bomb and a camera attached to its body. The bombs had the Automatic Remote release Switches instead of the manual release knots. He watched them fly away. About eight minutes into the flight his birds joined the flock of weather birds that were flying toward the stadium. Because the sky was overcast and dark, the birds were able to get very close to the stadium before anyone could see them. When they got about one hundred feet away from the stadium someone saw them and shouted, "Birds, Birds," The players began to run off the field as those in the bleachers started to run to the exits. There were two exits on this occasion, one of which was installed only after the chaos at the last game where the one exit was insufficient. People were running and screaming as the police, the National Guard and the soldiers were firing shots non-stop. Some of the birds landed on the field while Salerno's two birds flew over the stadium. As they flew over the stadium Salerno released the bombs automatically with the Automatic Remote Release Switches and the bombs fell right onto the top of the stadium building where the spectators were seated. The police were able to see the bombs falling because they were very close to the two birds. One of the policeman present cried out, "Oh my God. Did you guys see that?" Another officer shouted, "They are now dropping the bombs from the air like fighter jets. Run, let's get out of here." The officers ran to get as far away from the building as possible. The National Guard and the soldiers did not know why the police officers ran, so they stood their ground, still shooting at the now fleeing birds. The two birds managed to escape through the volley of bullets. About twenty seconds after the bombs were dropped Salerno put in the password and detonated the bombs. There was a huge explosion and the whole roof of the building blew apart as spectators began to scream louder and started pushing and shoving. Parts of the roof fell and injured and killed some of the spectators, and some other parts of the roof blew into the parking lot and around the building, killing some of the National Guards and soldiers. Although the birds were now out of sight, bullets were still being fired into the air.

Ambulances arrived and the paramedics rushed to render assistance to the injured. It was far worse than they thought. Bloodied bodies were stacked on top of bodies inside and outside the building. Guns were on the ground from the National Guards and the soldiers that were killed and their guns blown or fallen from their hands. The injured were crying, moaning and groaning from pain. Reporters were now on the scene and sending news feeds back to their respective television stations. Salerno was switching from channel to channel watching the carnage that he and his birds of terror had caused. For some reason he liked the term birds of terror because he wanted to terrorize the infidels, and that was just what his birds were doing. He watched the scene at the stadium as those who could assist the injured did what they could to assist them. Some policemen were crying openly and without shame because at least two of their officers were killed, because they could not escape from the scene fast enough. Salerno opened two beers and began to drink and celebrate his latest victory over the infidels. While he was laughing and rejoicing he thought about his ten birds that were killed and he began to cry. He then held a beer in the air and said, "This one is for you, my departed birds. May your souls rest in peace." Some of the athletes who were participating in the game had made it to the stadium building and were killed. The remaining players from both teams were crying and hugging each other as they mourn their missing friends. The teams' spirit of rivalry was now one of togetherness. One of the coaches was also killed.

The media covered the story of the bombing of the stadium and wondered how the security could not prevent that, especially after the first scare during the game prior to this game. People were calling in to the radio stations and television stations and venting their anger and frustration over the fact that law enforcement could not solve the bombing cases. Some of the callers said that they would leave this country and go abroad to live where there were no threats from birds bombing buildings and killing people. One caller said that he thought that the government was behind it and that it was a cover up, but he did not say how and why it was a cover up. It was obvious that his frustration level had got to him and caused him to speak unreasonably. However, the general sentiment was that law enforcement was not doing a good job in trying to solve the bombings.

It was good that they had found out that birds were carrying and depositing the bombs. On the other hand, it was not law enforcement that discovered it, it was the Leader of the Country's personal and private security that must take the credit for that. Law enforcement therefore, has not done anything worthwhile or deserving of credit when it came to solving the bombings, and it was about time that they knew that. Personnel in the media were now frustrated with law enforcement about the bombings still being unsolved. A female news anchor asked, "Will law enforcement solve these bombings, or will they have to admit that they are in over their heads and cannot solve them?"

The bodies kept being brought out of the stadium as Salerno watched with pride and satisfaction. Hundreds of curious on-lookers had gathered as close to the site as the police would allow, in anticipation of having a close look at the dead and injured. Some of the on-lookers were saying that one or more of their family members were supposed to be in the stadium and they wanted to know if they were alright. The police told them that they could not release any information at the time, but assured them that as soon as that information became available it would be released to them. Many in the crowd of on-lookers were crying and asking God to save their loved ones. One of the on-lookers said, "How can two little birds cause so much death and destruction?" Many present, especially the police, had seen the two birds, but no one was able to shoot and kill the birds, so the birds escaped. The fear was that the two birds would attack again some other place. The fact that the soldiers, the National Guard and the police could not shoot and kill the two birds was considered deplorable. The excuse for not being able to shoot and kill the two birds was that the birds were flying in a zigzag fashion, thus ducking or evading the bullets. Civilians wondered why in this day and age the military or some other governmental agency had not designed or manufactured some type of weapon to combat the zig-zag, evasive, movements of birds, animals and human beings.

The governor spoke the following evening after the bombing of the stadium. He said that he was sorry that a coward or cowards had bombed the stadium where spectators and players were enjoying the game. He extended his condolences to the families of the injured and those killed, and promised that they will get justice. He assured the public that the government and law enforcement were doing all that they could to solve the bombings, but because the method that was used by the terrorists was so novel, it would take some time before they were solved. He reminded the public of the huge reward for information leading to the arrest and conviction of those responsible. Finally he said, "It is estimated that at least three thousand innocent individuals perished in the stadium bombing. I pray that their souls rest in peace." From the expression on the governor's face it was apparent that he was stressed out and worried that law enforcement could not solve the bombings. On-lookers wailed and some threw themselves on the ground as bodies were being brought out of the bombed building constantly. Those who were bringing the bodies out appeared to be weary and tired from the constant movements of carrying bodies to and fro. Some of them took a break and were either sitting on something or leaning on parts of the structure that had not fallen, and wiping their faces. The heat from the explosion was having a negative effect on them and dust and soot had settled on their tired and worn faces.

On the street where Salerno lived traffic was normally slow. His house was situated at the end of the street on a Cul-de-sac with lots of tall trees on all sides of the house, which hid the house from the public. It was the ideal house for Salerno, because he could train his birds in his backyard and no one would know because the birds could not be seen from the street. Very few vehicles ventured as far as Salerno's house, and those that did were either lost or were looking for an address or had gone to the end of the street to turn around. His project required secrecy for the protection of himself and his birds. He had already lost ten birds and he was not prepared to lose any more. Thinking about those ten birds that he lost brought a wave of emotions on him and he began to cry. He wondered how the infidels could mourn the loss of infidels that his birds killed but not mourn the deaths of his birds that were waging a just war. He had not heard one single infidel say that he or she was sorry for the birds that lost their lives.

Salerno blamed the security guard who spotted the birds with the explosive devices strapped to them when his birds were about to attack the People's House. That guard was the epitome of evil and nothing less than a cruel infidel who was out to get in the way of the freedom fighters and their cause. Salerno wished that there was a way in which he could hunt down that guard and kill him in the same manner that the guard caused his beloved birds to be killed. He vowed that he would now wage a war on the infidels like he never did before, and would not let up even if it caused him his life. He saw his birds as avian martyrs who had done nothing wrong, and yet the worthless infidels took their lives, or caused some of them to lose their lives. His birds were flying away from the scene of the People's House when he was forced to destroy them. He would not have been forced to destroy them if the stupid, cowardly guard had not seen the explosive devices strapped to them and raised the alarm. If the guard had kept his big mouth shut when he saw the birds with the explosives, his birds would have been alive today.

It was just a few days after the bombing of the National Stadium, and the urge to strike another target was overwhelming and irresistible for Salerno. He knew that as the adage went, he had to strike while the iron was hot, so he thought of a suitable target for the next assignment. He chose the Parliamentary Building where what he termed, 'dirty politicians', who practiced politrics, would be. The streets surrounding the Parliamentary Building were very busy at all times. Soldiers, National Guardsmen and police were all around the building guarding it from attacks by the birds and any other forms of terrorism. It was always protected in this manner and by surveillance cameras, but because of the newest and latest threat that the birds created, the security was increased and improved. Those who were protecting the Parliamentary Building were not searching vehicles because the threat came from birds in the sky, not vehicles on the ground, so when Salerno drove by with three birds to scope out the building those guarding the building did not see him. He actually drove by on three occasions with three of his birds to familiarize them with the building. He figured that if he were seen with the birds and questioned he would say that the birds were his pets, but luckily, he was not seen with them.

The day arrived for the attack of the Parliamentary Building. It was a day when there would be a debate on a very important topic of national concern, so in addition to having all the politicians present, there would be many members of the community present. Salerno had chosen this day carefully because it would be a day that the death toll and injuries could be maximized. The weather was in his favor because the sky was dark grey with rain lurking. As a matter of fact, it had rained earlier, but only lightly. He believed that because of the overcast sky and because of how he planned to deliver the explosive device from the sky, the assignment would take those guarding the Parliamentary Building by surprise, and they would not know who or what hit them until it was too late. This strike would be about the element of surprise. He fed his three birds the usual stimulant laced meal with fresh water and watched them eat voraciously. After they had eaten he strapped the explosive devices to them and kissed them and sent them on their deadly journey. The birds flew off and headed toward the direction of the Parliamentary Building, flying higher as they went, like an airplane that has just left the runway and flying higher until it leveled off. They flew higher than any of the birds had flown on previous missions. They were out of Salerno's sight very early because of the overcast sky, however, when he sat at his computer he could see them as they flew toward the target. They appeared as little specs on a radar. Finally they arrived over the Parliamentary Building, and Salerno thought that he should release the explosive devices while the birds were still fairly high in the sky, so he pushed the buttons to release them. As soon as he released the explosive devices the birds made a bee line toward home. He immediately steered the devices toward the earth, and directly onto the parliamentary building.

Those guarding the Parliamentary Building were not expecting that the building would be attacked so they were somewhat relaxed. Maybe because there were so many of them guarding the building they became complacent. The discussion inside the Parliamentary Building had begun, and the room in which it was held was full to capacity with only standing room. The three bombs speeded toward the building as Salerno braced himself for the contact. Suddenly there were three huge explosions one after the other in quick succession, and the whole building shook as the roof came apart. One of the explosive devices fell directly on the roof over the room in which the debate was held, and it just about demolished that room. Almost everyone inside was killed instantly, and those who were not killed were seriously injured. Many soldiers, National Guardsmen and police men and women were killed or seriously injured. People were screaming and running, trying to get away from the area as quickly as possible. It was a scene that looked surreal. Nobody had seen any birds and nobody had seen any explosive devices, so they wondered if the bombs were set on or around the building prior to the debate. Those guarding the building did not believe that, because they had not seen anyone suspicious approached the building. Everyone who approached the building for the debate or any other reason was searched properly and nothing was found on them. Furthermore, the interior and exterior of the building was searched properly. The only logical explanation was that the explosive devices had literally fallen from the sky like manna that was mentioned in the bible.

More police officers arrived on the scene with paramedics and tried desperately to assist those who were still alive. The police were shocked to see the extent of the damage and the number of their own that were killed or injured. The guards that were still alive were pointing their guns toward the dark sky, and some of them were looking through binoculars to improve their vision. There was not a single bird in the sky, and that left them confused, because they believed that the explosive devices fell from the sky. It was difficult to keep the nosy public away. They were around the scene trying to find out exactly what happened, but apparently no one knew or if someone knew, he or she was not saying. The media was also already on the scene reporting about the incident and trying to find out what happened, but no one could tell them either. Photographs of the dead and injured were taken and transmitted to the television stations. The building was almost totally destroyed. People wanted answers from those that were supposed to be protecting the Parliamentary Building. One of the reporters asked a police officer, "How can something like this happen when there was so much security in and around this building?" The officer walked away without answering the reporter's question.

It was determined that two hundred and three persons died at the Parliamentary Building and fifty were injured. The investigation determined that no one saw any birds or explosive devices, but it was most likely that one bird carried three explosive devices or three birds, each carried one explosive device. The investigators believed that the second scenario was most likely because it was reported that three explosions were heard in quick succession. The Chief of Police spoke and gave his sympathies to the families of those killed and injured, and promised, like he always did, that the terrorist would be found and prosecuted. He said that the building was well protected with National Guardsmen, soldiers and police officers, but maybe because the weather was overcast no one could see the birds of terror. He admitted that there was no concrete evidence that the explosions were caused by the birds of terror, but it was most likely that they caused the explosions. A reporter asked him, "How in the world could this happen?" the Chief of Police apologized and said, "At this stage we do not know, but I can assure you, we will get to the bottom of it."

The detectives swore that they would leave no stone unturned, and they would solve this bombing and all the others. After the detectives had interviewed all Jayne's ex-students and searched their premises and found nothing of evidentiary value, they decided to return to question Jayne again, believing that maybe she forgot to give them all her students' names. She was surprised to see the two detectives again, because as far as she was concerned, she had given them all the information that she could on the subject. The detectives begged her to think harder than before and see if there were any other persons that she trained and she forgot to mention, or anyone that she did not train but who was in the bird training business. She thought for a few seconds then she said, "No, I think that's it." One of the detectives said, "Maybe someone that you trained years ago or whom you know has experience in the training and caring of birds."

She thought for a while again and said, "Well, there is one young man that I trained some years ago and he in turn trained birds, but he stopped training birds a long time ago, and I don't think he is the kind of person to train birds to kill people and destroy property." The detective that was closer to her said, "Who is he? We would like to question him." She replied, "I think you're wasting your time because he is an outstanding individual and a good Christian from what I understood." The same detective responded, "Who is he and what is his name?" She seemed to be thinking and trying to remember his name, and suddenly she blurted out, "I remember his name. His Christian name is Salerno, but I don't remember his surname." The other detective asked her, "Do you have a phone number for this Salerno?" She said that she did have a number but she did not know if he changed it. She then went to her address book and looked up the phone number. Surprisingly, she found Salerno's phone number and gave it to the detectives and told them where Salerno last worked. They thanked her and got up to leave to visit Salerno's work place to speak to his boss, and she said, "Detectives, I think you are wasting your time with Salerno, he is the perfect gentleman. He made the employee of the year on his job." They thanked her again and told her that it was just procedure. They left and went to visit Salerno's boss.

They knocked on the office door of the electronics business and were told to enter. As they entered they introduced themselves to a short, fat man, who in turn gave them his name and told them that he was the supervisor. The supervisor invited them into his office and told them to have a seat. After they were seated he asked them how he could assist them. They told him the purpose of their visit and asked if an individual by the name of Salerno worked there. "Yes, we have a Salerno Bondi working here," the supervisor replied. They asked him how long had Salerno been employed with the company, and he told them. He went on to say that Salerno was his best employee and that he was very reliable and dependable, and a big Christian in his church. "As a matter of fact, he was our employee of the year recently," the supervisor said. The detectives asked the supervisor,

"Have you noticed any violent tendencies in him or any radical traits in him?" and he replied, "Oh no, he could not hurt an ant. He is an ardent Christian who pays his tithes and gives good offering to his church. His best friend is Leon Chanley, who worked here also. Leon was severely injured when Leon's wife blew up his car. Salerno took that very hard, and is still finding it difficult to cope with it." They asked the supervisor if he knew if Salerno trains birds, and the supervisor said that he doubted it. The detectives got Salerno's house address from the supervisor and asked him not to mention their visit and what they discussed with him to Salerno. He promised them that he would not mention anything about their visit to Salerno. They asked him if Salerno was at work and he pointed Salerno out to them. As the supervisor was pointing Salerno out to the detectives, Salerno turned his head in their direction and noticed that they were watching him, and he wondered why they were watching him. He could sense that something was being said about him.

While Salerno was at work the detectives left his work place and drove to his residence, and from the road they looked into the yard. They noticed that the house was in an inconspicuous area, and the back yard was covered with overgrown bush and trees, which they thought could make a great hiding place for birds and birds' cages. They did not want to tip Salerno off in the event that he was the individual they were looking for, so they obtained a search warrant stating that they had probable cause because Salerno was a trainer of birds and he might be a radical because of his ethnicity. From the little that the detectives knew, they thought that he was a great match with the criminal profile that they had of the suspected terrorist bomber. The profiling issue was one of the problems that Salerno had with the infidels. He thought that it was so wrong to profile someone because of one's race or ethnicity or complexion. Salerno did not know if the detectives saw him looking at them when the supervisor pointed him out to the detectives, but he doubted that they saw him.

Salerno thought that the two men who were in the supervisor's office were law enforcement officers trying to get information on him, so as soon as they left he made an excuse to his boss to be away from work for about an hour. He left the building, got in his car and sped to his house, hoping to get there before the police arrived. His car had hardly stopped when he jumped out and rushed to his house door with his keys in his hand. He unlocked the door quickly and rushed into his bedroom and threw some clothing into a small suitcase. He got his passport from his drawer closest to his bed and put it in his pocket, then he rushed to the backyard, open the birds' cages and drove all the birds out of the cages. Some of the birds appeared to be puzzled and did not want to leave, but after Salerno chased them away they flew away from the cages. He then rushed back to the house, grabbed his suitcase and sped off toward his cousin Josef's house. He did not inform his cousin that he was visiting him, so his cousin was not expecting him. Salerno did not want to call his cousin because he was afraid that the police would have been able to track his phone from a cell phone tower that was close by or in the vicinity of his cousin's house. He knocked on his cousin's door and his cousin opened it, surprised to see Salerno. Salerno rushed in with his small suitcase in his hand as his cousin closed the door after he entered, and he said to Salerno, "Man, what's going on? Why are you rushing?" Salerno walked to the two windows in the front of the house and pulled back the curtains and looked out. His cousin asked again, "Man, what's going on?" Salerno sat on the sofa next to the front door, and every minute or two he looked through the window.

Salerno put his hands to his face, sighed heavily and said, "The police are trying to frame me for something that I did not do." His cousin remarked, "Wait a minute, frame you for what?" Salerno replied, "They're trying to frame me for those unsolved bombings." His cousin seemed to be surprised at what Salerno had just said, so he said, "My God, are you serious? Why would they accuse you?" Salerno got up, pulled the window curtain to the side a little and peeped out the window. He was beginning to perspire and started wiping his face with his hand as he said, "I don't know why they are trying to frame me. I guess they want somebody to blame." Salerno got up from the sofa and started pacing the floor as he shook his head in disbelief. "What are your plans?" his cousin asked. Salerno peeped through the window again, sat on the sofa closest to the window and replied, "I want to be here with you for a few days then I will work out an exit plan. Right now there is too much pressure." Josef was confused because Salerno denied any knowledge of what the police accused him of, yet Salerno was fleeing from the police. Josef decided to ask Salerno directly if he was involved in the bombings, but he decided to do it at a later stage.

The following day, the police, armed with a warrant to search, went to search Salerno's house early in the morning. They wanted to conduct the search before he went to work. As a matter of fact, they wanted to conduct the search by surprising him while he was still in bed, but something went wrong so they had to conduct the search later. When they arrived at the house they knocked on the door repeatedly, but there was no response. They decided to enter the house, so they turned the lock and to their surprise the lock turned and the door opened. As they entered the house they looked around and noticed that the bedroom door was opened and clothes were strewn all over the bed, and some were on the floor. It appeared as if Salerno had left the house in a hurry. The top drawer in the bedroom close to the bed was left open with some clothing hanging out the drawer. They checked the other rooms of the house and in the kitchen cabinets were boxes of what appeared to be ingredients for making explosives or bombs. In some other boxes was a type of hard plastic which is known to disintegrate when it is ignited. The detectives were now beginning to understand why there was no evidence left at the sites of the bombings. After the search of the house was completed they ventured to the back yard and began to search there. In the back yard they saw the empty birds' cages with evidence of recent occupation. There was fresh birds' stool, fresh water and fresh food for birds in the cages. While the detectives were searching the back yard five birds flew into the cages and began to feed and drink water. One of the detectives decided that it was best to lock the five birds in the cage and maybe use them as evidence if a trial ensued, so he rushed over to the cage that the five birds were occupying and locked them inside. They called in the Animal Care Department which came and took the cage with the five birds away.

The detectives left Salerno's property and returned to Salerno's workplace to arrest him if he were still there. When they arrived at his workplace they went straight to the supervisor's office and asked the supervisor if Salerno was at work, and the supervisor said that Salerno left early the previous day to take care of some private business, and he had not seen him since. The supervisor said that Salerno did not call him to say whether he would return to work or not, which was somewhat strange because Salerno took his job seriously. He said that Salerno was one of his best employees whom he valued a lot. The detectives told him that if Salerno showed up or called in to his job, he, the supervisor, must inform them. The police decided to make an announcement to the public, in which they sought information on the whereabouts of Salerno, reminding the public that Salerno was suspected of being the terrorist in the unsolved bombings and that he was considered very dangerous. The wanted announcement and the be on the lookout for Salerno Bondi, (BOLO) was aired on radio and television, and all points bulletins were put out for police on patrol to be on the lookout for Salerno. The descriptions of Salerno and his car were given to the public.

Airport ticket counters were checked and the agents were asked to be on the lookout for Salerno Bondi as it was feared that he would try to escape to another country. Employees at bus stations and bus drivers and taxi cab drivers were asked if they had seen Salerno and asked to be on the lookout for him after his photograph was shown to them. The photograph was one that was kept at the Motor Vehicles Department. Nobody had seen or heard from him after he left his job early to go home to take care of personal and private business.

The police reminded the public about the huge reward that was still unclaimed. It caused the public to call in many false sightings of Salerno and his car. Finally, law enforcement seemed to have a very good suspect, and surprisingly, they allowed him to slip right through their hands.

Salerno's cousin heard about the huge reward for the capture and prosecution of Salerno, and the cousin thought that if he had that money he would not have to work anymore. He was confused because in his culture it was unacceptable to rat or snitch on someone. He was conflicted, and decided to discuss the matter with Salerno, although he knew that it was not the smartest thing to do. Meanwhile, Salerno had parked his car inside his cousin's garage and locked the garage door, thus hiding it from those on the outside. When his cousin returned home from work he brought two dinners and two drinks with him, one for Salerno and one for him. They sat at the kitchen table to eat their meals, and while they ate Salerno's cousin said, "Salerno, would you consider me taking you in to the police? You are not guilty anyway." Salerno could not believe what he thought he had just heard his cousin say. He wondered if his cousin had forgotten that they were close family.

Salerno stopped eating, rose from the table, went to peep out the window and returned to his seat. He was obviously worried about what his cousin just said to him, and he was not certain how he should respond to his cousin. "Are you serious?" He asked his cousin. "Don't you realize that we are cousins?" Salerno asked him. His cousin was somewhat nervous as he began to respond to Salerno. "I'm just asking you. I could share the reward money with your family back home. It's just a lot of money", he replied. Salerno understood what it was all about, and he believed that his cousin was interested in money only and not his, Salerno's well-being. Salerno was angry on the inside and wanted to explode, but an idea came to his mind, and he said, "O.k., keep it a secret and tomorrow you and I would discuss how you would be handing me over to the police. I agree that money can go a long way with our families." Josef appeared to be happy with the answer that Salerno gave, and he thought that there was no point in asking Salerno if he was guilty, because Salerno would be turning himself in to law enforcement anyway, and he, Josef, would be getting a huge reward.

Salerno's cousin usually went to bed early. At 10:00 clock that night his cousin told him good night and retired to bed. There was only one television in the house, and that was in Salerno's cousin's bedroom, so Salerno decided to watch that television until he became sleepy, then he would turn it off and go to the living room and sleep on the sofa. Every night Salerno's cousin would fall asleep before Salerno, and tonight would be no exception. Salerno pretended to be watching the television, but his mind was on what his cousin said about turning him, Salerno, in to the police. He thought that his cousin lived among the infidels for so long that he had become an infidel and worshipped money and material things like the infidels. His cousin was now thinking like an infidel and was putting money above his family's interest. His cousin was a heavy sleeper who snored like a roaring lion. The following day was the agreed day that Josef would take Salerno in to the police. Salerno waited until his cousin fell asleep and began to snore heavily, and he sneaked into the kitchen, obtained a nine inch butcher knife and sneaked back into his cousin's bedroom. His cousin was lying on his back, with his mouth wide open and his hands to his side as he snored heavily. Salerno crept up to the bed where his cousin slept and started stabbing furiously at his cousin's neck and chest. The third stab was at the left side of his cousin's neck, and as soon as Salerno withdrew the knife the blood began to gush like a fountain from his cousin's neck. His cousin did not resist, he made a few twitches then lay still. He died instantly. By the time Salerno stopped stabbing Josef, Josef was almost beheaded. The bed was covered with blood. Salerno's hands were also covered in blood. During the frantic stabbing Salerno's hand had become slippery from the blood on his hand and his hand slipped down the blade of the knife and caused him to get a deep wound on his hand. He went to the bathroom and washed the blood from his hands and the knife and tied a small towel around his bleeding hand. He rolled his cousin's body up in the sheet on which his cousin's body lay and rolled it up in a piece of rug. After doing that he wondered what to do with his cousin's body, because he could not keep the body in the house too long. He went to the kitchen, brewed some coffee, and made a ham and cheese sandwich, and sat on the bed beside the body and ate the sandwich and drank coffee while he watched television.

The following day Salerno's cousin did not show up for work and he did not call in or send an excuse. Salerno knew that if an excuse was not given, his cousin's non-attendance at work would become suspicious, so he called his cousin's work place and pretended to be his cousin. Both he and his cousin had a very similar accent because they were of the same ethnicity and from the same country. He identified himself as his cousin and told the supervisor on his cousin's job that he had just had a death in his family back in his country and that he would be away from work for about three weeks because he was going to attend the funeral and be with his family for a while. The supervisor gave Salerno his sympathy, thinking that Salerno was Salerno's cousin, Josef. The supervisor said to Salerno, "I'll see you in three weeks, and please convey my sympathies to your family." Salerno was glad that he had successfully dealt with the problem of his cousin not showing up for work, and he was happy that the supervisor did not becoming suspicious. After speaking to his cousin's supervisor he went to the rear of the house and saw a utility shed in which his cousin kept tools and other miscellaneous items. While he was searching the shed he saw a shovel and a pick axe, so he took them out of the shed and began digging a hole under a huge avocado tree. After the hole was dug about three feet deep he entered the house, removed his cousin's body, dumped it into the hole and covered it with sand. After he covered the hole he spread some dry leaves on the top of it so that the grave could not be easily recognized.

Everything was going smoothly as far as Salerno was concerned. However, on the third day he had run out of drinking water, bread and cheese, which he ate day and night because no other food was available in his cousin's house. His cousin did not cook, but instead, would purchase food from fast food chains daily, which he thought was much cheaper than cooking himself. Salerno had no choice but to try to go in disguise and venture out in his cousin's car in search of food. He put a cap on and pulled it down over his eyes which were covered by a huge pair of dark sun glasses. As he drove he gazed around continuously hoping that no one would see him and recognize him or become suspicious, and hoping that the police would have no reason to stop him. When he got to the food store he purchased enough grocery to last him for a long time, so that he would not have to leave the house to purchase food for some time. Usually he would either watch television all night and day or play games on his cousin's computer or lap top. He would often peep through the curtain to see if anyone was lurking around the house or if the police were coming to the house. He was very nervous and restless, and it showed by his actions. He never saw anyone so he thought that what he had done to his cousin was flawless, and that no one would ever discover him. He decided that he would remain holed up in his cousin's house for as long as it took until the way was clear for him to leave. As it stood right now it was too risky to take a chance and leave.

As soon as Salerno arrived at his cousin's house two weeks earlier he realized that in his haste to escape he had forgotten to remove all the bomb-making materials and ingredients in his house, and he knew that it was a grave mistake. He knew that the police would search his house, find them and save them as evidence and use them against him at his trial if he were ever caught, although he figured that he would never be caught because he was too smart for the inept and inefficient police. While he was thinking of the police, the police decided to go and speak with Jayne again, and they told her that they caught some birds at Salerno's property and wanted her to interact with the birds to see if they were trained to some degree. She contacted the Animal

Rescue Department where the birds were kept and made arrangement to visit them. When she arrived at the Animal Rescue Department she noticed that the birds were the same type that she had used to do the training with Salerno, so she decided to try the same training programs that she used with him, and if the birds were familiar with those programs she knew that they were trained, and were not just pets. She started by giving the birds the simple commands to have them skip and sing. All that she taught Salerno during the training she did with the five birds and they mastered it. They appeared to be more advanced in training than the training that she did with Salerno. She told the detectives that the birds were well trained and much more advanced in their training than the training that she had taught Salerno.

The detectives had an idea that they thought that they could use to determine if these birds could be some of the birds of terror. They decided to strap two of the now defused improvised explosive devices that they found in Salerno's house to the birds and see if they would deliver the devices to an assigned target. It was a long shot but they had nothing to lose in attempting it. They asked Jayne to assist them and she agreed that she would do so. They wanted to know how the birds would know what target to drop the explosives on or if they dropped the targets at random. Jayne and the detectives examined the evidence that was collected from Salerno's house and noticed that there were photographs and sketches of the photographs of various buildings. The detectives had seen them before but they thought that it was a hobby of Salerno to take photographs of buildings then sketch them on his sketching pad. As they observed the photographs closely they noticed that the photographs and sketches were all photographs and sketches of the buildings that were bombed. Among the photographs and sketches were a photograph and a sketch of Leon Chanley's car. As one of the detectives looked at the photograph and sketch of Leon Chanley's car he said, "Oh my God, an innocent woman is in prison for bombing that car." The other detective rushed to that detective's side and looked at the photograph and sketch of

Leon Chanley's car and he said, "We screwed up. I could have sworn that she was responsible. We made a huge blunder." They noticed that there were red Xs on various locations on all the sketches. Jayne said that she figured out how Salerno might have communicated with the birds as to which buildings or targets to attack. She said that she thought that Salerno would take the birds to see the targets on several occasions then he would take photographs of those targets, which he later sketched and allowed the birds to familiarize themselves with. She went on to say that she thought that the red Xs on the targets were where the birds were supposed to release the improvised explosive devices or the bombs.

The detectives shook their heads in agreement. She agreed to spend a few days with the birds so that she and the birds could get to know each other, and afterwards she would take them out to see a target for a few days, and after that she wanted the detectives to strap the defused improvised explosive devices on three birds and send them out to the target to release the explosive devices at certain sketched locations on the sketched targets. One of the detectives wondered how the cameras that he found in Salerno's house were used. Jayne said that she believed that they were connected to Salerno's computer remotely. She and the detectives checked Salerno's computer along with an expert on electronics, and they found the password that would ignite or detonate the explosive devices remotely. They also found how to turn the remote cameras on. They could not believe how sophisticated and knowledgeable Salerno was in electronics and wondered why he used his knowledge and skills to do evil and inflict injury to others, as opposed to doing good.

Jayne located a target that would be most appropriate in the test for the birds. It was the detectives' headquarters in the downtown area. She took the birds by the headquarters to see the building and she took a photograph of the building. A police sketch artist who made sketches of criminals in an attempt to solve crimes, sketched the headquarters on a piece of paper, and Jayne placed a red X at the front of the building in front of the door and pointed it out to the birds. She decided that she would use one bird only in this demonstration for fear if she sent all five on the mission and they did not return or something happened to them, they would not be available in court as evidence if they were required. One of the detectives remained at the headquarters and one remained at the Animal Rescue Department where the bird was to fly from. The distance from there to the detectives' headquarters was about two and a half miles. Jayne rigged the bird with the defused explosive device and the mini camera and sent it off to drop it at the detectives' headquarters' front door. They called the detective who remained at the headquarters and informed him that they were about to release the bird and that he must be on the lookout for it. They released the bird and followed its path on the computer. To their surprise they watched the bird fly straight to the detectives' headquarters' front door. The detective who was on the lookout at the detectives' headquarters was struck to see that the bird landed at the front of their front door and released the dummy explosive device by loosening the knot with its beak and one of its feet. They jumped and shouted at their discovery and achievement. They could not believe that they had discovered exactly how Salerno executed his campaign to kill and destroy, using his birds of terror. The next step was to find Salerno, for they considered him armed and dangerous, and they feared that he could go some other place and set up his killing factory.

The police took to the airwaves immediately and showed a photograph of Salerno that they obtained from the Motor Vehicles Department. They urged the public not to approach him if they saw him, because he was considered armed and dangerous. They gave a description of Salerno's car and a number to call if he was seen. Meanwhile roadblocks were set up to see if he would be bold enough to be driving or in someone's vehicle when he knew that he was wanted. Some believed that he had already escaped and returned to his home country, while others believed that he was still in the host country where the bombing took place. Wherever he was the police were determined that he would be caught and punished. They knew that if he escaped and fled to his country of birth the chances of being caught and tried in a court of law were next to none. Their aim was to keep the pressure on him and hope that eventually he would make a mistake, which most criminals did eventually. They hoped that the constant pressure would flush him out from wherever he was hiding.

The public was warned that if they assisted in hiding Salerno they could be prosecuted and punished severely. The police were worried that it was two weeks since Salerno ran and there was not even a sighting of him or his car, which made them believe that maybe he had already left the state and gone to another state, or probably left the country. Even if that were the case, at least his car should have been sighted, but no one had reported any sightings of his car, in spite of searches made at the airport and bus terminals. Although they worried about that, nevertheless, it gave them some hope that he might be somewhere held up in hiding until the pressure cooled down. Law enforcement drove around in different communities looking to see if they would see Salerno's car parked on the road or in somebody's yard, but they found nothing. They tried to find out if Salerno had any friends or relatives, but they could find none. They went as far as contacting Salerno's home country to see if he had returned, but they were told that he had not. They had no choice but to sit out and wait to see if anyone would call in with a tip. Their efforts would soon pay off.

Salerno always chose late night to leave the house and go to the late night stores or restaurants, because he figured that by that time not too many people would be on the streets as pedestrians or commuters, and not too many police officers would be on the streets either. Tonight he would go to the twenty four hours convenient store to purchase some much needed items. The convenient store that he usually went to was just off a major highway with lots of trees and bushes on one side of the highway. He arrived at the convenient store at approximately 11:30 p.m., looking around him cautiously as he entered the parking lot. The store was practically vacant except for an old drunk who was a pan handler. Salerno exited his dead cousin's car, walked into the store and began to purchase his items. He did not notice that while he was in the store a police officer had driven up outside the store with the intention of entering the store to purchase a cup of hot coffee. This was the police officer's nightly routine, although he would normally come about 1:00 a.m. long after Salerno had left the store. Tonight the officer was feeling sleepy early because he had a rough day, so he was getting his coffee early.

As the office pulled into the parking lot he noticed the sole car parked in the convenient store's parking lot and he decided to run the tag. It came back to Salerno's cousin, Josef. Just then Salerno walked out of the convenient store with his bag of purchased items in his hand, and as soon as he saw the officer he became afraid and nervous. He told himself that he would try to remain calm. The officer was still seated in his car which was parked immediately behind Salerno's cousin car, blocking Salerno's cousin car from leaving. As Salerno walked towards his cousin's car the officer shouted to him, "Is that your car over there?" Salerno was not sure how he should answer the officer, or if he should answer him at all. Salerno looked around as if looking for an escape route that would be available if he made the decision to escape. He then turned to face the officer and responded, "Yes officer, this is my cousin's car. I borrowed it." The officer asked him his name and Salerno hesitated before answering. Before Salerno could answer the officer said, "May I see your driver's license?" Salerno put his hand in his back pocket and retrieved his wallet and passed the officer his dead cousin's driver's license.

The officer looked at the picture on the driver's license and looked at Salerno's face and said, "This photograph is not a photograph of you." On saying that the police officer began to exit his police cruiser, and as he opened the door and put his left leg out the vehicle, Salerno dropped the shopping bag with its contents and bolted off running across the highway toward the bushy area on the other side. The police officer pursued him on foot while calling in for assistance on his hand held radio. Salerno disappeared into the thick bushes running like a frightened deer from a hungry lion. After about five minutes three other police cruisers arrived with sirens blaring and lights flashing. One of the police officers had a K-9 trained dog in his vehicle. The police officer on the scene who questioned Salerno briefed the other officers and pointed out to the other officers the area where Salerno ran in the bush, and the officer who had the police dog entered that area with the dog. The other officers followed the officer with the dog. The dog had evidentially picked up Salerno's scent as it appeared to be pulling the skinny police officer who held the leash.

They followed the dog for an hour, and after that the dog appeared to have lost Salerno's scent, so the police officers returned to their vehicles. They called out a helicopter with heat sensors that could detect human beings from the heat that they released from their bodies. The helicopter flew around for a while, but once again the police were unsuccessful. They decided to leave the scene and check the area the following morning at the break of dawn to see if they could find the fleeing suspect. Salerno was travelling as fast as he could without taking any rest, because he knew that if he stood a chance of escaping he had to accumulate a good lead on them. Although he was tired he did not stop. He did not fear that the police dogs would catch him because he knew that what he did to affect them would prevent them from catching up to him. He was prepared for a situation like this, although he did not want it to come.

When the police officers returned to the police station, the officer who had demanded to see Salerno's driving license looked at the notice board on the wall in the police station and realized who had just fled from him, and he could not believe that he allowed a wanted suspected terrorist to escape. The officer knew that he still had a chance of catching Salerno if the owner of the car whose photograph and address that were on the driver's license that Salerno handed him could be located. The police looked up the address on the driver's license that Salerno gave him and sped off to that address to speak to the owner of the car. When they arrived at the address they knocked on the door but there was no answer. They looked around the property and through the windows, but they did not see or hear anyone. They noticed that a garage was on the property and that the door was locked, so they left and decided to return to the property the following day armed with a warrant to search.

The following day the police returned to Salerno's cousin's house with a warrant to search the whole premises including the garage. They entered the house first and saw evidence that Salerno was living there. However, no one was present. They noticed a huge dark brown stain on the mattress that appeared to be dry blood, and they began to fear for Salerno's cousin's life. After searching the house they moved to the garage, and broke open the door with the intention of searching it. After they broke the lock off the door and opened the door, they saw a car which they recognized as Salerno's car, the car that they had spent many weeks looking for. They made a cursory search of the car and broke open the trunk thinking that Salerno's cousin might have been inside it, but he was not there, so they decided to have it towed to the police station for a further and better search. Now the police realized why they could not find Salerno's car. They became more and more concerned about the fate of Salerno's cousin, Josef, who they feared was the victim of a homicide. They called a tow truck to tow the car to the police station. The bloody bed sheet was removed and sent to the lab for DNA testing.

A police helicopter was summoned to fly over the general area, and a police dog trained in detecting corpses was brought to Salerno's cousin's property to aid in the search for Salerno's cousin. At the same time another police helicopter and a police dog were employed at the site where Salerno ran from the officer by the late night convenient store. They searched that area for hours but they did not find Salerno, so the search in that area was called off. People who lived in the immediate area where Salerno escaped were warned to look out for

Salerno, the suspected terrorist, and not to approach him because he was considered to be armed and very dangerous. The residents of the area bought dogs and guns to protect them against Salerno should they come into contact with him.

The big concern for the police in addition to not being able to find Salerno was trying to find out where Salerno's cousin was. The dog that they took to Salerno's cousin's house had begun to search the cousin's property. When the dog was in Salerno's cousin's bedroom close to the area where the stain was on the mattress, it sat on its hind legs, indicating that a corpse was in the bed at some stage. The police were now certain that Salerno's cousin was not alive. Next they took the dog out to the back yard, and immediately the dog ran toward the avocado tree and began to sniff the ground under the tree then it sat on its hind legs. The police were now more convinced that Salerno's cousin was dead and was either buried under the avocado tree or his cousin's body had been placed under that tree and removed. They looked in the small shed at the back of the house and saw a shovel and pickaxe which they noticed had dirt on them as if they had been recently used. They removed the shovel and took it to the spot where the dog indicated that a corpse might be or had been and began to dig. After they had dug about three feet deep there was a pungent odor permeating the air and emanating from the hole. The police who were present were familiar with that odor as they had experienced it on countless occasions before. It was the unmistakable odor of decomposing human remains. After digging about six more inches, Salerno's cousin's body was found. Salerno had now added another body to his huge list of corpses.

The police were visiting the media warning the public to look out for Salerno, who was considered armed and very dangerous. The police told the public that if they saw him they should call the police immediately and not approach or confront him. They said that he was also wanted in connection with the death of another individual. The public was warned to keep their doors and windows locked at all times. Almost two days after Salerno escaped from the police at the convenient store's parking lot an old lady living alone sighted a stranger in her backyard acting suspiciously, and she watched him closely and noticed that he had moved to one of the windows of her house and was trying to pry it open. She had put window locks on all her windows making it very difficult, if not impossible, for a thief or burglar to enter through unless the window panes were broken. The old lady saw the man trying desperately to pry her window open to enter her house and she shouted, "Go away, I'm calling the police." She then got on her phone and dialed 911 and requested police assistance, telling the 911 operator that a strange man was trying to break into her house. As soon as she shouted to the man that she was calling the police the tired-looking man ran away. The police arrived about ten minutes later and she gave them a description of the prowler, which matched the description of Salerno. The police officer who responded to the old lady's call believed that the strange man was Salerno, so he summoned more officers at the scene.

The officers arrived with a police tracking dog, determined that they would not allow Salerno to escape again. The police helicopter was seen flying overhead as they searched for the strange man. By this time Salerno had broken into a vacant house a few blocks from where he was last seen, and he found among other things, a clothes closet with women's clothing. The occupant of the house appeared to be a female, and she was absent. Salerno quickly hid his clothes that he was wearing and dressed in some female clothing that he got from the house. Surprisingly, the dress fitted him well, except that it was a little too long. He put on a blond wig that he found in the bedroom, lipstick and a pair of woman's shoes and sat on the porch in a chair with a book that he appeared to be reading. The main road passed right in front of the porch of the house.

When Salerno left his cousin's house on the night when he ran from the police officer, he had put a tin of black pepper in his pocket. His reason for putting it there was to throw the police dogs off his trail in the event he had to run from the police and the police used dogs to track him. That explains why the dogs lost his scent on the first occasion. He sprinkled some that night when he ran from the convenient store, and did so again when he ran from the old lady's house. The police dog detected Salerno's scent at the window of the old lady's house, but after that the dog was going around in circles and sneezing a lot. The police brought another dog to the scene but the same thing happened with that dog, so they decided to go door to door asking the occupants of houses if they had seen a strange man any time lately. They showed the occupants a photograph of Salerno. The police advised the residents to call the police and do not try to take the law in their hands if they saw a stranger who did not fit in. Two police officers stopped their car in the front of the house where Salerno was sitting in a chair on the porch, and the police officer that was driving shouted to Salerno, "Lady, have you seen a strange man in the neighborhood recently?" Salerno was scared but he maintained his calm composure as he shook his head from side to side indicating that he had not seen the man, and he mumbled softly, "No officer." The other officer warned Salerno about the escaped terrorist, telling Salerno, "You must be careful. If you see a strange, suspicious man lurking in the area, please call 911." Once again Salerno shook his head, this time in the affirmative, and the police officers drove away.

What Salerno's next move would be, he had no idea. The masquerade that he had just pulled off was not planned, and had left him shaken and nervous. He could never see himself dressed in women's clothing and passing himself off as a woman, although he did not worry about it too much now because he knew that it was absolutely essential for his freedom. Anyway, he had to start thinking fast because he had no idea when the homeowner of the house that he was presently occupying would return home. In the house he found cereal and other canned food like corned beef, sardines and spam. He ate a good meal and took a shower while thinking what he would do next. He figured that if he could fool two police officers into thinking that he was a woman, he could fool the general public also. He spent more time putting on makeup, earrings and other accessories, and shaved with a razor he found in the bathroom, and afterward he called a taxi cab to take him to the airport. His plan was to go to the airport, purchase a plane ticket and travel to another state as a woman. He knew that he was taking a huge risk of being identified but he had no choice. It was something that he felt that he had to do to try to avoid being captured. Once he arrived in another state he figured that it would be easier for him to make his final escape.

The taxi cab arrived driven by an elderly man who wore thick eye glasses. Salerno got into the cab and the driver asked, "Where to young lady?" Salerno was glad that he had tricked the old man so far, and that gave him courage and confidence that his plan would work. Feeling over confident he replied in a feminine voice, "The airport." In spite of his over confidence he decided to speak as little or infrequently as possible for fear that the taxi cab driver might detect that he was a male. The driver began to drive off, and as he drove off he said, "Lady, you should be careful because there is a damn mass killer somewhere in this area. When I got the call to come to your address at first I decided against it because I was afraid that I might come in contact with that bastard, but I have not made a fare for the day so I had no choice. They should torture him to death when they catch him. We don't need scumbags like him in our country." Salerno did not respond, but after he saw the old man looking at him in the rear view mirror, Salerno shook his head in agreement with what the old man said. The driver drove slowly as he listened to country and western music on his radio in his taxi cab. They arrived at the airport and Salerno paid the fare and walked slowly into the terminal building, almost twisting his right foot from having trouble walking in the high heel shoes. He was forced to make slow, deliberate steps to avoid falling and creating a scene. He wished he had found a pair of woman's shoes that had a lower heel. He wondered how women could walk in shoes like the pair that he was wearing.

At the ticket counter Salerno bought his ticket to another state, and everything went smoothly. The ticket agent did not show any signs that she knew that Salerno was a man. After he purchased the ticket he headed to the bathroom to urinate. Impulsively, he headed for the man's bathroom, forgetting that he was supposed to be a woman. As he entered the men's room, an elderly man was exiting, and he said to Salerno, "This is for men, lady. Can't you read?" Salerno realizing that he had made a huge blunder, said, "My body is here but my mind is elsewhere." He then headed for the ladies' room marked 'Women', and rushed into the only toilet stall that was available. By now he could hardly hold the urine any longer and he had begun to wet himself. As soon as he entered the toilet he stood in the front of it and began to urinate directly in the centre of the toilet bowl, and it was making a loud sound. A lady on the toilet next to him looked under the stall that Salerno was in and saw feet in women's shoes facing the toilet, when the feet should have been facing away from the toilet if the person were a woman sitting on the toilet seat or stooping over the toilet bowl. The lady also noticed that Salerno's feet were big for a woman's feet, and his toenails were not painted and needed clipping.

The lady was confused and wondered if the person in the toilet next to her was a female with a male's sex organ, or a male disguised as a female. She believed that the latter was the case. She went to the basin to wash her hands and decided to linger at the basin until the person emerged from the toilet to see what was going on. While she waited she thought of the possibility of the individual having both male and female sex organs, but if that were the case, the person should have used the female organ, she thought. Just then Salerno exited the stall and walked over to one of the basins to wash his hands as the lady looked at his face and down at his groin area and back at his face. She looked at his hands which appeared to be rather large for a female, and noticed that his fingernails were not manicured. She was convinced that Salerno was a male. Her belief was strengthened when Salerno started to walk out of the ladies' room. She noticed that he could hardly walk in the high heel shoes. She walked out behind Salerno, and as she did so, she noticed an airport police officer close by, so she approached the officer and said, "Officer, that thing wearing the beige dress is not a woman. It's a man, and it used the ladies' bathroom where other ladies and I were." The officer asked, "What are you talking about?" and the lady replied, "It was in the ladies' room peeing like a man and it cannot walk in high heels. I think that it is disguised like a woman because it has something to hide." Before the officer could respond, the man who saw Salerno entering the men's room and who turned Salerno back was standing close to the officer while the other lady spoke to him, and he told the officer that he agreed with the lady who just spoke to him. The man then told the officer that he had to prevent Salerno from using the men's room because he thought that Salerno was a woman. The officer decided that he would have a word with Salerno because what the lady and the man told him sounded suspicious.

Salerno was seated while he waited for his flight to be announced so that he could board the plane. As he sat he watched the police officer walking in the direction where he was seated, and he became fearful. He stood up and decided to walk off just as the officer said, "Just a minute lady." Salerno stopped and said, "Are you speaking to me officer?" The officer replied, "Yes. May I see your I.D.?" Salerno knew that he was in trouble because he had no identification card with him that would show that he was a woman. He had paid for his ticket with cash and gave the ticket agent a fictitious name. He pretended to fumble in his little purse that he had taken from the house where he got the female's clothes, and he said, "Officer, I don't have it with me. I forgot it at home." The officer asked him his name, and he gave the officer the name Rosemead Hai. The officer said, "Come with me, I have a few questions I would like to ask you." The officer was about to escort Salerno to the office that was used by the airport police. Salerno thought that the police would make him undress, remove his makeup and wig, and would discover his true identity, so he bolted. He could hardly walk in high heels, so running in them was out of the question. After he ran about fifteen feet his right foot twisted in the shoes and he fell on his face with his legs wide apart and the dress over his head. Would be travelers could not help laughing at the spectacle as the police officer straddled him and placed his hands behind him and handcuffed him. Salerno tried to resist but he was eventually taken to the office at the airport for questioning.

In the police office the police officer asked Salerno, "Who are you?," but Salerno refused to answer. He sat staring at the ceiling of the office. The officer then said to him, "What is your real name?" Again Salerno refused to answer. The officer told Salerno that he would be taken to the private room and searched by a female police officer. Salerno did not want to be insulted by having a female search him. He looked at the male officer and said, "I am Salerno Bondi." At first his name did not ring a bell to the male police officer, but the female police officer present whispered something in the male officer's ear, and the male officer quickly drew his weapon and said, "Get on the ground now." Salerno was about to comply, but before he could comply the male and the female officers grabbed him by his arms and pushed him to the floor and handcuffed him. They then lifted him from the ground, sat him in a chair, and called for backup, stating, "We have the escaped terrorist." In a short time about a dozen other police officers arrived with weapons drawn. The media, which have police scanners, were also on the scene. Most likely they had heard what transpired between the two police officers who captured Salerno and the 911 operator when they called her for backup. As the police brought Salerno out of the room to take him to the jail downtown, the media was snapping photographs of him in drag and shouting out questions and remarks to him. One of the reporters shouted, "Are you the person who killed all those people with bombs?" Another reporter shouted, "Why did you do it Salerno?" A third reporter asked, "Did anyone assist you?" The reporter who asked him the first question asked him, "How did you train the birds of terror?" Salerno did not respond to any of the questions that the reporters asked.

Every news channel was showing Salerno dressed as a woman. One of the reporters asked, "Is this the feminine monster that terrorized our community for so long?" Some television programs and radio talk shows had listeners calling in and expressing their gratitude and elation over the fact that the individual who killed so many people and destroyed so much property by using birds of terror was caught. Some of the callers praised the police and others criticized them. One caller said that had it not been for a vigilant civilian, the terrorist might have escaped the country and might have never been caught. The Chief of Police went to the media and said, "We got him. The terrorist that is responsible for all the bombings, using his birds of terror, is now in custody. We have plenty evidence that he is the individual responsible and soon he will be brought to justice." People drove by the County Jail honking the horns of their vehicles and shouting various phrases. Extra police were put on guard at the jail for Salerno's protection. It was ironic that at some point, the public was protected from him, but now he was being protected from the public. He was afraid that if the public got to him they would lynch him.

On the day that Salerno was caught a miraculous thing happened. That morning about 6:00 a.m. the nurse on duty at the hospital where Leon was, entered Leon's room to ensure that he was alright and all his tubes were still in place. As she entered the room with some gloves and other things in her hands and humming a gospel song entitled, 'God is good' she saw Leon sitting up on the bed and smiling. She was so shocked that she dropped everything that she had in her hands and ran out of the room screaming as she went to look for the doctor on call. Other nurses saw her and heard her screaming and wondered what happened. They saw a terrified look on her face so they ran behind her to find out what was wrong. By the time they got to her she had already approached the doctor and was trying to talk to him as she panted out of breath. The doctor told her to take a deep breath and take her time and tell him what happened. After a few seconds and after taking the doctor's advice, she calmed down. The nurses who followed her were standing around her as if to protect her as she told the doctor what happened. She said, "Doctor, the patient, Leon Chanley, oh my God." She was trying to catch her breath when another nurse said, "Has he died?" The doctor was holding the nurse by the shoulders as she trembled and began to cry again. She had not answered the other nurse's' question when she was asked if Leon Chanley had died, so the doctor asked her, "Has Mr. Chanley died?," to which she shook her head in the negative. The doctor asked again, "Well, what is the problem?" She said, "Mr. Chanley is sitting up in bed and smiling. Oh my God is good!" The doctor looked surprised and said, "Are you sure? Are you alright?" She shook her head indicating that she was sure and that she was alright. The doctor removed his hands from her shoulders and literally ran to Leon Chanley's bedroom with the nurses in hot pursuit.

When the doctor and the nurses arrived at Leon's room Leon was still sitting up and smiling. The doctor rushed over to him and said, "Mr. Chanley, can you hear me?" Leon shook his head affirmatively. The doctor then said, "Can you raise your arms?" Leon raised both arms. The doctor removed the sheet that covered his legs and asked Leon to wiggle his toes. Leon tried to wiggle his toes but he could not do it. The doctor then scraped the bottom of Leon's feet with a sharp object and asked Leon if he could feel it, and Leon shook his head in the negative. He did not move his feet when the doctor scraped the sharp object at the bottom of his feet. The doctor removed the tubes from Leon's mouth and asked Leon if he could speak, and Leon spoke. The doctor mumbled, "Indeed, this is a miracle that I am witnessing today." The nurses present were wiping tears from their eyes. They knew that because of the extent of Leon's injuries he was not supposed to come out of the coma and move any part of his body or talk again.

They surely believed that their God was involved in what was now happening to Leon. He appeared to be paralyzed from the waist down, but in spite of that it was incredible that he was alive. He was given breakfast which he ate all by himself for the first time since his car was blown up and he was injured. All the nurses began to talk to him, telling him how happy they were that he could communicate with them. He asked them where his friend Salerno was, and there was silence in the room for a moment. He asked them again and one of the nurses told him that Salerno and his other co-employees visited him on a couple of occasions. He wanted to know if he could use a phone to call Salerno to give him the good news personally, but he was told by the doctor that it would not be safe for him to engage in much conversation at that stage. The doctor and the nurses knew that Salerno was on the run as a suspect in the bombings, including the one in which Leon was injured, but they did not want to tell Leon that; at least not as yet.

A member of Salerno's cousin's family was found and a DNA sample was taken from him and compared with the DNA of the body that was found under the avocado tree in Salerno's cousin's yard. It was confirmed that the body was that of Salerno's cousin, Josef. It was determined that he had died from stab wounds caused by a sharp instrument like a knife, and his death was determined to be homicide. The knives in the cousin's house were tested and blood was found inside the handle of one of them, which was later determined to be Salerno's cousin's blood. Also, there was evidence of blood at Salerno's cousin's house that was not the blood of Salerno's cousin. Now that Salerno was caught the DNA from that unexplained blood would be compared to his DNA. The police now had an insurmountable case against Salerno, and they were going for the death penalty. They felt that the evil acts that Salerno committed cried out for the death penalty. He maimed and killed too many people to allow him to live. They realized that because of the many lives lost and the brutal manner of taking those lives, the trial would last very long. They prepared for a long, drawn out trial.

After Salerno was captured and it was made known that he was responsible for the bombing of Leon Chanley's car, Leon's wife,

Daksy Chanley, retained a lawyer to represent her, who made a habeas corpus application for her release from prison. The prosecution did not oppose the application, stating that they agreed that mistakes were made and they were sorry about that. The judge said that what happened to Mrs. Daksy Chanley should have never happened and that she should bring a law suit against those responsible. He went on to say that to add insult to injury, Mrs. Chanley sustained a serious lasting injury. He then spoke directly to Mrs. Chanley as everyone listened intently. He said, "Mrs. Chanley, I am sorry that you had to endure what this system did to you. It should have never happened and I hope that it never happens again. I hereby grant this application. You are now a free woman and you are free to leave." All the time the judge was speaking Daksy Chanley was crying uncontrollably and wiping the tears from her face with a small wash cloth. Her attorney patted her on her back as he kept whispering something in her ear. As the judge arose to leave the courtroom Mrs. Chanley let out a piercing scream which permeated the courtroom. It appeared that she could no longer contain the pain and anguish. She put her head in her hands as she sat in her wheel chair and shouted, "Thank you Lord." She was wheeled out of the courtroom still crying. The family member who wheeled her out of the courtroom was crying also. The reporters were outside the courtroom and began to take photographs of her as she left. One of the reporters asked her, "Mrs. Chanley, how do you feel?" She was now smiling as she said, "All I can say is that God is good. God is good."

The police decided to bring Salerno in for questioning to see if he would confess to the bombings. One of the investigating officers had an idea. He decided to have the five birds present in the interrogation room and watch their reaction and Salerno's reaction when Salerno was brought into that room. That would also be compelling evidence against him if the birds seemed to know and recognize him. The police had the birds brought to the interrogation room about forty five minutes before Salerno was brought to the police station from the jail. The birds were gloomy, lethargic and not friendly before Salerno entered the investigation room. All stayed in one corner of the cage stooping low at the bottom of the cage. The two interrogating officers entered the room and the birds remained in the same crouching position as if they were sad. While the two detectives were seated in the room the door was opened and Salerno was allowed to enter, and as soon as the birds saw him they got up from the crouching position and began to chirp and sing and move around flapping their wings. They could hardly remain still. The transformation was instant, remarkable, and incredible. They tried desperately to get to Salerno but the door of the cage was locked and they could not get through the bars. In unity, they started chirping as if they were singing for Salerno. At first Salerno appeared not to notice the birds because he knew that the detectives were up to something when he saw his birds in the room, but it was difficult not to respond in kind to his birds' loving gesture. He arose from his seat, walked over to the cage and placed his fingers through the bars of the cage. The birds came to his fingers and started playing with them. Salerno could not pretend any longer, and he could not hold back the tears, so he began to cry. He could not understand why the infidels were treating his innocent birds like criminals. After all, he wondered, the birds were only carrying out orders, and the orders that they were carrying out were justified.

The interrogators watched the interaction between Salerno and the birds and came to the conclusion that it was irrefutable evidence that the birds were some of Salerno's trained killers. One of the detectives told Salerno that it was time that he sat down, and Salerno returned to the small desk and sat in the chair that was prepared for him. He wondered if he cooperated with the interrogators if they would free his birds. There was no doubt in his mind that he would eventually go to prison and most likely receive the death penalty, but he did not want anything to happen to his birds. He did not trust the interrogators with his birds. He believed that the interrogators would want to euthanize his birds because the birds were viewed as killers. He wondered how the interrogators could be so mean that they would put his birds to sleep and keep them in cages like they were criminals. He kept them in cages also, but it was only for their training, and it must be remembered that he freed all the remaining birds. He asked them, "Why are you so mean and cruel? How can you treat my birds like they are criminals?" One of the detectives told him that they would be asking him some questions, and if he answered those questions truthfully, they would answer some of his questions.

The interrogators introduced themselves to Salerno and began to question him. They asked him a series of questions and put certain allegations to him.

Detective: "Is your name Salerno Bondi?"
Salerno: "You know my name, why do you ask me my name?"
Detective: "Whose car were you driving when you ran from the police at the convenient store?"
Salerno: "You know whose car it was, so why do you ask me?"
Detective: "Your cousin's body was found in his back yard. Did you kill him?"
Salerno: "You do your work and you should find out who killed him."
Detective: "Did you train birds?"
Salerno: "Maybe."
Detective: "Did you use your trained birds of terror to kill and maim people and destroy their property?"
Salerno: "I'm not answering any more of your questions, and I'm not taking any part in this one-sided interview."

The detective ceased questioning Salerno after Salerno stopped cooperating, and took him back to the jail. While he was being led away he turned around and blew kisses to the birds, and they skipped and jumped up and down in the cage as they made excited noises as if they did not want Salerno to leave. He was obviously sad as he left the interrogation room, and it showed on his thin face. He was sad not because he was being interrogated or was in jail, but because he was leaving his birds behind, and he believed that the infidels were not treating his birds as well as he treated them, or as well as they should be treated.

Some residents from Salerno's country visited him and advised him that he should request a public defender because his alleged crimes were very serious and he could be sentenced to death. He laughed aloud and said that it would be a pleasure if he were made a martyr for the cause. They told him that there was no point in losing his life if he could avoid it. Later on during that week Mary, an employee from his former workplace visited him and asked him why he did those things that he is accused of doing. He replied, "A man has to do what a man has to do." She said to him, "I remember what Leon used to say to you. He never thought that you were the one killing so many people. How could you hurt him?" Salerno appeared not to be listening to what she was saying, but he was. It was just that he did not want to hear what she was saying. He bit his bottom lip as he said, "I'm not ready for this now," and he turned away from her. She left feeling sad and dejected. She still did not believe that Salerno was capable of doing what he was accused of doing. Although he refused to talk to her about the accusations, she had a feeling that in the end the police would be proven to be wrong in their accusations against him. She had a feeling that she knew the young man that she worked with, and he was a gentle, quiet and law-abiding person. As far as she was concerned, the police would have to have clear, cogent evidence for her to believe what they were saying about him.

The jail guard took Salerno's breakfast to him at 7:00 a.m. on the following morning. He was one of the last prisoners to receive breakfast. All the prisoners who received their breakfast before him were eating theirs by the time the guard reached Salerno's cell. Salerno was kept in isolation for his own safety because he was considered very dangerous and not a citizen of the host country, and because he had allegedly killed women and children. The warden handed Salerno his breakfast through the small window that was used for that purpose, but Salerno refused to accept it. The warden tried passing the breakfast to him again and again, but he still refused to accept it. The warden then asked him, "What happened, are you not hungry this morning?" but Salerno did not respond. The warden placed the breakfast back onto the dinner cart and moved away to give breakfast to another prisoner.

The warden took Salerno his lunch at lunch time when all the other prisoners were given theirs, but he refused to accept his lunch also. The warden asked him, "Don't you like the prison food?" Salerno did not reply. When it was supper time Salerno refused to accept the supper from the warden. The warden asked him if he was alright, but Salerno refused to answer. After the third day of not accepting food from the warden, Salerno was approached by the officer in charge at the jail who asked him if something was wrong. Salerno was now getting weak and he really did not want to die, but they would not know that. He decided that he would speak with the officer in charge of the jail, but he would make it appear as if he wanted to die or that he would remain on his hunger strike until his wishes were granted. The officer in charge asked him again if something was wrong, and he said, "I am on a hunger strike and I will not eat until law enforcement free my birds." The officer in charge responded, "I have no control over that, but will you kill yourself for some birds?" Salerno replied, "Those birds are very important to me." The officer in charge said, "I will forward your request to the proper authorities," and he left and went to his office and called law enforcement and conveyed Salerno's request to them. The officer that responded to the call from the officer in charge said, "Good riddance. We don't need people like him in this world." The officer in charge of the jail asked the officer who received the call from him to pass the message on to his superior, and he did.

One week passed without Salerno eating anything. He was living off water only, and he was becoming thinner and thinner and weaker and weaker each day. The officers at the jail were worrying because they did not want Salerno to become sick and die at their jail and afterward they would have to be answering questions in an inquiry, so they called law enforcement again. This time law enforcement decided to speak to Salerno, fearing that if they did not speak to him he would surely die and those maimed and killed by him would never receive justice. They believed that an individual who would maim and kill as many people as Salerno did would do anything, including taking his own life. They also knew that Salerno was one who thought that to die for his beliefs would make him a martyr, and as a martyr, he would one day return as a hero.

Law enforcement decided to make an application to the court to force feed Salerno in order to save his life, because under no circumstances they would free the birds, because the birds were crucial evidence against him in the up-coming cases. A doctor visited the jail and assessed Salerno's condition and came to the conclusion that Salerno was extremely ill and if he were not fed by force it was a foregone conclusion that he would die. The doctor said that the intervention of feeding Salerno forcefully had to be done immediately because if it were not done immediately his condition would soon be irreversible. Salerno was prescribed vitamins and other medication but he refused to take them. The court granted the application to force feed Salerno, and the police along with a doctor, rushed to the jail to force feed him. As weak as Salerno was he still put up a fight and clenched his mouth shut in order to prevent food being forced into it. They fought with him in an attempt to get food into his mouth, and finally they were successful, but he refused to swallow the food. Finally they managed to get some food down his throat and he tried to regurgitate it, but he was unsuccessful. Each day the police and the doctor had to follow the same procedure in order to get food into Salerno's stomach, and gradually he began to regain his strength and weight. He told them that he would not take part in any trial because the court would be nothing but a Kangaroo Court, and he could not receive justice. Furthermore, he told them that by force feeding him they were doing it against his will, and therefore, they were assaulting him every time they forced fed him. They told him that they disagreed with him because they had a court order to force feed him.

Law enforcement was concerned about the birds that Salerno once owned that are still at large. Their fear was that Salerno might have been working with other criminals, or that another terrorist or other terrorists may obtain possession of the trained birds and use them to engage in terrorism like Salerno did. Bird traps were set all over the place, including in the yard that Salerno once lived. Some birds were caught, but none proved to be any of the birds that Salerno trained. They had already eaten all the food that was left in the open cages in Salerno's yard. Law enforcement believed that the remainder of the birds that Salerno turned loose probably showed up on Salerno's property, but Salerno was not around when they showed up. They believed that maybe he could assist in catching them because the birds knew him. They asked Salerno to assist them by visiting his property and remaining there a few times, but he refused to do so. He begged them to release the five birds that they held in captivity, stating that if they did that he would tell them everything that they needed to know about the making, transporting and detonation of the bombs. They knew that the proposition that he made sounded good, but they did not believe that Salerno could be trusted. It was strange that he did not trust them and they did not trust him. They believed that if they set the birds free Salerno would renege on his part of the deal to reveal what he knew about the bombings. Nevertheless, they told him that they would have to consider his offer carefully and get back to him. Law enforcement discussed the matter and decided that if they went along with Salerno's offer they would be taking a big risk, so they turned down his offer.

The police made a final news release in which they informed the public that they would not be saying anything further about the Birds of Terror case until after the trial. They said that the terrorist that was responsible for the bombings was under arrest, and that they had an insurmountable amount of evidence against him, in spite of his attempt to trick and lie to his friends, his employer, his church and everyone with whom he came into contact. They said that the DNA from the unknown sample of blood that was found among Salerno Bondi's cousin Josef's blood, belonged to Salerno Bondi. The Chief of Police gave the public a list of things that law enforcement and the public should do in the event someone engaged in similar attacks. He said that Law enforcement would be investing in a better radar system; one that could detect very small objects like birds and what might be attached to them if something was attached to them. Also, the Multi Spray gun, or MSG, would be a common feature for law enforcement in cases similar to this case. He said that all electronic communication equipment would be monitored where possible for security reasons, and security would be enhanced in and around government buildings. The Chief of Police ended by saying that he and law enforcement on the whole, apologize to Mrs. Daksy Chanley for the pain and suffering that she experienced as a result of her arrest, conviction and sentence.

Salerno was now in custody for several months. After he was captured and placed in custody there were no incidents of bombings, which, coupled with all the other evidence, pointed undoubtedly to Salerno as the sole person responsible for the bombings. The detectives did not think that they needed to strike a deal with Salerno about releasing the birds, because as far as they were concerned they had a rock solid case against him. They decided to continue building their case against him until it was time for the trial, at which time they believed that convictions would be a virtual certainty. As the trial date drew nearer and nearer Salerno thought that it would be best to apply to have a public defender assist him in court, as he had thought about the martyr concept, and he decided that he no longer wanted to be a martyr. He wanted to remain alive and continue fighting for the cause of the freedom fighters. He believed that if he were convicted, regardless of the sentence, so long as it was not the death penalty, he would or may eventually be released, or he may escape and he could continue the fight for freedom. Even if he was not freed or he did not escape he could still convert prisoners to his faith and belief. Life, therefore to him, was more precious and more worthwhile and meaningful than death.

A message was sent to the prosecutor on behalf of Salerno that he would like to have a court appointed lawyer, and subsequently one was appointed to represent him. The court appointed lawyer for Salerno was given all the evidence by the prosecution that they had accumulated and planned to use against him. The court appointed lawyer read the evidence carefully and decided that it was strong and compelling, and would be very difficult to overcome. The prosecutor told the court appointed lawyer that the prosecution would be aiming for the death penalty and that it was because of the many people that Salerno killed with the improvised explosive devices. The prosecutor informed the court appointed lawyer that there would most likely be many death penalties imposed on Salerno, and more likely than not he would be put to death. Salerno's court appointed lawyer explained the evidence to him and also told Salerno that the prosecutor would be fighting for the death penalty on several counts. As he spoke Salerno sat quietly and ingested every word that the court appointed lawyer said. After the court appointed lawyer was finished speaking he said to Salerno, "Do you understood everything that I just told you?," and Salerno told him that he did.

The court appointed lawyer told Salerno that he would scrutinize all the evidence in detail and would return to speak to him in seven days, and that he wanted Salerno to think about the overwhelming evidence against him, and decide if he would like to take a plea bargain. After the attorney left Salerno contemplated trying to escape from the jail, but he decided that it was too risky and too difficult to escape from that jail. Security was too good, and a failed escape attempt would only attract harsher punishment on him by the authorities. Everything that he tried or thought about trying lately seemed to fail. His project with the birds was going on well until the guard at the People's House caused that to be stopped. He escaped at the convenient store and was already at the airport with his ticket, only to be caught later. He thought that his capture at the airport could have been avoided if he had remembered that he was actually a man but he was supposed to act as a woman. At times he blamed his penis for his downfall. He wondered why his luck was now so hard and everything appeared to be working in favor of the infidels. Soon he would have to face trials in courts dominated by people with different beliefs than his, and people that he hated with a passion. He believed that although he was caught and had some set-backs yet he was already victorious, for he had maimed and killed many of his enemies on their own turf and without their knowledge for a very long time of who had done it. He knew that one day in his next life he would be rewarded for that, but he was not yet ready for the next life.

One week later, the state appointed lawyer for Salerno returned to the jail and explained the charges and procedure to Salerno again. He then told Salerno that he read all the evidence and he was satisfied that the evidence against him was overwhelming, and that it would be almost impossible to beat the charges. He asked Salerno, "Will you consider pleading guilty to the charges if the prosecution takes the death penalty off the table?" Salerno did not want to be looked at as being a coward and a person that was afraid to die, although the truth is that he was afraid to die, but on the other hand he wanted to be alive so that one day he might be able to fight against the infidels again, if only in prison. The public defender told him that he did not have to give an answer at that time, but that he could give the answer on his next visit to the jail. Salerno replied, "I'll tell you the answer now. I will plead guilty to everything and save the government a lot of money and time, but only if my five birds are freed, and they must be freed prior to any guilty pleas." The lawyer assured him that the matter would be raised with the prosecutor, but that at this stage there could be no guarantee that the prosecutor would accept his offer, because the evidence against him was very strong, and the birds could be used as evidence against him. The lawyer left the jail and called the prosecutor and made an appointment to see the prosecutor the following day.

The following day Salerno's court appointed lawyer met with the prosecutor and informed him that Salerno would plead guilty to all the charges if the five birds were released immediately. Salerno's lawyer continued, "There's one catch, the five birds must be freed prior to Salerno pleading guilty to all the counts, and they must be released in Salerno's presence." The prosecutor knew that they had more than sufficient evidence to convict Salerno of all the counts against him, but if the matter went to trial, it would be time consuming and would cause the government a lot of money, so he asked the court appointed lawyer, "If I agree to that, what is there to prevent Salerno from reneging on his part of the bargain after the birds were released?" Salerno's lawyer rubbed his hands together and replied, "The truth is that there is nothing to stop Salerno from reneging on his part of the deal if that is what he wants to do, but I guess we'll just have to trust him. I have a feeling that he is very serious and he will not renege on it." The prosecutor responded, "Some of those people like Salerno are elevated when they are perceived as martyrs; what if this is a case like that?" Salerno's lawyer remarked, "Like I said before, I think he is serious, and we may just have to take the risk. Life is all about taking risks and chances." The prosecutor told him "I would have to take some time to consider Salerno's offer, and I would have to discuss it with the District Attorney, after which, I would get back to you." The court appointed lawyer notified Salerno of what transpired between the prosecutor and him, and Salerno thanked him.

The prosecutor discussed Salerno's offer with the District Attorney, who appeared to be not too pleased with it. The district attorney felt that the evidence against Salerno was very strong, cogent, and overwhelming, and that Salerno deserved the death penalty. The prosecutor told the district attorney that he agreed with what he said, however, he, the prosecutor, believed that the case would be inordinately long because of the many counts against Salerno. He continued by stating that it would take a lot of time and money if the matter went to trial. Finally, it was agreed that the prosecution would take the chance and draw up the agreement for Salerno to sign. The deal would include the birds being freed on the day before the trial commenced, and on the day set for the commencement of the trial Salerno would plead guilty to all the charges and say exactly how he planned and executed all the offences. If it were discovered that Salerno lied about what he said in the agreement the deal would be off the table and Salerno would be eligible for the death penalty. The agreement was explained to Salerno and he agreed to it. He believed that he was man enough to honor an agreement that he entered into. "It was the infidels," he said, "who did not honor agreements." Law enforcement wanted to know how he made the bombs and the exact materials that he used so that they could prevent other similar bomb attacks.

Daksy was visiting Leon in the hospital frequently, and they were laughing and touching each other more than they ever did when they were married. Somehow they both seemed to have grown in maturity after their near death experiences. On one occasion when Daksy visited him at the hospital and they were laughing and touching and smiling, suddenly Leon became serious as he held her hand. She was nervous and became serious also as she looked straight into his face. He had tears streaming down his face as he squeezed her hand and said, "Daksy baby, will you remarry me?" Suddenly she began to cry and she pulled her wheelchair closer to him as she said "Yes I will." They hugged and kissed each other as they told each other, "I love you, I love you." Two weeks later a Justice of the Peace attended the hospital and officiated in the wedding ceremony for Leon and Daksy. Two of Leon's nurses took part in the wedding ceremony. Three weeks later Leon was discharged from the hospital and he and Daksy lived in a specialized house for persons with disabilities. They constantly reminded each other that out of evil came good, because if the evil Salerno did had not caused their disabilities they might have never remarried, so what Salerno meant for harm turned out to be something positive.

The day before the trial was to begin Salerno and the prosecutor signed the agreement, and the birds were set free in the presence of Salerno, his lawyer, the prosecutor and some police officers. Salerno was crying as the door to the cage was opened and they flew out and came over to him and stood on his shoulders. One of them perched on his head, which made him laugh through the tears. He kissed each bird on its forehead and said, "Go, you're free." The birds flew in a circle around him then flew off together as if they were going on an assignment. Salerno smiled as they flew off. It was hard seeing them fly away knowing that it might be the last time that he would ever see them again, but it felt like he was being freed as he watched them fly off. He looked at the prosecutor and the court appointed lawyer and said, "Now I'm ready. You kept your end of the bargain, now I'll keep mine." He was ready indeed because the following day he was brought into the packed courtroom to plead to the many counts lodged against him. As the counts were read to him he kept saying 'guilty', until the last count was read to him. The judge asked him if he pleaded guilty because he was guilty and he said, "Yes sir." After Salerno made the guilty pleas he went into detail about how he traveled to his home country and met with a man called AB who taught him how to make and detonate what he called untraceable explosive devices, or UEDs, and when he returned to this country he trained the birds to deliver and detach the bombs at various sites. He said that he chose those sites at random and wanted to inflict as much injury and as many deaths as possible.

Salerno became thirsty after he had spoken for so long, so he was given some water. After drinking the water he continued with his confession. He told the court that if he was not caught he would have continued killing and destroying property. He was asked why he tried to kill Leon Chanley and he said that Leon was praising the host country too much, and he thought that Leon was just like all the other infidels. When Salerno finished speaking the judge asked him if he had said all that he knew about the bombings, and he said that it was all. Some witnesses were called from his job and the church to give good character evidence on his behalf, but the judge did not seem too impressed when they were giving their evidence. When they were finished the judge permitted Leon and Daksy to give victims impact statements. Leon made his statement first. He said, "Salerno I trusted you and I had you for my best friend. I would have done anything for you. You may recall how happy I was for you when you got the award on the job. I never knew that you were so evil and had so much hatred in your heart. I told you one time ago that whoever did the bombings was not a human being but a humonster. Do you remember that? When I said it you asked me what I meant by humonster? Well I'll say it again. You are a monster in human skin. Do you recall that I once told you that when those terrorists, whom I call dogs, are caught I will be right there to see them in court and I will shout, God bless this host country, and down with the forces of evil?" Salerno responded, "Yes, I remember that." Salerno continued, "Well, I say, God bless this host country, and down with the forces of evil."

Leon wheeled his wheel chair back to his seat with tears in his eyes. Almost everyone in the courtroom was crying after Leon spoke. The judge was seen wiping his eyes with Kleenex tissue. The next to speak was Daksy Chanley. She was already crying as she wheeled herself to the front of the room to the microphone and faced the jam packed court. She was handed some Kleenex which she used to wipe the tears from her face and the cold that had run down her nose. Her mascara was coming off and staining her pink powdered face. She looked directly at Salerno as he tried to hold his head down to avoid direct eye contact, and she commenced by saying, "Salerno, hold your head up and look at me and be a man for once. I forgive you. I want you to know that you may kill my body or try to destroy my body directly or indirectly, but you cannot kill or destroy my spirit and my soul. I love you but hate what you did to me, my husband, and all the others that you killed and maimed. I leave you in the hands of a higher and mightier power." When she was finished she wiped her face again and wheeled herself to her position where she was prior to giving her victim impact statement. Spectators were crying and wiping their eyes. A lady at the back of the courtroom whispered to another lady sitting beside her, "I couldn't do what she and Leon just did. I would have hung him up by his toes and everyday give him little electric shocks until he died." The other lady said, "That is too good for him."

When Daksy was speaking there was hardly a dry eye in the huge courtroom. Even the judge was still wiping his eyes, which had turned red. The courtroom reporter stopped typing for a moment to wipe the tears from her face. The prosecutor blew his nose loudly which caught the attention of everyone in the courtroom, who saw when he wiped tears from his face. Salerno's court appointed attorney was shaking his head from side to side as Daksy spoke. The whole atmosphere was so solemn and serene, for surely she was an innocent victim. Now she was back beside Leon she held his hand and they both cried. For a moment the court was silent except for the sniffling of noses and sighs coming from those present. Leon and Daksy hugged each other and started crying aloud as their families took them away from the courtroom.

Everyone was waiting to see what would happen next, as the courtroom procedure was new to many present. Many had attended court for the very first time in their lives. Outside the courtroom was as packed as inside. People were standing outside because they could not get a seat inside. The judge gave Salerno the opportunity to speak, and at first Salerno refused to speak, but he changed his mind and stood up and said, "I worship the sun, the moon and the stars. They are my god. Nature is my god. That is why my birds are so important to me. My birds and I did what we had to do because infidels like you and those who lost their lives try to destroy nature. Everyone makes noise about infidels that lost their lives, but what about the lives of my ten precious birds? No one is saying anything about them. I cried for those birds on many occasions. I have to live without them. Who are more important, infidels or my birds?" Murmuring and curse words were coming from the spectators in the courtroom in disagreement with what Salerno was saying. An old man present stood up and shouted, "Murderer, you should be stoned to death; you devil." A police officer rushed to where the old man was sitting and ushered him out of the courtroom. While the old man was speaking, others in the courtroom began to clap and make remarks in support of what he was saying. The court clerk had to ask for order in the court. Salerno's court appointed lawyer appeared to be embarrassed as Salerno spoke. He had no idea what Salerno would say. He had a look of disbelief on his face when Salerno was speaking, and a look of relief on his face when Salerno stopped speaking and took his seat.

/

The judge looked around the courtroom and wiped his face a couple of times and blew his nose before he began to speak. He looked at Salerno and the court appointed attorney and said, "Salerno stand." Salerno and his court appointed attorney stood and looked directly at the judge as the judge blew his nose one more time and began to speak. "Salerno Bondi, you are the most despicable, depraved, and selfish creature on the face of this earth. I have done a lot of cases during my tenure as a judge and I have never come across anyone like you. You are a heartless devil. You destroyed many lives of people whom you did not know and who did you nothing. I was minded to rescind the agreement between you and the prosecutor, but in order to avoid further waste of the court's time in appeals I decided to honor it. I now sentence you to a life sentence without the possibility of parole for every one of these crimes. I think prison is too good for you, but that is the worst I can do for you under these circumstances. Officers, take him away. I do not ever want to see him again."

Two burly police officers handcuffed Salerno while six police officers walked before them and four other officers walked behind them with guns drawn. It was obvious that they regarded Salerno as a high risk. As Salerno was taken away he turned his head with a smirk on his face and said, "All of you in this courtroom can go to hell where you belong." When they were outside the courtroom people were shouting insults at Salerno. An elderly woman whose husband was killed when the post office was bombed shouted, "You damn dirty bastard. I hope you rot in hell." Another individual who was standing on the outside of the courtroom shouted, "Hand that skunk over to me. I'll show you what I will do with him. I will pull out one of his fingernails and toe nails each day and cut a small piece of his flesh off him until he dies." Leon was very close to the police car that Salerno would be put in. Leon looked up toward the sky and saw a bald eagle flying gracefully above. When Salerno got close to Leon Salerno tried to avoid looking at him, but Leon turned in his wheel chair and said, "This country will always prevail because we are united and it stands for what is right and what is good, and right prevails over wrong and good prevails over evil."

Printed in the United States
By Bookmasters